RAW

Also by Mark Haskell Smith

Fiction
Moist
Delicious
Salty
Baked

Nonfiction
Heart of Dankness: Underground Botanists,
Outlaw Farmers, and the Race for the Cannabis Cup

RAW

A Love Story

Mark Haskell Smith

Black Cat
a paperback original imprint of Grove/Atlantic, Inc.
New York

Printed in the United States of America
Published simultaneously in Canada

ISBN: 978-0-8021-2201-8
eBook ISBN: 978-0-8021-9299-8

Black Cat
a paperback original imprint of Grove/Atlantic, Inc.
154 West 14th Street
New York, NY 10011

Distributed by Publishers Group West

www.groveatlantic.com

13 14 15 16   10 9 8 7 6 5 4 3 2 1

For Jamison Stoltz and Morgan Entrekin

1

Seattle

Did you really hook up with Roxy Sandoval?"
Everywhere he went people asked him the
same question. Like it must have been fake. Like
they couldn't believe their eyes even though it was happening
right there on the TV. Twenty-five million people tuned in
and saw the white sheets tented over their bodies as Roxy's
head bobbed up and down and Sepp moaned and thrashed
like a porn star being electrocuted, but they still had to ask.
He'd been aware of the cameras for sure—you don't go on a
show like *Sex Crib* and not know that there are cameras in
every single room. The place was totally wired for video and
sound. They would've put a minicam inside the toilet if they
could get the footage past Standards & Practices.

Did he really hook up with Roxy Sandoval? Dude. Sepp
and Roxy had hooked up in about every way a man and a
woman could attach to or insert their various body parts in
each other. They did it backwards, forwards, upside down, and
sideways. And then they did it again. And again. Everyone
had seen it. And the footage that didn't make the show? The
raw stuff? That was available for only $39.99 on the special
adults-only DVD; it was like a network-authorized amateur

sex tape with real production value. Sepp especially liked the way his eyes looked in the night-vision cameras, that weird inside glint that shined out, like he was some kind of night-stalking Roxy-banging jungle cat. A puma, maybe.

"Didn't you watch the show?"

The guy asking about Roxy must've weighed three hundred pounds—a mass of pasty flab cloaked in a fluorescent-green Seattle Sounders jersey.

"For sure. I've seen all your shows. My favorite was *Love Express*. But I always wondered about Roxy. Was she as hot as she looked?"

Sepp reached up and dragged his fingers through his spiky brown hair. A stylist on the show had spent hours giving him a razor cut so he'd always look like he'd just climbed out of bed; she'd shown him how to apply a dab of product and tousle it just right, so he could do it anywhere. He blinked his blue eyes at the guy—eyes that some snarky reporter on *E!* had said looked a little too close together. Sepp didn't think so, but whatever, dude. Let the haters hate. You don't get named one of *People* magazine's sexiest men alive with scrunched-up eyes.

Sepp looked up from the book-signing table. "What do you think?"

The guy smiled. "Yeah. I think she'd be hot."

Sepp flashed his freshly veneered teeth and took the book out of the guy's clammy grip.

"TV doesn't lie." Sepp rapped his knuckles on the cover of the book. "And the rest is all in here, amigo."

Sepp said this with confidence, as if he'd actually written his book, but the truth was that he hadn't had much to do with it except wasting a couple days hanging out with the ghostwriter, listening to him whine about how he couldn't meet women and nobody liked him and Brooklyn was overrated and the world was just a big bucket of shit. Sepp didn't know why the book wasn't the true story of his life, but it had something to do with the network owning his life rights or something, so the book was a novel, some made-up stuff that was like his story but not exactly his story. It was close enough; the hero was a reality TV star with a tight body so it was like, only part fictional. That's pretty much all Sepp knew about it and, really, he looked amazing on the cover and his name was the same size as the book's name so, like, how cool is that? His agent said it was all part of their overall brand strategy for him. Plus they'd paid him a lot of money.

Sepp opened the book to the title page, the part that said *TOTALLY REALITY: A Novel.* Underneath that it said Sepp Gregory. So awesome.

"Would you like it personalized?"

Brenda had told him to ask that. She was the publicity person at his publisher and she knew everything about selling books. She told him it would keep people from selling the book on eBay if their name was written in it.

The guy nodded. "Make it to Blake."

Sepp personalized it, then signed his name, making a dramatic swooping *S* followed by a few tight loops to create the double *pp*. Brenda had made him practice this signature, over and over again until it looked cool, but was still readable. Sepp had never thought about his autograph before but Brenda had told him that it was important to have a clear, stylish signature. Sepp handed the book back and smiled.

"Thanks Blake. Keep it real."

Sepp offered his fist and Blake bumped it with his, grinning the stunned smile of someone who's just come into close personal contact with a real live celebrity.

Blake shuffled off and Sepp looked at the line. If a line snakes, as the cliché goes, then Sepp's line was an anaconda, fat with fans, winding through the signing area and up some stairs, past the coffee shop, through the length of the Elliott Bay bookstore, and out the door into the gray drizzle of Seattle. They were all clutching his book, some of them with more than one copy, juggling it with their lattes and umbrellas and what Brenda called memorabilia. Brenda had made it clear that if anyone wanted memorabilia signed they had to buy one book for each DVD or poster or calendar or T-shirt or whatever it was that they wanted him to autograph. He was on tour, she reminded him, to sell books.

One of the bookstore employees, an attractive middle-aged woman with frizzy dark hair and a woolly cardigan, came up to him.

"Can I get you something? A coffee? Water?"

The bookstore people hadn't acted all that happy to see him when he first rolled in. Some guy with a beard behind the counter even gave him the stink-eye. Brenda had told him that a lot of bookstore owners blamed television for declining readership so they didn't love TV stars and he might get some attitude. Sepp understood that—no hard feelings—because given the choice between a cool show and a dumb book, dude, that's a no brainer.

While the folks who worked at the bookstore had acted all snooty when he arrived, now that they were watching a couple hundred books fly off the shelves—hardcover copies at $26.99 a pop—they wanted to make sure he was hydrated; now they were super delighted to have a TV star in their store.

Sepp smiled up at the woman.

"Can I get a latte? With low-fat soy?"

It was his private joke to ask for low-fat soy. It was like asking for a decaf unicorn.

She nodded. "Of course. I'll be right back."

Sepp turned and smiled at the next person in line. He was delighted to see it was a fresh-faced young woman coming toward him with a book in her hand.

"I'm such a fan."

She smiled, revealing a tangle of braces in her mouth like she'd just chewed a handful of paper clips.

Sepp couldn't help it, he grinned back at her. "Thanks. Would you like this personalized?"

"Can you make it 'for Madison'?"

"Sure."

He looked up at her. She was cute. "You go to school, Madison?"

"Yeah. I'm at the U-Dub."

"Awesome. It's good to stay in school."

One of the things Sepp liked about being a celebrity was that he got to be a role model for young people. He wanted to be inspirational. He liked to tell them to go to school, use condoms, and have good personal hygiene. These things are important.

Madison cleared her throat. "Mr. Gregory? Can I get a picture of me and your abs?"

Sepp didn't consider this an unusual request. He'd spent a lot of time on various TV shows with his shirt off and he was justifiably famous for his six-pack. How many crunches did he do a day? Five hundred. And then he did other stuff too. Some Pilates. Some work with medicine balls and kettle bells. His abs were toned to perfection with state-of-the-art personal trainer technology and sweat. *Men's Health* had named him the "#1 Summer Bod" last year and done an article about his ab regimen. And when he was on *Sex Crib*? Dude. All any of the other guys could do was ask about his workouts. His abs were stars, that's why he was wearing his shirt unbuttoned on the cover of the book.

"The line's pretty long. I don't know if I can flash my abs to everyone who asks."

She bit her lip in a practiced bit of coy. "I'll let you autograph my boob."

Sepp grinned. She was totally cute.

For her part, Madison sensed something in his hesitation and slipped out of her padded down vest and pulled her sweater off, over her head. She dropped her clothes on the floor and fumbled with the buttons on her flannel shirt.

"Do you have a camera?"

Madison's shirt opened to reveal a thermal cotton camisole. "My phone has a camera."

The bookstore employee returned with Sepp's latte just as Madison lifted her camisole, pulled down her bra, and revealed a perfect cocoa-colored breast.

"What's happening?"

"He's autographing my boob."

The bookstore employee handed Sepp his coffee. "Of course he is."

Sepp took a Sharpie and gently put his looping signature across her breast. "You have a nice body."

"Yeah?"

The bookstore employee put a hand on Madison's shoulder. "We need to keep the line moving."

"But he promised me a picture with his abs."

The bookstore employee looked at Sepp. "You did what?"

"It's no big deal."

And with that, Sepp lifted his T-shirt and revealed just what all the fuss was about.

2

New York City

Curtis poked the olive with his finger. The little green orb bounced in the glass, floated to the surface, and then sank. The bar didn't have any craft beers so he decided he'd drink what locals drank. He was in Manhattan, the bustling home of serious people doing serious things, so he might as well have a serious drink. Curtis sucked the gin off his finger, getting a taste of something slightly medicinal mixed with grit that had accumulated under his fingernail. He recognized that this was a very good martini. At these prices it better be.

Curtis caught his reflection in the mirror behind the bar. Did he look like a writer celebrating his debut on *The New York Times* Best Sellers list? He had the thick glasses and rumpled hair of a writer. He wore an old checkered shirt that clashed stylishly with his skinny tie and the rust-colored corduroy sport coat he'd found in a vintage store in Bushwick. And even if he wasn't roguishly handsome, at least he was roguishly unshaven. He looked like he could be a successful writer. But really, what did it mean to make the bestseller list? Nowhere in *The New York Times* did it mention his name. Even if they said the book was ghostwritten, the paper of record wouldn't identify Curtis Berman as the ghostwriter of *Totally Reality*. Which, he realized, was maybe just as well.

He adjusted his glasses, pushing them up his nose, over the bump he got when his college girlfriend threw a German-English dictionary at him, and took a deep, anesthetizing gulp. It was too much, too strong, and he nearly gagged as the icy firewater sluiced down his throat. He spluttered and let out a gasp.

"There you are."

Curtis felt a soft hand pat him on the back and turned to see Amy, his literary agent, smiling at him.

"Hey Amy."

He tried not to sound pathetic, wanted to keep the ooze of self-pity out of his voice, but he saw from her expression that he'd failed. She plopped her oversize purse on the barstool next to him and let down her hair. She hung her denim jacket on the chair back, revealing a loose vintage dress and a mass of curls and cleavage. Curtis reminded himself not to stare at her breasts, but then he wondered if that was a biological impossibility. The male DNA is programmed to stare down dresses. He'd read that in a scientific journal.

Amy snapped him out of it. "You should be happy. You're on the list."

Curtis sighed. "Sepp Gregory is on the list."

Amy gave his arm a squeeze. "Curtis. Look. Everybody knows you wrote that book."

"Everybody in publishing."

"Those are the people who matter."

Curtis popped the olive into his mouth. "Tell that to my parents."

"Listen, Eeyore, the news gets better."

Amy signaled the bartender, pointing to the empty martini glass. "Can we get two of those?"

Curtis was curious. How could the news get better? "What?"

Amy looked around for the hostess. "Do you want to get some dinner? I'm starving."

"Now you're teasing me."

She smiled and pulled out her iPad. "Your publisher sent these. There's clips from *People*, *Entertainment Weekly*, *Newsweek*, *The Washington Post*. They're all raves."

She flicked the screen with her finger, sending the images flashing by. She stopped on one and enlarged it. "Here. This'll cheer you up."

As the bartender strained two martinis in front of them, Curtis took the iPad and looked at the screen. He was surprised to see that the review was by the book critic of the *Los Angeles Times;* usually a critic of his caliber wouldn't waste his time reading a book by a celebrity. Then there was a picture of Sepp—shirt off, of course—standing with a wall of books behind him, as if he actually knew how to read, a dumbass grin plastered on his face. Curtis imagined that would be what Tarzan looked like if he ever tired of living with monkeys and sat down and wrote a bestseller.

"Maybe I need to start working out."

Amy picked up her martini and took a sip. "It couldn't hurt."

Curtis skimmed the review, until his eyes landed on this:

One of the most brutally vivid and stunningly emotional accounts of the search for the essence of humanity and the revelation of the sublime soulfulness unlocked by sexual encounters I've read in years. Joseph Conrad have you heard the news, this is a *Heart of Darkness* for the reality TV generation . . .

Curtis reached for his martini and took another giant gulp. This time the gin burned his throat in a good way and caused his eyes to water. Amy must've thought he was getting emotional because she gave him a gentle pat on the hand. "It's good, Curtis. It's really good. Don't think I won't make this count."

He wiped his mouth on his jacket sleeve and looked at her. "How?"

"You'll see."

She chinged her glass against his.

. . .

Amy had offered to give him money for a cab, but Curtis insisted on taking the train home. He'd eaten something, some kind of grilled chop, but mostly he'd had martinis and then, to really celebrate, a glass or three of champagne. He was susceptible to car sickness when he'd been drinking and the last thing he wanted to do was vomit in a cab. So he took the train.

Although the subway seemed more blurry than usual, it was still early—only ten—and the cars were crowded. Curtis saw two people reading *Totally Reality*. And the other people he saw with Nooks and Kindles and Kobos and iPads and Androids? He could only assume that they were also reading Sepp's masterpiece. Curtis swelled with a confusing mix of gin-sick pride and drunken rage. He wanted to go up to them and confess that he'd written the book, that the prose that was dazzling them was his own, it was his heart and soul on the page. He wanted to tell them that Sepp Gregory couldn't spell the word "novel," much less construct a sentence. How could they doubt him? Had they watched any of those shows? But then he was struck by a different emotion—the chilling fear that people would think that he was a hack, a sellout, someone who was uncool.

He watched a young woman reading the book. She looked like an office worker, a smart one, perhaps even someone in publishing. She laughed at something on the page, some bon mot that Curtis had written. There was an expression of delight on her face that enraged him. He wanted to grab the book out of her hands and tear it into pieces.

Curtis reached for a handrail. He realized that he was unsteady, light-headed, suddenly a bit nauseous, and in no shape for a confrontation.

The train screeched into a station and he contemplated getting off and walking home, maybe stopping along the way to throw himself off the Brooklyn Bridge, but who was he kidding, he wasn't in the mood for a hike, and besides, who knew how many people above ground were sitting in cafés or on park benches smiling knowingly as they clutched copies of *Totally Reality.* The bars were probably full of people reading excerpts out loud, sharing the brilliance of Sepp Gregory with their friends. *Can you believe a reality TV star could be such a prose stylist? The dude's a genius!*

He let his head droop. The weight of his gin-swollen brain too much for his aching neck.

Curtis had dedicated the last five years to researching and writing a historical novel about a family of Ethiopian Jews who came to New York City in the late 1940s. It wasn't your typical assimilation story; this family claimed they were the direct descendants of Moses, and Curtis's book had a kind of Jewish-immigrant magic-realist quality that the professor in his MFA program said reminded him of Bernard Malamud. And yet, despite his agent's best efforts, nobody was interested in publishing lengthy Malamudesque novels. They peppered him with compliments. His writing was "luminous" and "lyrical" and had "velocity" and everyone who passed was "positive they were making a big mistake." One editor made an offer, but only if Curtis was willing to make the family Haitian and cut out all the "mystical Jewish stuff." He was praised and admired by the publishing elite, but no one would take a chance on him. Not even the hip, indie publishers who were sprouting up all over the country. He was literally typing an email, asking his parents for a loan, when Amy called with the offer to ghostwrite a novel for a reality TV star.

The fact that this book was now on the bestseller list made Curtis want to kill something. Normally he was the kind of guy who wouldn't hurt a fly, but today he craved the crunchy satisfaction of crushing something small and nonhuman under his shoe, like, for example, a cockroach. Maybe he wouldn't hurt a fly, but he could fuck up a roach. But he didn't see a bug on the train and there was no detectable insect life on the platform when he got off the G train at Flushing Ave.

When he emerged from the station Curtis saw a paper coffee cup from a Greek diner lying on the street. He gave it a kick and it skittered across the sidewalk and bounced against a wall. He walked up to it and gave it a good stomp. That felt good. Curtis sighed with pleasure. It felt so good he stomped it again, harder. And then he did it again, putting all his weight into it, adding a shouted expletive, because the cup wasn't completely flattened. That felt even better and suddenly he was jumping up and down on it, shouting at the top of his drunken lungs as he crushed the living shit out of that fucking paper cup.

3

Seattle

A cab dropped Sepp back at his hotel, a cozy boutique-style hotel at the bottom of a steep hill in the Pike Place Market. He'd spent more than three hours signing books, chatting with fans, and posing for pictures with his T-shirt pulled up around his neck.

He'd never done a book signing before. This was just the first stop on his seventeen-city, thirty-five-day North American tour, and he was already beat. Not that he would complain; he really liked meeting his fans. It was so much more awesome than being at some TV premiere with a bunch of suits or some VIP after-party with actors and their entourages. At the bookstore he got to get face-to-face with real people and hear how much they liked him. And they really liked him. They thought he was cooler than shit. They said so.

He didn't go to his room to change clothes. He went straight to the fitness center in the hotel. It turned out to be a tiny gym, just a treadmill, a stationary bike, a bench, and some free weights. It was after ten and he didn't expect to see anyone else in the gym, so he shrugged off his shirt for like the nine thousandth time that day and stripped out of his pants. It didn't bother him to work out in his boxer briefs. They don't really look like underwear.

He found a yoga mat, rolled it out, and began doing a series of abdominal exercises that had been designed by his personal trainer to keep him looking abtastic while on the road.

Sepp had finished his ab work and was just starting to do some bench presses when he heard the door to the gym swing open. He looked up from the bench and saw someone who looked kinda familiar enter the room. Sepp gave her a friendly nod.

Madison grinned and walked toward him. "Remember me? You wrote your name on my boob."

Sepp remembered. "That's kinda hard to forget."

She stood there staring at him. Sepp wondered if she was angry about it.

"You're not mad are you? It'll wash off."

Madison began unbuttoning her shirt. "It was my idea." She took her flannel shirt off and hung it on a treadmill.

"Want me to spot you?"

Sepp shrugged. "Sure."

He positioned himself on the bench, making sure that the bar was exactly right. He turned to see if she was ready and saw that she'd removed her camisole and bra and was now topless, his autograph clearly visible. Then he noticed she'd taken off her pants too. She walked over to the bench and straddled him, standing over his rippling torso. It wasn't really the correct way to spot someone, but he wasn't lifting that much.

It occurred to Sepp that her finding him in the hotel gym wasn't an accident. "How did you know I was staying here?"

"I've got a friend who works here."

Sepp nodded and lifted the bar with a sharp exhale. He was only lifting one hundred ten pounds, but he was going for twenty-five reps. Madison counted as he pressed. Sepp didn't even try not to stare at her breasts. I mean, really, what's the point of not looking? It helped his workout, that was for sure; he didn't even think about it and the reps flew by. Madison grabbed the bar at twenty-five and helped him rack the weight. Not that he needed any help. He could've done forty or fifty reps. Sepp wondered if he should always work out with a topless trainer. Maybe that could be like some kind of cool new business. Topless gyms. Do they have those?

"Wow. You're really strong."

Sepp lay on the bench and looked up at her.

"This is more for endurance. You know? I'm not trying to bulk up."

Madison nodded. "I don't like bulky guys."

She grabbed a towel and began wiping the sweat off his face, moving the towel down to his rippling abs.

"Wow. These are hard as rocks."

"Yeah. Well. I work 'em a lot."

She worked the towel down to his crotch and began massaging his penis. "What else is hard down here?"

Sepp squirmed, but she sat down on his stomach, pinning him to the bench while she reached behind her, no longer using the towel, and fished his cock out of his underwear.

Sepp cleared his throat. "I don't think this is a good time."

"It'll be a good time, don't worry about that."

"What if someone comes in?"

Madison made a pouty face that Sepp knew girls thought was sexy.

"Are you nervous? Need a little help?"

She stood up and turned around, bending forward so that she could put his cock in her mouth. Sepp looked at her ass as it moved to the rhythm of her sucking.

"I'm sorry. You're a really hot girl but I've been traveling a lot and I'm, like, really, really totally tired."

Sepp hated the way he sounded. But the truth would've been too weird. The truth was that he hadn't been able to get it up since Roxy had dumped him and it's not like he hadn't tried. He'd been with four or five other women since Roxy but every time, he got nothing. No matter what they'd done or how they'd tried or what dirty words they'd said or sexy outfits they'd worn or kinky toys they'd used, it always ended in failure. His cock wouldn't rise. At best he'd get a kind of squishy half-masted thing. It was totally humiliating. Sepp had been to see a doctor but there was nothing wrong with him physically; the fact that most days he woke up with morning wood that felt like ten inches of rebar proved that. The problem was in his head. The problem was Roxy. Roxy was in his head.

Madison stopped and sat up. She flicked her head and her hair flew out of her face. "It's okay. It happens."

He could tell from the sound of her voice that it was not okay and that it didn't really ever happen to her and she really hadn't been expecting it to happen right now, not with him.

"I really do think you're hot. Super hot. It's just, you know, we're in a public place and all."

"Sorry if I bothered you."

She grabbed her clothes and scurried out of the gym.

4

San Francisco

Harriet felt her hand tremble. She put down her mug of tea—an Earl Grey from England with real bergamot in it—and steadied herself.

She was sitting in her reading chair, a knockoff of an Eames lounger, listening to National Public Radio's *Bookish*. Taped in Seattle and hosted by renowned literary critic Titus Goldberger, *Bookish* was the only nationally syndicated program devoted exclusively to literature and literary culture. If you asked Harriet, Goldberger was more influential than all the top critics at the *London Review of Books*, *The New York Times*, *The New Yorker*, the *Los Angeles Times*, *The Guardian*, and even the *Los Angeles Review of Books* put together. He operated on the cutting edge, discoursing on authors like Roberto Bolaño, Steve Erickson, John Banville, William Gaddis, David Foster Wallace, and Don DeLillo, and he didn't just review books or interview authors, he "engaged with the text" and had the ability to "limn psychological truth" from the most impenetrable subtext. He often referred to writers he admired as "saviors of the sentence" and was quick to denounce writing that was not up to his standards with his catch phrase "utterly pedestrian." While Harriet wished that *Bookish* had more female writers on the program, she couldn't argue with the capacious intellect of the host. It was her favorite show and she would often download podcasts of the interviews and listen to them over and over.

But today something unusual was happening. Today a reality TV star named Sepp something-or-other was the guest on *Bookish*. Harriet didn't own a television—why would she?—but even she knew, in a vague pop-culture-trivia way, who Sepp was. His passionate romance with another reality star and their subsequent breakup had dominated the media when it happened. You couldn't go out of your house, you couldn't go online, without hearing about them. Harriet felt that these kinds of people, the *Real Housewives* and *Kardashians* of the world, were responsible for the dumbing down of American culture and should be, well . . . exterminated is probably too strong a word, but they should be marginalized in some way.

Harriet had lately become obsessed with the downward spiral of intelligent discourse and literary culture. Ideas and original thought were now taking a backseat to some celebrity's "baby bump." The world was drowning in drivel. She liked that word, "drivel." It was from *dreflian*, an Old English word meaning to "dribble or run from the nose." That pretty much summed up celebrity culture: a constant drip of snot.

She'd been writing about this a lot lately in various columns and reviews. She was a frequent contributor to literary websites like *The Rumpus* and *The Millions,* and was a freelance book critic and essayist working on assignment for a number of newspapers, including the *San Francisco Chronicle, The Seattle Times, The Globe and Mail* in Toronto, and on occasion *The New York Times Book Review*. She was, essentially, a brain-for-hire and somehow—with the help of the occasional job teaching private writing workshops—managed to piece together enough money to survive on. To cap off all that, she also had her own blog, *The Fatal Influence,* and tried to tweet as many times a day as possible.

In the elite community of literary critics and commentators —full disclosure, they were all aspiring authors—Harriet was a rising star. Like Titus Goldberger, Harriet admired books of quality and seriousness, and authors who shared her devotion to what she liked to call "the higher mind." She wasn't afraid to slam a book that didn't rise to this level—and, honestly, that meant most of the books currently being published; she wasn't a chickenshit or a PR fluff service like some reviewers. She told it like it was, called out the pretenders, and, well, if it destroyed a young novelist's career, then maybe she was just doing the world a favor by getting them to quit writing and start taking their day job seriously. In the book world she attracted attention for her outspokenness, high standards, and intellectual rigor, and occasionally she was asked to be on National Public Radio's *Fresh Air.*

Of course not everyone loved her reviews or her blog. She had rivals; one of them—a complete asshole and pothead author of several collections of "humorous" essays—mocked her in print and referred to her blog as "The Influential Flatulence." But she'd been published—two years ago a novel she'd written was put out by the University of Central South Dakota Press. It had only sold three hundred and twelve copies, but it was a start.

She ran a hand through her hair, pulling a longish strand behind her ear, and pushed her chunky eyeglasses up so they rested on the bridge of her nose. She leaned in toward the radio. She didn't want to miss a word. Titus Goldberger wasn't the kind of person to suffer fools and Harriet couldn't wait to see what he would do to this unsuspecting doofus. She imagined Goldberger leading him down a path, giving him just enough rope to ensnare himself on the bough of his own stupidity. Then Goldberger would mercilessly flay him.

Apparently the reality star had written a novel, which was unusual for a television personality. Don't they usually write memoirs or guides for picking up women? Harriet hoped that Goldberger would use this opportunity to rail against the dimming of American culture. That's what she would've done.

But today Goldberger—who usually seemed so aloof and erudite—was positively gushing.

"When I think of debut novels, and I've read many, many fine books by preternaturally talented young tyros, but when I read them, I rarely find language worth relishing. Sure, there is a captivating raw quality, a brutality of freshness if you will, to the wordplay; but in your book, *Totally Reality,* I have to admit that I found myself in awe of the maturity of voice and the perfect precision of the narrative."

There was a long pause and then Harriet heard the author speak.

"Awesome."

"That's what I'm trying to say. You see. You have a knack, an incisive, pithy quality. You cut to the heart with the perfect word, the mot juste. I see that over and over in your book."

"Yeah. I'm like, you know, just, let's get to it."

Harriet thought the author sounded like a moron and she kept waiting, hoping, for Titus Goldberger to spring the trap and take him down. How could a reality television star write a book? Had he even written it? Don't celebrities use ghostwriters?

But Goldberger didn't spring the trap.

"In your other career, your television career, you're well known for having an impeccable physique, a torso, if I'm not mistaken, that could've been crafted by Michelangelo, it is so similar in appearance to his statue of David."

"I work out a lot. If that's what you're asking."

"What I'd like to do, and I apologize to my audience because there is no picture in radio, only the aural world, but what I'd like to do is, if you're willing to indulge me, is to see this body, this majestic abdomen, in the flesh."

"You want me to take my shirt off?"

"Is that asking too much? Have I crossed a line of propriety?"

And that's when Harriet's hand began to twitch.

5

Brooklyn

Curtis woke up to the sound of hammering coming from the kitchen. It wasn't loud, not like a hammer hitting a nail. It was more of the persistent and highly annoying *tap tap tap* of careful carpentry. Curtis took a quick inventory of his body; the *tap tap tapping* wasn't helping the pounding headache that was reverberating through his cranium, and there was a taste in his mouth that reminded him of licking nine-volt batteries when he was a kid. He blinked and the sound of his eyes flapping caused a stabbing pain in his head to ping from front to back and awaken an unpleasant sensation in his stomach. Curtis couldn't tell if he needed to vomit or take a dump or both, so he just lay there, hoping the sensations would subside. He shifted in bed and felt a sharp twinge in his right ankle, like it had been dislocated or just wasn't hooked on to his leg properly.

Tap tap tap. Tap tap tap.

Curtis inhaled and, using every single ounce of strength he could muster, pulled himself to a sitting position. The sensation of being upright caused him to gasp and choke back a rush of hot bile rising in his throat. It was acrid and sudden and tasted distinctly of olives. He waited for his guts to settle.

Curtis put on his glasses and looked at his foot. It was slightly swollen, nothing too serious, and there was a ring of soft purple bruises caressing the bones around his ankle.

Testing his ability to put weight on his foot, he stood tentatively, and noticed the Arts & Leisure section of *The New York Times* with Sepp Gregory's moronic face staring back at him. It was the author photo that went with the review. It was above the fucking fold. The photograph itself was beautiful, unmistakably Marion Ettlinger's work, and it sent a toxic spasm through Curtis's body. Why would the most famous literary portrait photographer in America take a picture of Sepp Gregory? Wasn't that some kind of betrayal?

Curtis read the first line of the review and realized he'd read it last night. Other bits and pieces of the previous night began to fall into place. The martinis. The rave reviews flooding in from every corner of the country. The celebratory champagne. The unmistakable feeling that he was doomed.

A bleary memory emerged from his gin-shriveled hippocampus, a warning buzz that he'd done something incredibly stupid. He'd made a pass at his agent. He was sure of it. A drunken lunge of parted lips and slobbery tongue. She'd parried it skillfully enough; he remembered the powdery taste of the makeup on her cheek. But had he really copped a feel as they'd hugged good night? Yes, he realized. Yes, he had.

Curtis hobbled into the kitchen, where his roommate, Pete, was bent over, focused on hammering small nails into the sole of a shoe he held clamped between his knees. Pete had been working as an apprentice cordwainer, learning the art of making bespoke shoes for discerning Brooklyn hipsters. Curtis thought it was an unusual thing for someone with a degree in philosophy from Princeton to do. Who wants to make shoes?

Wasn't that the kind of thing that the first immigrants to Brooklyn did so that their children could go to good schools and study philosophy? Why the reverse evolution? But Pete was into all kinds of goofy stuff like that. He enjoyed reading steampunk fiction and wore suspenders to hold up his wool pants. He almost always wore a tie and jacket when he went out and Curtis didn't even want to think about all the hats. Pete had wanted to become a milliner before he heard the siren song of cordwainery and the tiny apartment they shared was cluttered with hats and molds and forms and all kinds of arcane tools. Curtis had thought about basing a character in a story on someone like Pete, but then he'd be living with Pete in his imagination and it was hard enough to live with him in the apartment.

Curtis put a plastic capsule into the automatic coffee-maker and pushed the button to start it. He took a bag of frozen Indonesian stir-fry out of the freezer and a bottle of coconut water out of the fridge and sat down at the table across from Pete. The smell of leather and lanolin caused Curtis's stomach to growl.

"Do you have to do that in the kitchen?"

Pete looked at Curtis. He put down his hammer and twirled the ends of his handlebar mustache into tight little points. "Late night?"

"Something like that."

Curtis chased a couple of Advil with the coconut water and then gingerly elevated his foot onto a chair and placed the frozen vegetables on top of his ankle.

Pete nodded. "What's with all the coconut water in the fridge?"

Curtis considered the coconut water. It didn't taste that great, but was supposed to contain all kinds of beneficial vitamins and minerals.

"I thought I'd try it."

The coffee sputtered in the machine. Curtis didn't make a move to get up. Pete noticed the frozen vegetables on his ankle.

"What happened to your foot?"

"I jammed it on something. Took a martini step."

Pete twirled his mustache ends again. "You need better shoes."

. . .

The digitalized chime of a ringtone jolted Curtis back into consciousness. He'd gone back to bed and now a version of AC/DC's *Highway to Hell*, a song he'd assigned to his agent as a joke, was causing his phone to rattle and buzz on the bedside table. He didn't know how long he'd been asleep, but now he clawed at the air, blindly reaching for his iPhone.

"Hello."

"Hey! Have you gotten used to the idea that you're a big-time famous author?"

Curtis took stock of how he was feeling. His headache was gone, and he did feel a little bit better, but he was covered in sweat, as if his body had pushed all the booze out his pores. *That coconut water is powerful.* He looked out the window; it appeared to be late afternoon.

"Uh. Yeah. About last night. I think I owe you an apology."

"Later. Right now, I've got news."

The excitement in her voice caused Curtis to sit up, which caused his stomach to lurch and send a bubble of acid up his throat. Curtis gagged.

"I hope you're sitting down."

"I am."

"They want a Roxy Sandoval novel."

"You're fucking kidding me. There's no way in hell I'm—"

She cut him off. "Let me finish. They've made a serious offer."

"No. I don't care."

"Two hundred thousand dollars."

Curtis looked at the phone, momentarily at a loss for words. How could they offer that much for what would undoubtedly be a shitty book? "Is this some kind of joke?"

"No joke. They want you to get started right away. You'll need to deliver the manuscript in six months."

"But what about my novel?"

Curtis had tried not to sound petulant but realized he'd failed. There was a pause on the line.

"Curtis. I think you're really talented. That's why I represent you. But your novel . . . Let's just say it's a bad environment for fiction right now."

"And it's a good environment for dreck?"

"Yes. It's a fantastic environment for dreck. Everybody wants dreck."

Curtis shifted in bed, the sheets releasing a slight animal funk.

"I don't know."

"Right now, you've got a track record with this kind of thing. You're hot. That's why the offer is so good. You want my advice, take the money, knock out the book, and then you can spend the next couple years working on your novel."

"I have a track record for writing dreck?"

"Hey. Not everyone does."

Curtis sighed. "Can I get some kind of credit? Like 'as told to Curtis Berman' or something?"

"Why do you want that?"

"I just want some proof that I exist. Otherwise it just doesn't seem real. Is that asking too much?"

Now it was Amy's turn to sigh. "You realize that offers like this are rare, right? This doesn't happen in publishing anymore."

Curtis didn't try to hide the petulance in his voice. "Just let me think for a minute."

He thought he heard her curse under her breath, but wasn't sure. "Call me when you decide. Oh, and never touch my breasts again."

She hung up before he could respond.

6

San Francisco

Sepp closed his eyes and felt the cool, moist touch of a sponge as the makeup artist applied some foundation under his eyes. He let out a contented sigh and settled back in the chair. It felt good to be back in the makeup room, getting ready to go in front of the cameras. Sepp realized that the best moments of his life had followed a touch-up by a makeup artist. Meeting Roxy for the first time. Making love to Roxy. Had he ever spent time with Roxy when he hadn't had makeup on?

He felt a soft brush dust his cheeks and opened his eyes to see the makeup artist, a stylish black woman with dreadlocks, looking at him, her brows furrowed in concentration.

"I'm just adding a little color. You're looking kind of pale."

"I got up early."

"You flew in this morning?"

Sepp wanted to nod, but knew not to move his head.

"From Seattle. First flight out."

She chuckled and patted his leg.

"Well, don't worry. Sit back and relax and I'll make you look beautiful. Every woman in the Bay Area is going to want you."

Sepp closed his eyes and let out a soft exhale. As he relaxed, her words turned into a vision in his head. He was standing naked in front of millions of women. Tall, beautiful, short, plump, young, and old, they were lined up as far as he could see—across the Bay Bridge, through the streets of downtown, all the way down the Embarcadero, waiting for a turn with him. But they weren't holding his book. They didn't want an autograph or a photo. They were horny. They wanted his cock. Millions were waiting. He was standing on some kind of elevated platform, his penis flaccid and dangling in the crisp San Francisco breeze. He was having trouble breathing. The women began to chant his name, calling for him, urging him to begin. All he needed to do was get it up, sport some wood, rise to the occasion and be a hero like Superman, like those dudes in the movie about Sparta. But as the chants grew louder, his penis began retracting into his body, like a periscope going down, un-telescoping until it disappeared into his skin and he was left cockless and smooth, like some mutant toy, buff and tan and sexless.

An involuntary shudder rocked through his body and he gasped. His eyes popped open and he began breathing hard, hyperventilating.

The makeup artist put her hand on his shoulder, a look of real concern on her face.

"You okay? Want me to get you a coffee or something?"

Sepp felt his heart pounding harder than usual, like he'd been running sprints. A sudden tightness seized him and he began to tremble. He took a deep breath, fighting to keep his composure.

"A coffee would be awesome." His voice was croaky, like he was on the verge of sobbing.

"You're a pro, honey. You got nothing to worry about."

She put her brushes down and left the room. Sepp closed his eyes and tried to control his breathing. What was wrong with him? It was like Roxy had put a voodoo curse on him or something. Since when did thinking about sex cause him to freak out? Dude, he thought about sex all the time. He wondered if he was having a panic attack. He remembered that one of the other contestants on *Sex Crib,* a big bodybuilder guy, had panic attacks and took pills to make them go away. Sepp looked at his hands. They were shaking like he had some kind of old person's disease. Maybe he needed to start taking panic pills.

If his inability to get a boner hadn't been so alarming, Sepp might've seen the irony in his situation. *Sex Crib* was kind of like *The Bachelor* and *The Bachelorette* only instead of looking for true love by going on dates and skydiving and horseback riding and taking French cooking lessons until you're the last man standing, *Sex Crib* was about hooking up as much as you could. The person with the most successful hookups was the winner. The fact that he and Roxy had fallen in love just made the whole experience beautiful. Sepp was not without a sense of humor, and if someone else had been crowned king of *Sex Crib* and then couldn't get it up, well, dude, that would be funny. Only it was happening to him and it wasn't really all that funny.

The makeup artist came back holding a small Styrofoam cup of coffee.

"I forgot to ask how you take it, so here's a sugar and some creamer."

"Thanks."

He took the cup from her and took a sip. The warm liquid made him feel a little better and he began to calm down. She tilted her head, looking at him.

"You sure you're okay?"

Sepp nodded. "You want to touch up my abs? They'll probably ask me to take my shirt off."

. . .

They were classic morning show hosts. The female of the species was a buxom and frothy blonde wearing a tight orange top that made her breasts pop on camera. The male was a slightly older dude with hair that was graying at the temples. He had a kind of world-weary grin that comforted viewers and made them feel like he was one of them, that he was in on the joke.

The commercial break came and Sepp was hustled into a seat at the "coffee table" and quickly wired for sound. The stage manager gave him a last look, satisfied that she'd hid the microphone wires.

"Remember. You're just having a conversation with Mike and Anne."

She pointed to the hosts to make sure Sepp knew who Mike and Anne were. Sepp smiled.

"Got it."

There was a countdown, some music, and then the hosts started blabbing. They chatted for a moment, mentioning something about Sepp's "amazing bod," and then they turned and looked at him. Sepp didn't know what they were going to talk about. They'd held up a copy of his book and so he assumed that was what they'd be discussing, but Anne threw him a curveball.

"So Sepp, who are you dating? I mean, Roxy might've let you get away but you can't keep a bod like yours off the market for too long."

Sepp blinked. "Um. I'm not dating right now. It's kinda hard when you're on tour, you know?"

Mike shook his head in disbelief. "C'mon! You're like a rock star. You don't expect us to believe that."

Mike turned to Anne. "Authors get groupies. Don't they?"

Anne nodded and said, "John Grisham's a hunk."

Mike looked at the camera and smirked. "And who doesn't remember having a crush on the school librarian?"

Sepp didn't know what to say; he'd never had a crush on a librarian or, now that he thought of it, been in a library, and he didn't know who John Grisham was, although he seriously doubted he had abs like his. Sepp shrugged.

"The tour's just started, so you never know. I'm keepin' my options open."

Anne smiled. "San Francisco won't let you down. Not after they see your body."

Mike nodded along with Anne. "You look great in that T-shirt. I wish I could get away with that."

Anne gave Mike a good-natured nudge. "I keep telling you to go to the gym." She turned her attention to Sepp. "Is that Ed Hardy?"

The best thing about being a celebrity was all the free clothes he got. And, dude, he didn't even have to pick them out, a stylist did that for him. Sometimes he'd open the door to his walk-in closet in his condo in Cortez Hill and there would be all these cool T-shirts and new tennis shoes and all kinds of free stuff already hung up and put away. The only catch was that he couldn't tell anyone he got the stuff for free. He was supposed to get people to think he shopped for the stuff himself.

Sepp nodded. "I get most of my shirts from there."

Anne turned to the camera. "And we'll see what's under that T-shirt right after traffic and weather."

...

Sepp sat in the passenger seat of an older, well-kept Toyota Camry as a guy named Len drove from the TV studio to a talk radio interview. Len was the media escort Sepp's publisher had hired to drive him to all his events and interviews while he was in the Bay Area. Sepp thought that it was kind of a weird job to drive authors around. Len was a cross between a publicist, a stylist, a personal assistant, and a chauffeur. How did you get a job like this? I mean, seriously, could you just apply for it? And why call them escorts? That made it sound naughty.

Len had a shaved head and trim goatee and wore a black leather jacket. Sepp liked him instantly; he looked like a bodyguard and Sepp thought it would be cool to actually need a bodyguard. Like they always say, you're not really famous until you've got a stalker. That's what Sepp's talent agent had told him and she knew everything about being a celebrity.

Sepp looked out the window. The people on the street were a pretty rad-looking bunch. They were way more into fashion in San Francisco than in San Diego. Here they wore cool leather shoes instead of flip-flops and they had, like, jackets and scarves instead of T-shirts and trucker caps. But then S.D. was more of a beach town and San Francisco was like a city in a movie with subtitles.

As the car maneuvered through the traffic of Market Street, Len cleared his throat and looked over at Sepp. "Can I ask you something?"

Sepp nodded. "Sure."

"How do you break into reality television?"

It was a good question and Sepp didn't have a great answer. His story was pretty simple. He was just in the right place at the right time with the right physique. Before he became a huge celebrity, Sepp had been a semiregular amateur beach volleyball player and mostly irregular construction worker. Hey, no big deal, he just preferred doing the dig, set, spike on the beaches of San Diego to hanging drywall. Nights were spent chillaxing at local clubs, drinking vodka sodas, and hooking up with girls with tan lines. Back then sports and sex came easily to him. He was tall and blond and could rock a puka-shell necklace like nobody else. He wasn't a professional beach volleyball player, not yet, but he was a good enough amateur to be invited to play against the pros at tournaments. That's where a TV producer spotted him and asked if he'd like to come in and audition. Most people don't know this, but even reality shows have auditions and casting sessions. It's just like a show that's not reality, if you can wrap your head around that. Sepp got lucky. Really. In fact, he'd had to make the most difficult choice of his entire life by choosing between being on *Sex Crib* and playing in a traveling tournament sponsored by El Vivo Tequila.

Sepp looked at Len. "I was an athlete and they were looking for athletes."

Len snorted out a laugh. "I was a mathlete. You think they'll give me a shot?"

Sepp shrugged. "You never know, man. Anything can happen."

That's something his father told him. Anything can happen. Life is nothing but a chain of random decisions. Sepp went on *Sex Crib* and met Roxy and then she broke his heart and he tried to get over her, but now here he was, an author having sex-panic daydreams in San Francisco.

7

San Francisco

arriet walked into the bookstore and felt her hands clench and begin to strangle the yoga mat she was carrying. This involuntary homicidal impulse was directly related to the tower of *Totally Reality* stacked on the front table. Harriet turned to her friend Isabelle. "I need my bite guard. This makes me grind my teeth."

Isabelle, an attractive woman who worked as a chef in a vegan restaurant, looked at the books. "I know, what does he do to get those abs?"

Harriet glared at her friend. "Don't encourage it."

Isabelle laughed, then caught herself when she realized Harriet was serious. "What?"

"This shit."

Isabelle smiled and nodded. Harriet recognized it as the kind of nod you give crazy people; it looks as if you're agreeing with them, but really you're just trying to keep them from getting crazier. Harriet knew she wasn't crazy, she was sure of it, so why was her friend giving her that look? Isabelle changed the subject. "How about a nice cup of tea?"

Harriet knew that people only offer a nice cup of tea when they're trying to calm down someone who's on the verge of going postal. Harriet liked the word "postal." It was a new-ish word, coined after a series of violent workplace shootings by postal service employees who'd lost their marbles. Harriet looked at her hands and noticed her knuckles had turned white. "Sure. Tea sounds nice."

As Isabelle walked toward the bookstore café, Harriet stood glaring at the stack of books. There it was again, in all its glory, a perfect example of what Harriet thought of as the stultification and amok-crapalizing of literature. Books like *Totally Reality* weren't just another sign of the end of Western civilization, they were actively accelerating the culture toward the trash heap.

Harriet cleared off a table in the café section. She found a copy of *The New York Times* and saw that they'd reviewed *Totally Reality*. Harriet felt a sense of relief. The Gray Lady wouldn't let her down. The newspaper of record would set the record straight.

By the time Isabelle brought the tea—and a couple of pistachio biscotti—over to the table, Harriet was seething.

"Did you see this?"

"What?"

"The *Times* reviewed that stupid book."

Isabelle smiled at her. Again, with the expression of someone who is a little alarmed but doesn't want to show it. She put the tea in front of Harriet and spoke in a soothing voice, the kind of tone a veterinarian might take while treating a wounded rottweiler. "Have you thought about internet dating? I mean, you're online all the time anyway."

If she were being honest, Harriet would admit that she thought about internet dating frequently. Of course she thought about it. She'd even tried to put up a profile but could never get her picture to look right. She was attractive in an intellectual-with-chunky-glasses sort of way, with soft brown hair cut into a severe bob. She was pretty, with plump lips and a roundish face that was sprinkled with freckles. If pressed she would say her eyes were her most attractive feature, even though she refused to manicure her eyebrows into topiary or whatever it is that women do, and besides, they were always behind her glasses. She knew she had a nice figure, maybe not a feline yoga silhouette like Isabelle, but she wasn't a tall person, she was petite with petite curves. She could look sexy, she was confident of that, but there was no way in hell she was going to wear some low-cut dress and dangle her tits for a dating profile photo; that would attract the wrong type of man. Besides, they never gave her enough room on those sites to fully express her interests, hobbies, and turn-ons. Why limit her interests to four hundred words? That's barely enough to scratch the surface on David Foster Wallace, let alone describe her interests in Jonathan Lethem, George Saunders, Margaret Atwood, or the dozen or so other living authors that she considered important to her.

"When was the last time you went on a date?"

"I've been on dates. Just not recently."

Isabelle nodded thoughtfully, then leaned forward. "When was the last time you had sex?"

Harriet ignored that. She didn't want to admit to anyone that it had been over four years since she'd last been intimate with a member of the opposite sex. It's not a crime. It was nothing to be embarrassed about. She just hadn't met anyone she wanted to do that with.

Harriet slapped the newspaper with her palm. "They compare a reality television show to Jane Austen. That's just moronic."

Harriet had always like that word, "moron." It was an ancient word, probably some combination of sanskrit *murah*, meaning "idiotic," and the Latin *morus*, which meant "foolish."

Isabelle stirred some agave nectar into her tea and nodded. "You know there are lots of nice single men out there. You work so hard, it wouldn't hurt you to go on a couple dates."

"Seriously? Are you fucking kidding me?"

Several other customers looked over and saw Harriet waving the Arts section of *The New York Times* in the air like some kind of ersatz semaphore. Isabelle took a tentative sip of her tea. "Oh, don't be so dramatic. It's not the end of the world."

Harriet dropped the paper to the table and looked at her friend. "That's where you and I differ."

Isabelle looked slightly offended. "Have you even read this supposedly terrible book?"

"Fuck no."

Isabelle spread her hands in a gesture of open-mindedness. "Well, maybe it's amazing."

Harriet smacked her hand on the table, causing some tea to slop out of the cup. Isabelle leaned forward and put her hand over Harriet's fist.

"Relax. You'll ruin your yoga buzz."

Harriet looked at her friend. It was true. Whatever calm and spiritual glow she might've earned from doing yoga had evaporated the second she saw the books on the front table. Harriet closed her eyes and took a deep breath. She exhaled, feeling only microscopically less angry.

Isabelle patted her hand. "The bookstore needs to make money. You've gotta remember that."

Harriet sighed. "I'm not blaming the bookstore, but it just kills me. I mean, I worked my ass off on my novel, for, I don't know . . . years. I got rejected by almost everyone and instead they publish this drivel."

"But your book came out and it was a good book. That's all that matters."

Harriet smiled. "Do you think so?"

Isabelle opened her eyes wide, displaying her absolute conviction, and nodded her head vigorously. "You're a West Coast writer. You're too avant-garde for New York." Isabelle took a tentative bite of the biscotti before continuing. "You know how those things go. They probably hired a ghostwriter."

There was something about the way Isabelle said it that gave Harriet an idea.

"You know what? This is perfect. I'm going to use this."

"To do what?"

"I'm going to expose this book for the canard it is. I'm going to bring the whole stinking apparatus down."

Isabelle bit into her biscotti. "Canard?"

Harriet smiled, suddenly feeling energized. "You know. Sham. Fabrication. Fake. Big fat bamboozle. Pick one. But that's exactly what this is." Harriet pointed at the picture of Sepp in the paper. "How can he write a book? He can't even wear a shirt."

8

San Francisco

Sepp followed Len out of the building. He'd just been on a San Francisco public radio station and it had gone okay, or as good as they ever went. They asked the usual questions, like "What's it like to write a book," and Sepp had given his usual answer, "It's totally cool." It wasn't a lie, exactly. He didn't say he'd written the book, he just said that writing a book was totally cool. It probably was. Right?

Just like on the TV morning show, the DJ asked if he was seeing someone. Sepp thought it was sweet that people in San Francisco were so concerned. They probably felt a little guilty, since it was on the San Francisco episode of *Love Express* that Sepp rebounded from Roxy with the woman who would break his heart for the second time on national television.

If Roxy Sandoval had driven a stake through his heart and left him ground up like fresh hamburger meat on the set of *Sex Crib*, then it was Caitlin Hartman who threw the burger on the grill and torched it until there was nothing left but crunchy carbon.

The premise of *Love Express* was simple: famously spurned reality TV star travels the country in a tricked-out bus with a team of stylists and relationship experts to find a new love and mend his broken heart. The ratings for the series finale of *Sex Crib* had broken all kind of records for a reality show—even those singing shows didn't score this high—and with the country still reeling from Roxy's betrayal, it made sense to roll out the *Love Express*.

The producers sorted through thousands of video auditions for blind dates with Sepp, interviewed the finalists, and then scheduled the tour. The bus would arrive in a city and the crew would film every moment of the blind date from both sides. The primping and prepping with the stylists, the date itself, and then a "debriefing session" with the experts. There was also a confessional for the women to spill their guts before, during, and after the date.

If Sepp and his date hit it off, he'd offer her a "ticket to ride" and she could come on the bus to the next town. Then her challenge would be to try to disrupt Sepp's next date. The producers liked this format because it added conflict and competition to the show, plus a healthy dose of evil scheming and compulsive lying that, as everyone knows, are the most important ingredients for successful reality television. There was a lot of duplicity and dysfunction on the bus, but no one could come close to Caitlin.

She was as sweet as a praline, with a syrupy cotillion-queen accent and the perky figure of a high school cheerleader. Caitlin wore her blond hair perfectly perfect and she could dress in jeans and a button-down shirt and somehow make it the sexiest outfit he'd ever seen. Sepp spent a lot of time watching reruns of the old TV show *Gilligan's Island* on late-night cable, and thought of Caitlin as the Mary Ann to Roxy's Ginger. Sepp had always thought Mary Ann was hotter than Ginger anyway, kinda like how in *Three's Company*

Janet was sexier than Chrissy, even though Chrissy was played by Suzanne Somers and she was supposed to be super hot.

His confidence at an all-time low, his self-esteem shot through the heart with a Roxy-size hole, Sepp was hooked by Caitlin right away. It was understandable—people often bounce from one extreme to the other, and Caitlin turned out to be the mother of all rebounds.

In the game of *Love Express*—if human relationships and love can be considered a game—Caitlin was a boss, kicking ass on every date up and down the West Coast. She had a firm grip on her man, only her man wasn't that firm. Sepp was ashamed to admit it, but it was with Caitlin that he discovered his Roxy-based erectile dysfunction. Luckily *Love Express* didn't show any between-the-sheets action—the network wanted it to be a show about finding love and not hooking up—so to the country it looked like Sepp had finally found his perfect match. It was a fairy-tale coupling, a magical affirmation of true love, proof that you could get your heart broken, bounce back, and find "the one." The story had resilience, redemption, and a happy ending. Stories about their love gushed forth from *Entertainment Weekly, People, Us Weekly,* and all the other supermarket tabloids. The network even floated the idea of doing a two-hour wedding special and following them on their honeymoon.

But once the *Love Express* rolled in to Albuquerque, well, Sepp didn't see it coming—no one saw it coming—but like he heard somebody say, it's not a twist if you see it coming.

Sepp had a date with a lovely young neurosurgeon. Smart, beautiful, and with a great sense of humor. Some reviewers wondered why a woman like this would want a date with Sepp Gregory; others wondered why she would agree to appear on a reality show. *USA Today* suspected that she was a fake, an actress-for-hire. Sometimes reality shows would do that, throw in a ringer to mix things up, but the lovely young doctor was the real deal, a bona fide drop-dead gorgeous brain surgeon with a great rack. Everyone thought she might be the one to capture Sepp's heart and knock Caitlin off the bus, but it all went awry when Caitlin and the lovely young neurosurgeon hit it off in a big way and left Sepp sitting at the bar watching his frozen margarita turn to slush.

The show, which was meant to be a celebration of love and a sexy frolic in the dating world, took a dark turn and Sepp plunged into depression. The dates that followed this betrayal became awkward and hard to watch; gone was the free spirt from the beaches of San Diego and in his place was a moody, pained, and slightly pathetic mope. One of the last episodes featured Sepp eating a pint of Ben & Jerry's "What a Cluster" ice cream and talking to a real therapist, Dr. Jan, for an entire episode. The producers tried to cheer him up—they plotted surprises and brought in some of his best beach volleyball bros—but it didn't work, and turned out to be more than America could bear to watch. The show ended a few weeks later with the official excuse that Sepp had been hospitalized for exhaustion.

...

Len honked at a van and cursed as he tried to maneuver through the traffic. Sepp realized he hadn't been back to San Francisco since the time he met Caitlin. He wondered if she still lived here. Had she stayed with the neurosurgeon in Albuquerque or had she moved back? Sepp pulled out his iPhone and turned toward Len.

"Do you think I'll have time to meet someone for coffee?"

Len shrugged. "It's your tour."

9

Brooklyn

Curtis walked into the kitchen and saw that Pete had set up a giant pot of water and was simmering a half-dozen glass jars. A Post-it was stuck to the range hood that said, "Pickling. Be back soon." Several heads of cabbage were sitting on the counter and a mound of peeled garlic cloves was stinking up the kitchen from a bowl on the counter.

Curtis opened the fridge and poured himself some more coconut water. He had to admit the water was working; his nausea had subsided. But the idea of Pete pickling something was disturbing. What was he making? Sauerkraut? Kimchi? Why did he leave a pot boiling?

Curtis went back to his room and lay down on the bed. He felt tired, washed out. Even his tattoos—the long medical sketch of an ulna that stretched down his inner left forearm and Samuel Beckett's famous advice, "Fail Better," emblazoned in a font called American Typewriter on his right inner bicep—seemed slightly faded after his boozing. He wondered if his body might be suffering from some kind of imbalance.

He swallowed a glug of coconut water and, as he habitually did, scanned the real estate section of the *Times*. It wasn't as if he could afford a fabulous co-op in a doorman building in Tribeca, but that wasn't him anyway. He wouldn't want to live with a bunch of stock market hotshots and trust fund socialites. He wanted to stay in Brooklyn, surrounded by bohemians. His people. The artists, musicians, writers, chefs, and intellectuals who made Brooklyn the only place to be in America.

Still, he enjoyed reading through the real estate ads, and looking at the grainy thumbnail photos gave him license to imagine a better life. And then he found an ad that made his heart jump. He read the copy out loud.

"A two-bedroom two-and-a-half-bath with a large living room, wood-burning fireplace, sunroom and garden in a landmark brownstone. $2,190,000."

Curtis looked at the photo of the building; it looked stately and important. It was his dream home. Just the kind of building a super-successful novelist would live in. Someone like Paul Auster or Jonathan Safran Foer or Jhumpa Lahiri.

Curtis closed his eyes and began to imagine the dinner parties and improvised literary salons he would host in his new brownstone. He'd make bruschetta in the modern kitchen with fresh basil and heirloom tomatoes from his garden. There would be wine, of course, but also a house cocktail, something bespoke, handmade, and unique, like a Negroni or a Blood and Sand.

He'd read about a guy who made his own bitters. Maybe he could do that too. Berman's Bitters. That actually sounded like a real thing. He could bottle it himself and give it out to people in publishing or maybe supply the cool new cocktail bars that were popping up across the city. He could see one of the new breed of mixologists inventing a cocktail that featured his bitters. It would be a signature libation; a drink people would talk about, maybe the subject of a "Talk of the Town" piece in *The New Yorker* or dropped in a short story as a subtle homage—an in-joke that only the in-crowd would get. It sounded like something Elissa Schappell might do.

His new friends and comrades, all famous Brooklyn writers and editors, would gather in his living room and talk about writing and ideas and publishing-world gossip. Maybe he would get a turntable and spin some vinyl. Curtis imagined eclectic modern paintings dominating the walls, maybe something by Cory Arcangel or one of Aaron Young's motorcycle paintings. He would get offers for the art—Salman Rushdie was desperate for the one over the mantel—but Curtis wouldn't sell. They meant too much to him.

Best of all, he wouldn't have a pickling cordwainer for a roommate.

Curtis blinked. Something strange was going on in his boxers. His real estate fantasy had given him an erection. He began to muse on the nature of arousal as he toyed with himself, but then he stopped in midstroke, smacked by the realization that, with his share of the royalties from Sepp's bestseller, and the huge advance to ghost the Roxy Sandoval novel, he could actually afford to buy a place. Maybe not this dreamy brownstone, but definitely a bigger apartment.

Curtis picked up his cell phone and dialed his agent. If he was going to sell out, he wanted to get as much money as possible.

10

San Francisco

Brenda, the publicist, had scheduled a series of drop-in signings for Sepp and that meant he and Len would spend the better part of the day driving from bookstore to bookstore, Len cursing at the traffic while Sepp tried not to get carsick. The drop-ins were simple: They would enter the store and Len would introduce him to some random employee who would then have to go round up all the copies of *Totally Reality* they could find for Sepp to sign. Sepp was surprised by how many bookstore employees didn't know who he was. What was wrong with them? Don't they watch TV?

Brenda had assured him it was good for the book and good for the stores to have signed copies around. "A copy signed is a copy sold," she'd said. But Sepp didn't understand why the bookstores didn't raise the price of the books once they were signed. Like, what was the point? Shouldn't an autographed book cost more?

Len found parking on Second Street right in front of a small bookstore called Alexander Books. It was the one thing Sepp thought was cool about the bookstores in San Francisco: They looked like how he thought bookstores were supposed to look—kinda funky, with windows piled high with books and community bulletin boards layered with flyers for bands and protest marches and announcements for lectures by Chilean poets and sublets for cheap. It wasn't the kind of place where Sepp and his friends would hang out—they preferred gyms, juice bars, and the beach—in fact, he'd only been in one or two bookstores before his book hit the bestseller list and that was because he'd been dating a girl who went to UCSD.

They entered the store and headed toward the counter where two men, a tall handsome black man and a slightly scruffy-looking guy, stood. Len held up a copy of *Totally Reality.*

"Hey guys. I'm here with Sepp Gregory."

The black man nodded and looked at Sepp.

"Dude. Take your shirt off."

Sepp smiled and, without thinking, pulled his T-shirt over his head. The black guy burst out laughing and applauded.

"That's what I'm talking about."

Sepp couldn't tell if they wanted him to keep his shirt off or not. He watched as the scruffy guy shook his head and handed the black guy a ten-dollar bill.

...

It was a bit of a schlep according to Len, and they really should drop in at Booksmith on Haight Street and Book Passage in the Ferry Building, but Caitlin would only agree to meet Sepp at a café near her apartment on Potrero Hill. While Len sat in the car and checked his email, Sepp entered a ramshackle storefront named Farley's.

The café was cool and cozy, mostly filled with with people peering intently at their laptop screens. Sepp didn't understand that. Why go out and read your computer? Shouldn't you go out and talk to people? That's what he did. He had a computer but he hardly used it. He didn't like porn and otherwise, really, it just seemed like a waste of time. For sure it wasn't something he'd haul around to look at in public.

There was only one table without a laptop and that was where Caitlin Hartman had parked her tightly packed jeans.

When he saw her—he couldn't help it—his face sparked into a broad smile. Her blond hair was swept back into a tight ponytail, giving her a casual sporty look like she'd just come from a yoga class. And her makeup was all natural, so she had a healthy glow, with bushy brows and bright hazel eyes. She still looked like the girl next door, as wholesome as a glass of milk. That was what made her so popular on the show. She was fresh-faced and innocent and somehow that made her way sexier than your typical reality TV skank. Sepp remembered one producer who said she was hot because she was so clean you wanted to make her dirty. That fantasy was the secret of her appeal.

Caitlin stood and gave Sepp a quick hug. "You look good."

For some reason Sepp found himself blushing at the compliment, a rush of emotion and heat rising through his body. He couldn't tell if he was happy or angry or sad. "Thanks. So do you."

Caitlin sat down. "You want a coffee?"

Sepp shook his head. "I'm good."

He sat across from her and stared. He couldn't help it. All the emotions that he'd thought he'd processed and dealt with in the care of Dr. Jan, his network-appointed psychiatrist, began to reawaken and percolate inside him. Caitlin sat there grinning and nervously sucking on one of her fingers, a habit she picked up when she quit chewing gum on Season 3 of *Celebrity Vice Busters*.

"So? How are you?"

She pulled her finger out of her mouth, letting a thin strand of saliva shimmer in the light as it bridged the gap between a plump red lip and a manicured pinky. "I'm not very happy about your book."

It had never occurred to Sepp that someone might not like being mentioned in his book. It's cool to be mentioned in a book. Isn't it? Besides, they hadn't used her real name. Although, if you knew anything about what he'd been up to, it wasn't hard to figure out.

"Why?"

She laughed. "Are you joking?"

From his expression it was clear that he was not joking.

"You made me look like a slut."

There were so many things Sepp wanted to say to her. He wanted to tell her that, yes, she probably did look like a slut in the book—not that Sepp knew for sure—but that was because she'd acted pretty slutty in real life.

"It's not really you. It's a fictional novel."

Caitlin pouted. "It didn't seem that fictional to me."

"Well it is."

"Doesn't seem that way."

Sepp shrugged. "What do you want me to say, Caitlin? That I'm sorry a made-up person seems like you?"

"I'm not a made-up person. And I'm not a floozy."

"I never said you were."

Caitlin glared at him and, for a brief second, he thought she might throw her coffee on him or do something dramatic, but she didn't do or say anything.

Finally, Sepp asked, "Are you still seeing the doctor?"

"Screw you, Sepp." Caitlin began rooting through her purse for something. "Is that all you care about?"

He held his hands up. "I'm just curious. You guys seemed like you were in love."

Caitlin pulled a tissue out of her purse and delicately blew her nose. Then she turned to Sepp.

"The producers needed me off the bus for the sake of the show and it seemed like a good twist."

Sepp's expression changed. His jaw dropped, baffled. "Who told you that?"

"It was in the script."

Sepp tried to process this new information. "So you weren't in love?"

Caitlin laughed. "We're still friends, but that whole thing was something the writers came up with. You never read the script, did you?"

Sepp didn't think he needed to read the scripts. The producers and director always told him what to do and what to say so, like, why waste his time? Wasn't it better if he was at the gym? He looked up at Caitlin. "I thought we had something special."

Caitlin reached over and patted his hand. "We weren't in love. We were on TV. There's a big difference."

11

San Francisco

arriet sat at her desk and stared at her laptop screen. It amazed her, really, the things people said when they heard she was a writer. Like it was easy. Fun. Something you did on a whim. People just didn't get it; they didn't appreciate the level of difficulty, they couldn't fathom the amount of energy required to pluck thoughts and imaginings out of the ether and craft them into deep, soulful explorations of the human condition. Does that sound easy? Does it?

People are fucking stupid.

Harriet had been convinced of this fact for years. For a long time she thought it was because of where she'd grown up, that people in Sacramento were stupid, but as she got older and traveled more, she realized that it was generally true of all people, except maybe people in France; they read books in France.

She'd had a normal-enough childhood. Both her parents worked for the State of California in various minor bureaucratic positions that kept them immune from changing administrations and they provided her with a stable middle-class life. She'd been a bit of a tomboy when she was younger, playing AYSO soccer on a coed team and scrabbling up trees in the park, but everything changed when she turned twelve and, seemingly overnight, morphed from a scrawny girl into a young woman. The boys who'd been on her soccer team, her tree-climbing colleagues, suddenly acted weird around her, and older teenage boys, the kind of boys who drove cars and smoked cigarettes, began talking to her, asking her questions and staring at her chest. Her girlfriends weren't much help either. They became distant, jealous, weird.

Looking back on it now, Harriet realized that she kind of freaked out when she hit puberty; awkward, a mutant. At least that's how she felt.

She began avoiding the other kids and went to the one place where no one would find her—the library. It was there that she met a librarian, a friendly young woman who was obsessed with books. The librarian was stylish in a way that Harriet had never seen, with short hair and thick glasses and capri pants, and she was friendlier than any of Harriet's teachers had ever been, which was weird because Harriet was always a straight-A student. The stylish librarian used to take Harriet by the hand and lead her into the stacks to show her books she might like. She would stand close to her, so that Harriet could feel the heat coming off her body, and tell her why she liked certain books, why they were important to read. Looking back on it now, Harriet realized it was a kind of seduction. It began simply enough with *The Awakening* by Kate Chopin and *Annie on My Mind* by Nancy Garden and took off from there. Harriet enjoyed the books—some were better than others—but she loved the experience of sitting alone, lost in a story, not worrying about being talked about behind her back or having boys stare at her in the weird way teenage boys stared at girls, so she came back for more.

By the time she was fourteen she'd read *Lolita* and most of Tolstoy, with passing glances at Henry James and D. H. Lawrence. She read Flaubert and Balzac and Hugo and kooky West Coast authors like Richard Brautigan and Tom Robbins. But it wasn't until she was sixteen and sat down with Thomas Pynchon's *Gravity's Rainbow* that Harriet's life changed. Finally she'd found an author who could give her a jolt of something that felt totally exciting and new. It was like a drug and she was hooked. Sadly that discovery coincided with the librarian's taking her into the special collection room and planting a kiss on her lips, complete with tongue.

Harriet got a job at a bookstore, which seemed like it would be the most awesome job in the world until she realized she spent most of her time helping people find the newest Grisham or Stephen King or Danielle Steel. That's when she figured out that people were fucking stupid.

...

Harriet checked to see how many hits her blog had gotten that morning and was pleased to see the number already over two hundred. She had a loyal following: People looked up to her and checked in on her site several times a day. The numbers weren't huge—she got about five hundred unique hits a day, and then she'd be linked and tweeted and retweeted across the virtual world. The comment threads on her blog were justifiably famous for being well written and lively. She was obviously reaching a very select, sophisticated group of readers and fellow writers. It was what they call in the publishing world a "platform," something that was supposed to translate into robust sales of her novel, that's what her editor said, and she was encouraged to blog relentlessly. In the end, she couldn't do it—she didn't want her blogging or her reviews and critical writing to become some kind of sales tool. That was too cynical. Her novel would have to stand on its own. Her sales might suffer, but she had integrity.

Harriet had been working on her new project; it was a novel, although she didn't really think the word "novel" fully captured the epic scope of her work in progress. Currently the manuscript was a lean nine hundred pages and she was finding it difficult to cut anything. Her agent had said the story was "Byzantine," but Harriet didn't know what her book had to do with the machinations of the royal court of Constantinople, so she and that agent parted company. Was it really too long or were readers getting lazy? How can you edit such an intricate work? Pull one thread or remove one character and the whole thing would collapse. A friend in her writing group had suggested she turn it into several distinct books, similar to Proust's *À la recherche du temps perdu*. Harriet liked this idea.

So far thirty-six agents had politely passed. Harriet didn't hold it against them. She knew that it was a combination of laziness on the agents' part—how could they engage with her work when their submission guidelines only let her send thirty pages and a one-page synopsis?—and she understood their fear when they passed. They were all looking for a beach read or thriller, a paranormal teen romance or a story about gargoyles, any entertainment crafted to be easily digested. One agent went so far as to tell Harriet that her book was a "commercial impossibility." Harriet took that as a compliment.

She began composing a new entry for her blog.

The pages herewith have been slavishly devoted to the exaltation of literature, the celebration of writing as a noble art and the writer's life as an exalted quest to enrich the soul of civilization. At times we are harsh critics of books and writers that, frankly, just aren't good enough. It's a dirty job, but we are the speakers of truths, members of the resistance, the rare few to speak the words that must be spoken.

Alas, such is the weary state of intellectual discourse in these times that we are forced to take action. To woman the battlements and storm the ramparts, to shout the truth and put an end to literary frauds perpetrated by commercial publishers for the sole purpose of making money.

If you are, like us, a warrior for literature, a crusader for culture, then you will help us put a stop to these outrages, this callithump of fraud, this spectacle of flimflam masquerading as a novel written by a reality television actor. Now is the time to say *ça suffit!*

12

NYC

The thing about living in New York City that really bothered Curtis was the lack of easy access to bathrooms. He'd knocked back a couple mugs of coffee at home, then grabbed a third at Café Grumpy to drink on the train and now found himself stuck on the G at Court Square in Long Island City due to some track fire farther up the line. Curtis couldn't really follow everything that crackled and fritzed over the loudspeaker, but the news wasn't good, he could tell by the world-weary, no-reason-to-panic inflection in the conductor's voice. The delay meant that by the time he changed trains and pulled into the Seventh Avenue station, his skinny jeans were pressing on his full bladder, causing him to stare out from under his porkpie hat with a panicky squinch.

As he hustled toward the building on Broadway he scanned the street for a restaurant or coffee shop, someplace, anyplace, that would let him urinate before he had to go to the publisher's office, ask for the bathroom key, and suffer the humiliation of knowing that everyone was waiting, looking at their watches and silently judging him.

Which is exactly what happened.

Curtis strode into the foyer and, trying to keep from sounding hysterical, asked for directions to the restroom.

He walked down the hallway, moving as quick as he could without breaking into a sprint. For some reason, the closer he got to the bathroom door the more his bladder shrieked, and by the time he stood over the urinal, watching several cups of recycled coffee hit the porcelain, his eyes welled with tears of relief.

He studied his reflection in the mirror as he washed his hands. Was this the face of a sellout? Or was this the look of a man who could put a down payment on a two-bedroom in Brooklyn? Maybe there wasn't a difference.

It had always annoyed Curtis that, no matter how scrupulously he attempted to dry his hands—and he used multiple paper towels—they never quite got dry. There was always some residual moisture, an aura of clamminess that clung to his fingers long after he'd tried to dry them. He'd shake hands with whomever he was meeting and see the look on their faces, a microbial fear flickering in the eyes, as their smooth, dry hands clasped his moist palms.

Curtis returned to the receptionist's desk and noticed a stack of promotional bookmarks heralding a bestselling mystery author famous for writing books with baked goods in the title: "crumpet," "scone," and "muffin," to name a few. He remembered a joke he'd read about the author on a blog about the series being "toast." He started to repeat it, just as the editor came out to greet him. "Curtis?"

"Hi."

She looked like an editor. In other words, she looked smart and decisive and stylish, and she had cool glasses. She extended her hand. "So nice to meet you. We loved what you did with Sepp Gregory. That was amazing."

Curtis had wanted to make a good first impression. So after rinsing, he had really made an effort. He used four paper towels and then flapped his hands around in the air, like a shadow puppeteer controlling spastic pterodactyls, before wiping them on his shirt and jamming them into his trouser pockets.

Curtis hoped for the best and shook hands with the editor. "Thanks."

"C'mon. The team's waiting."

She turned and strode down the hallway. Curtis saw her discreetly wipe her palm on the side of her skirt.

. . .

After having his moist hands clasped halfheartedly by everyone around the table, Curtis slipped into a chair and the meeting began. It was unusual for a publisher to throw together a meeting like this, but Amy had told him that they were fast-tracking this project. They weren't screwing around, and wanted him to meet the team who would be guiding the book from concept to the bookshelves of America. It would be his team, he was the quarterback, and it was important that he went into the meeting with a positive attitude.

Around the conference table sat the fresh-faced future of the publishing industry. The editor introduced them, but Curtis wasn't good with names and they entered and exited his consciousness as soon as they were mentioned. There were a couple of publicists and marketing people who all looked friendly and professional and surprisingly peppy, a woman from sales who looked about eighteen, and a slightly scruffy art director. They were all young and hip and Curtis felt like he was in a room full of overachievers, AP honor students eager to prove themselves.

The art director lifted a mock-up cover of what a Roxy Sandoval novel would look like. "This is just something we threw together yesterday."

Curtis looked at the cover. There was a very revealing photo of Roxy Sandoval nearly topless at the beach, with only a light coating of sand covering her breasts, enough to make it somehow palatable for the general public in much the same way a chicken fried steak is somehow more acceptable than raw meat. The title, *Sandy Panties,* was sprayed across the top in a hot pink graffiti-style font that looked like a calculated attempt to reach the edgy urban market. Curtis leaned forward and squinted. He saw the words "as told to Curtis Berman," in a microscopic and stunningly dull blue on the bottom. "You put my name on it?"

The editor smiled at him and folded her hands in front of her. "What do you think?"

Curtis looked up. "Wow."

"Wow is right. This is the book America is waiting for."

...

To celebrate being the writer of the forthcoming and sure to be runaway bestseller, *Sandy Panties,* and to ease his deep sense of shame and personal failure, Curtis walked out of the publisher's office and across midtown to the Apple store on Fifth and Fifty-Ninth. He'd considered going to a bar and getting trashed; that's what a lot of writers do when they sell their souls, that's what he imagined Faulkner or Franzen or Bret Easton Ellis would do. They would salve their wounded—but greatly enriched—pride with a few doses of pricey firewater. But he could get drunk later. Instead he pulled out his credit card and purchased a top-of-the-line, ultrathin MacBook Air. If he was going to produce dross, he'd at least write it on a nice laptop.

13

San Francisco

Sepp had given his talk—Brenda called it a "spiel"—and now he was sitting at a makeshift table at Green Apple Books signing books. It was way more fun than the drop-in signings because his fans were here. There were a lot of them too. There must've been a hundred. At least. They were mostly female, which normally would've been totally cool, but now it kind of freaked him out. Not that they were like the women in his panic-attack day terror—these women weren't outwardly horny or chanting his name or doing anything scary—mostly they were waiting patiently for a turn to have him autograph their copies of *Totally Reality*.

Sepp wasn't what you'd call superstitious, but he sometimes felt like he was psychic. You know, you get a vision or a feeling or a premonition that something's going to happen and then, like, it totally does, like when you're swimming in the ocean off Swami's and you just feel that you're about to get munched by something so you haul ass out of the water and then the next day some surfer gets his board chomped by a big fish. That kind of thing had happened to him before and so now that the women of San Francisco weren't screaming for his cock, well, Sepp felt relieved. It was bittersweet, for sure, because normally who wouldn't want the women of San Francisco screaming for their cock?

After his coffee with Caitlin, Sepp had done something he hadn't done in months. He called Dr. Jan in Los Angeles. He told Dr. Jan about the panic attack and his conversation with Caitlin, and how he was worried that he had cancer or some kind of brain tumor that was causing his erectile dysfunction. Dr. Jan told him to stay calm and said that he might be having trouble processing something she called the "cognitive dissonance" that can occur from being on a reality TV show. That's exactly how Dr. Jan said it. It made Sepp's head spin to think that there was a danger of going crazy from being on a reality TV show. Seriously, right? You think they'd warn you. Dr. Jan told Sepp to stop by when he got to LA. Just making the appointment made Sepp feel better.

Sepp signed another book and smiled. The women in San Francisco were a lot different than the women in Seattle. Gone was the snugly wool and cozy flannel. In San Francisco they seemed to be into expensive denim and stylish cotton blouses. Their shoes were different too. There were no waterproof boots in the San Francisco crowd. Sepp remembered the *Love Express* blind date he'd had in Seattle: a beautiful dark-haired software engineer with cool glasses that made her look like the winner of a Miss Science contest. Sepp had really liked her until he discovered that she didn't shave her legs or under her arms. That was too European for him. At the time it had grossed him out, but now that he thought about it, maybe she was just trying to stay warm.

As the line moved forward, Sepp smiled, shook hands, posed for photos, and turned on the charm. He realized that his fans could be divided into three different groups: the hot young women who were attracted by his celebrity and rippling abs, the chubby romantics who wanted to help him find true love, and dudes.

"You've had bad luck with women."

Sepp looked up and saw a tall, blond woman smiling at him. Lankily limbed with her hair yanked back in a ponytail, she had the look of a former college volleyball player. Sepp couldn't help but notice that she'd used some kind of glitter-infused makeup; her cheeks sparkled like a disco ball.

Sepp shrugged. "It happens to everyone."

What could he say that hadn't been said in every gossip column and magazine, and on *Entertainment Tonight, Access Hollywood,* and all those late-night talk shows? The blonde handed her copy of *Totally Reality* to Sepp, making sure she brushed her fingers against his hand. "Are you still looking?"

"For what?"

"For the one?"

Sepp thought about it. "Yeah. I guess I am."

The blonde beamed. "That's the spirit. You'll find that special someone." She leaned over and whispered. "She might even be right under your nose."

Sepp smelled her minty-fresh breath and looked up at her. He was struck by the fact that behind her cheerleader-meets-raver exterior she had crazy eyes. Or maybe she was stoned. But whether they were baked or insane, her eyes were definitely giving him psycho signals. There was something about them that made him freeze, like she was putting him in a trance. He wondered if the fish he'd eaten at lunch was fugu. That was the Japanese blowfish. He'd heard a surfer buddy who'd been to Japan talk about it once. It's like you eat the fish and then you can't move, but your brain still works, but you can't talk or anything, and then you die. Which was fucked up. That's how this glitter cheerleader was making Sepp feel. Fugu.

The blonde leaned in even closer and Sepp suddenly wished Len was a real bodyguard. "The universe has plans for you."

A voice from the line broke the spell. "Are you fucking kidding me?"

Sepp felt power return to his body and turned toward the voice. He saw a petite woman with chunky eyeglasses standing there with her arms crossed impatiently, a snarl twisting her lips. She was dressed in black jeans and a black cotton blouse, like a beatnik or, maybe, Johnny Cash.

The woman in black glared at the blonde. "I haven't got all fucking day."

The blonde smiled at Sepp. "Why don't you sign my book afterwards."

She attempted a wink, just to make sure he understood exactly what she had in mind. But Sepp didn't want a rerun of his failure in Seattle. Besides, this woman scared him.

"They've got stuff planned for me. I'd better sign it now."

The blonde smiled wistfully. "One door closes, another opens. Just make it out to Lisa Starflower."

Sepp signed the book and handed it back. She let her fingers touch his again.

"Good luck on your quest, Sepp. I'll pray for you."

"Thanks."

The woman in black stepped forward, not so subtly body-checking the blonde out of the way, and slammed her book on the table.

"Can you inscribe it for me?"

Sepp was taken aback by her aggressiveness. There was something about this girl that he'd never seen before. He actually felt flustered, and not in a good way.

"Sure."

"Write, 'I'm ashamed that I wrote this so-called book.' And then sign it 'fallaciously yours.' I'll help you with the spelling. 'Fallaciously' is a big word. But a good one. It's from *fallacia*. That's Latin for 'deception.'"

Sepp looked at her. She was definitely a hottie, but she should really try to improve her attitude. Sepp turned on the charm. "What about 'fellatio'? Do you know where that comes from?"

She gave him a look that reminded him of his teachers in school when he said something stupid. "From *fellatus*, also Latin."

Sepp went to his default setting with women and apologized.

"I'm sorry you had to wait so long."

"Oh. It's worth it."

Sepp nodded. "I have the best fans in the world!"

Several women who were listening in the line cheered when he said it. From the back one shouted, "We love you Sepp!" Another voice said, "Show us your abs!" This was followed by a wave of nervous laughter. Sepp stood up and looked down the line of fans. "Are you ready?"

A cheer rose from the crowd. Sepp lifted his T-shirt. There was a flurry of clicks and whirs and snaps as various digital devices captured the moment.

The woman in black turned and fumed at Sepp. "Great. How many fucking Facebook pages will this be on?"

Sepp grinned at her. "A whole lot."

"Make them delete the photos."

She seemed serious and it caused Sepp to drop his shirt and sit back in the chair. Brenda had warned him about freaky people he might meet on his tour, but this was the first one he'd encountered who was so angry. "Hold on a sec. What did I ever do to you?"

"You've denigrated the culture of words and ideas."

"How'd I do that?"

"With this. Your so-called opus." She waved the book in his face. "Did you even write it, or did they have a ghostwriter churn out the pablum?"

Sepp tried to hide his expression. He wasn't going to admit that he hadn't written the book. He couldn't. In his contract he'd had to say that, if asked, he would say that, for sure, he'd written every single word. But his face betrayed him. He was never a good liar.

She stopped and looked at him. "You didn't, did you?"

Sepp didn't know what to say to her, not really. What was up with the women of San Francisco? One minute they're fugu-hypnotizing you and the next they want your nuts on a stick. But he'd looked her in the eye and now he knew that she knew and, really, now that she knew he didn't really have to say anything.

There was a long pause and then, finally, she said, "Make it out to Harriet."

14

San Francisco

Harriet sat on the Muni and flipped through her freshly signed copy of *Totally Reality* as the trolley wobbled up Folsom Street. She was looking to see if there was any acknowledgment or credit for a ghostwriter, but there was no mention at all. Maybe they got a real ghost to do it. Or maybe they got a real literary writer to do it—some midlist writer who was so ashamed by their greed, so embarrassed by how low they'd fallen, that they made sure their name didn't appear anywhere on the book.

A young woman leaned over from the row behind her. "That's the best book I've ever read."

Harriet turned and narrowed her eyes at the woman. "Then you need to read more books."

...

The first thing Harriet did when she got home was feed her cat. She opened a can of cat food—the organic kind that the vet had recommended from the specialty pet shop—and, as the slightly acrid smell of whatever they put in boutique cat food assaulted her nose, it dawned on her that Sepp Gregory wasn't the culprit. She hated to admit it, but with his sun-stoned Beach Boy smile and his ripped body, he had a certain innocent charm, a wild and free naïveté that stirred her in ways that made her feel slightly uncomfortable. It was the kind of emotional response you'd have for a slightly retarded puppy, torn between cuddling it and having it put down.

It was the publisher and their proxy, the ghostwriter, who were committing crimes against humanity. Sepp Gregory was the beard, the patsy, the fall guy.

Often Harriet would write about her responsibility as a critic; she wasn't afraid to step forward and take the mediocre to task for their simplemindedness or to banish terrible writers to critical oblivion, but picking on Sepp was too easy; it would be intellectually lazy. If she was going to do her job as a literary critic then she should identify the true writer and hold him or her responsible. After all, if no one agreed to ghostwrite this utterly useless shit, then those books would never see the light of day. If it weren't for ghostwriters, publishers would have to look for new writers, new voices to discover. Writers like Harriet. It was the avaricious and greedy ghostwriters who were facilitating this endless stream of mind-numbing text-feces. They were the ones she needed to stop.

She picked up her cell phone. Harriet had friends in publishing, especially some of the smarter publicists and marketing gurus who kept her mailbox filled with advance copies of forthcoming books for her to consider reviewing. Even though it was after eleven in New York, she called the mobile number of the publicist for *Totally Reality*.

"This is Brenda."

"Hey, it's Harriet Post from San Francisco. Sorry about the time difference."

There was a pause on the line and then Brenda said, "What's up?"

"I'm reading Sepp Gregory's book and I wondered who ghosted it. I mean, the writing is great."

This time the pause was so long that Harriet thought she might've dropped the call, but then Brenda said, "This is off the record?"

"No. On the record."

This time there was no hesitation.

"Sepp Gregory wrote the book. And I'm going back to sleep."

Harriet heard the line click off. She sat there for a moment staring at her phone, then realized she was grinding her teeth. She put her bite guard in and considered her next move. Why hadn't she asked him when she had him cornered in the bookstore? Surely he would know the name of the person who wrote his book.

She opened up her laptop and googled her way over to the *Totally Reality* website. She wanted to check to see where Sepp was appearing next. She was miffed to see that he didn't have any more public appearances in the Bay Area and was going to be in Los Angeles. Harriet didn't really have the money to go flying around after people, but she knew she was on to something. Not just a review or essay or blog post, but an exposé about ghostwriters and celebrities and their fans, the whole culture that encouraged them. It would be an important book, like Upton Sinclair's *The Jungle,* only instead of a slaughterhouse for meat, she'd be in the slaughterhouse of ideas and originality. She'd be there in the first person, on the abattoir floor, watching the publishing-industry spam-

spewers making sausage out of the belly buttons and assholes
of pop culture. If she couldn't swing a book deal, maybe it was
a piece that would appeal to *The New York Times Magazine*
or *Byliner;* maybe *The Paris Review* or *The New Yorker*. At the
very least *Gawker* would be interested.

Harriet had wanted to crack open Roberto Bolaño's new
book, the fourteenth posthumous novel of the talented Chilean writer to be published—at only four hundred pages, it
was also one of his shortest posthumous books—but decided
she should do her research. If she was really going to get to
the bottom of this and take down the ghostwriter, she'd better read some of the book. She didn't want to be accused of
not reading it, of making assumptions, of judging a book by
its cover. Even though, in this case, the cover was a full-color
glossy of Sepp and his amazing torso, which was pretty fucking easy to pass judgment on.

She curled into her reading chair, her cat immediately
jumping up to sit on her legs and clean itself, and cracked
open her copy of *Totally Reality.*

Surprisingly, it didn't suck.

By the second page Harriet involuntarily gasped. She
couldn't believe what she was reading. It wasn't the story that
caused the convulsive spasm in her lungs—she couldn't care
less about the travails of some jughead sweating in a gym—it
was the writing. The prose was gorgeous. Every line sang with
luminous precision. The language was knowing and direct,
and yet also elegant and clever. There were echoes of Nabokov
mixed with a touch of the contemporary; a little Michael
Chabon and Dana Spiotta ignited with the street argot of
Junot Díaz. And yet it was distinctly original.

Harriet couldn't keep her critic brain from marveling, from spinning out adjectives of praise for the work. And because the writing was so delicious, she found herself reading compulsively, turning the page to see what would happen next; the story of a buff and burnished beach volleyball player's crush on a hot Latina becoming epic and deeply moving.

15

In Transit

Curtis looked down at his new shoes. Pete had made them and, though they had some kind of steampunk perforated design along the sides, they were incredibly stylish. Comfortable too. They only real drawback was the soles weren't scuffed up enough to provide traction and Curtis had almost fallen on his ass in the airport. Still, it was an incredibly nice gift and Curtis found himself thinking that Pete wasn't such a bad roommate, even if his odd hobbies sometimes stunk up the kitchen.

Curtis pulled his backpack out from under the seat in front of him, lowered his tray table, and set his new MacBook Air down on it. The plane offered wi-fi so he keyed in his credit card number, glancing to his right to make sure that the heavyset businesswoman sitting next to him was engrossed in the crossword puzzle inside the in-flight magazine. Normally he would've read a book, but he wanted to do some research before he met with Roxy Sandoval and felt justified paying for the wi-fi. Besides, now he could put it on his expense account. Curtis knew a bit about Roxy from his chats with Sepp, but he didn't really know what had happened to her since *Sex Crib*. He began with a simple Google search.

There were a surprising number of photos of Roxy, spreads of her pouting and posturing in *Maxim, Esquire,* and even nude shots from *Playboy's* "Girls of Reality TV" special edition. He skimmed articles about her diet—"lean protein, vegetables, and lots of tequila"—her exercise regimen—"squats for a tight ass, and then lots and lots of sex"—and her new-age approach to spirituality—"when the spirit moves you, move your spirit." She had a *Wikipedia* page with her basic biographical information—where she was born, what cities she'd lived in, her parents' names and occupations—and he found a copy of Roxy's old high school transcript that was put online by a fan. He wasn't surprised to learn that she'd been a straight-C student with a history of disciplinary problems.

Curtis googled on. He scoured in-depth interviews covering Roxy's ambivalent feelings about stiletto heels because they "mangled her feet, but made her ass look awesome," how silk made her feel more like a woman, how she would never ever dye her hair red, and how she "identified as bisexual."

He bookmarked some pages, not the ones about Roxy or her fitness tips, but a list of famous sushi bars he wanted to eat in now that his publisher had given him a corporate credit card to cover his travel expenses while he researched the book. He couldn't fly first class, but he could stay at a groovy hotel and eat sushi every night. They wouldn't begrudge him that. The success of *Sandy Panties* was riding on his happiness.

He surfed over to his favorite lit blog, a site called *The Fatal Influence,* to see what was happening in the literary world. He was surprised—and secretly a little thrilled—to see that the blog was discussing *Totally Reality.* Curtis didn't think the serious and hyper-intelligent Harriet Post would even bother discussing commercial fiction, but there she was, cutting to the core of the problem with a rapier-slash of insight. He'd always thought of her as a kindred spirit. He'd been inspired by her novel, *The Huntress of Ecstatic, Oregon,* which really deserved a wider audience.

Curtis was interrupted by an email from a real estate broker he'd contacted. He followed the links and began reading intently about various carriage houses, convertible 1 + 1s, brownstones, and whatever else the broker could find in his price range. There were listings for a brand-new boutique condo project in Vinegar Hill, and a classic co-op in Cobble Hill. There were so many fantastic choices. This was way more exciting than writing a book. Curtis closed his eyes and smiled, letting the possibilities dance in his head. He'd always wanted to be a part of the home-owning cult and now it was within his reach. He felt a gush of happiness fill his chest. Soon he'd be spending his weekends testing colors on the living room walls and complaining about the cost of curtains to his friends. This was almost as good as a MacArthur genius grant. In fact it was better. He'd earned it. Curtis felt his pants tighten.

"You must be quite a fan."

Curtis opened his eyes and saw the big-boned businesswoman in the seat next to him—he'd been inhaling her perfume for a couple hours—pointing to his computer screen and an image of Roxy Sandoval in a bikini, bent over and ready to hike a football to some famous quarterback. He cursed himself for not putting his headphones on. Nobody bothers you if you've got your Bose QuietComfort clamped over your ears. Now he had to make conversation.

"Oh, um, I'm just doing some research."

She smiled, revealing bright white teeth framed by orangey-red lipstick.

"You must have an interesting job."

She seemed to say it without judgment, but it ruined his real estate buzz. Curtis sat up, his penis pushing against his pants. He felt a rush of embarrassment, like when he was in high school fantasizing about the faint outline of the bra of the girl in the seat in front of him and the next thing he knew, he was called to the blackboard to stand in front of the class, hoping nobody noticed his raging teenage boner.

"I'm writing a book."

The woman laughed. "A book about her?"

Curtis adjusted his glasses and nodded. "According to my publisher, it's what America's waiting for."

16

Los Angeles

Sepp entered the green room and surveyed the offerings. There was a bowl of fresh fruit sitting on the table by a couch, a thermos of coffee with one of those pump squirters, and a little fridge filled with cans of Red Bull. Sepp was reaching for a Red Bull when he saw himself in the mirror. He groaned and lay down on the floor.

LA's version of Len was a media escort named Kathryn, an attractive woman in her early forties with a wild poodle of blond hair framing a face that now looked down on Sepp with real concern.

"Are you okay?"

Sepp nodded and began doing sit-ups. "Count for me."

"I'm sorry?"

"Count my crunches."

"Out loud?"

"Yeah."

Sepp began to crunch. Kathryn began counting. "Thirteen, fourteen, fifteen, sixteen . . ."

A young woman wearing a walkie-talkie headset entered the room. She saw Sepp on the floor, then looked at Kathryn.

"What's he doing?"

"Crunches."

Sepp looked up at Kathryn. "Don't stop counting."

"Sixty-three, sixty-four, sixty-five . . ."

The woman looked at a clipboard. "We need to go over a couple things."

Sepp exhaled and began to bicycle his legs as he did crunches. "Go ahead."

"Sixty-seven, sixty-eight, sixty-nine, seventy . . ."

The woman was obviously flustered. "Why are you doing this?"

"They're going to ask me to take my shirt off . . ."

"Eighty, eighty-one, eighty-two . . ."

". . . and I want my abs to look super cut."

"I can assure you that they won't ask you to take your shirt off. It's not in the script."

"Ninety, ninety-one, ninety-two . . ."

Sepp didn't stop. He knew that you couldn't trust the script. Life wasn't scripted, you know, or it shouldn't be because if it was scripted then it was boring like his friends who went to college and then got out and took stupid jobs and got married. Dude, that's the script. That's what they want you to do. Sepp felt better improvising. That's what you do in a volleyball game. You don't know where they're gonna hit it so you got to be on your toes. That's what was so awesome about reality TV. You don't know what's going to happen until you get there and sometimes you still don't know what happened until the show airs. Isn't that why people watch? For the unscripted moments?

The count hit one hundred and he switched to alternating his crunches from side to side. The young woman with the clipboard listened to something on her headset, then turned to Kathryn. "I'll come back. How many of these is he going to do?"

Kathryn shrugged and kept counting. "One twenty-one, one twenty-two, one twenty-three . . ."

Sepp looked up at the producer. "I usually do about five hundred."

. . .

It was going to be a busy day. Sepp had already done two phone interviews with East Coast radio stations—Brenda called them "phoners"—as Kathryn drove like Richard Petty, careening through the morning gridlock, to get him from the hotel to the studio on time. Considering the fact that he was being bounced from side to side as the car ricocheted through traffic jams and raced down obscure side streets—the motion causing Sepp to feel slightly carsick—the phoners had gone okay.

The first was with one of those wild and crazy morning shows where the DJs said outrageous things, played goofy sound effects, honked horns, and peppered him with questions about the true heft of Roxy Sandoval's breasts—"They're not real, are they?"—and asked if a bisexual woman's vagina tasted different than a straight one's. One of the hosts was obsessed with anal sex and kept making jokes about Roxy's "back door" while the other host kept calling Sepp "Play-yuh" and banging a cowbell every time he said it.

The DJs wanted to know who was riding in the limo with him. Was it another reality star? Pamela Anderson? Kim Kardashian? Kimberly from the LA episode of *Love Express*? Sepp had to laugh. People who thought that being on book tour was some kind of glamorous babe-magnet all-night rock 'n' roll party didn't know what they were talking about. Dude, when he was promoting a TV show it was all fancy champagne, *America's Next Top Model* wannabes, and five-star hotels. The network would send over a stylist to dress him, a hair person to put product in, and a town car to take him to all the fancy parties. The book business was totally different. Sepp had to fly business class and didn't get a limo; he'd be picked up at his destination by media escorts who, while being perfectly nice people, drove Toyotas and Hondas, not banana-yellow super-stretch Hummers.

At first Sepp thought his publisher was just super cheapo, but then he learned that he was getting actual star treatment for an author. This, it seemed, was as good as it got, the book business operating on more of a "Go Greyhound" philosophy than Hollywood.

Sepp didn't want to tell the DJs that he was driving in a Honda Accord with a middle-aged woman. Although if he were being truthful it wasn't so bad; the car was probably only six or seven years old and Kathryn was hot in a distinctly milfy way. So when the morning DJs pressed him for details, Sepp said, "More cowbell, amigo."

That got a big laugh.

Sepp's next phoner came five minutes after the first. A women's show about women's issues. You wouldn't think it, but this was way easier. He just told them he was looking for love, hoping that someday he'd find a woman who was authentic and real; someone who would "fit" with him. Sepp wasn't just saying that because chicks like to hear it, he actually believed it. He'd thought he'd found that woman a couple of times, but it hadn't worked out. That didn't mean he was going to stop looking.

Sepp's sincerity was totally genuine and always had an effect: It made women say "Aww," and it made them look at him with big, sympathetic eyes and reach out to touch him, maybe to see if he was real, because he was almost too good to be true, a genuine romantic with the body of a Chippendales dancer.

Sepp hung up from the phone interview and sat in the passenger seat staring out the window. He let the commercialized clutter—all that signage shouting for attention—of Hollywood roll past. Normally it would've excited him. The energy of commerce, the vibe of the metropolis. But today he wasn't feeling it.

Kathryn must've been able to tell that he was in a funk, because she tried to cheer him up.

"That was a good interview. You were great."

Sepp smiled. "Thanks."

But despite the smile on his face, he was starting to get a terrible feeling in the center of his stomach. It wasn't indigestion or acid reflux or anything that you could treat with bicarbonate; this sensation was some kind of anxiety-spewing jellyfish-of-fear spreading its icy tentacles through his body, making his heart pound, twisting his bowels. It was another panic attack. This one came with the creeping realization that maybe, just maybe, he was the butt of some massive joke, a conspiracy to ridicule him, and the whole entire world was in on it. It was not a great feeling. Dude. Not at all.

Sepp wished the Honda Accord had a confessional. That's the one thing Sepp loved the most about being on a reality TV show—besides all the hooking up with hotties, the free booze and stuff. The confessional was that little private room where you could bare your soul. It's just you, a chair, a camera, and one of the producers. You just take a seat and start talking. Spill your guts, let it all hang out. Totally tell it like it is. You can be conflicted, upset, bewildered, betrayed, happy, hurt, or ecstatic; you can be a churning ball of confusion and misplaced emotions. You can shout, you can cry, you can make fun of the people who upset you or threaten to punch them in the throat. Over-the-top emotion is encouraged; tantrums, fits, and blubbering like a jilted teenager on prom night are the currency of the confessional and the producer is there to help keep you talking. Sometimes the producer would say stuff to make you mad, like how Bryce or Oscar was hitting on Roxy; other times they'd make you feel great, tell you that you were "King of the Crib." It was all about getting in touch with your feelings. When you finally saw it on TV, the editors had somehow made sense of it. They made sense of you. It's like they know you better than you know you. Dude. It's so weird. There you are on TV and you actually look like you know what you're talking about. Like you know who you are and all your emotions and feelings and thoughts actually add up to something. It's not like that in real life.

He was glad he'd made the appointment with Dr. Jan. She'd know what to do.

. . .

Sepp took the elevator up to the third floor and found Dr. Jan's office. He opened the door and went into an empty waiting room. The office was in Beverly Hills and looked fancy, like some of the houses he'd seen in Newport Beach when he was working for a catering company—they always had to be super careful not to spill any red wine or drop any salmon mousse on the carpet at those places. There was a nice painting on the wall, a picture of some fields with a barn in the distance.

He sat down and started to read a magazine about golf, but couldn't concentrate. His nerves were still jangling from the panic he'd had in the car. Dr. Jan opened the door to the waiting room.

"Come on in."

Dr. Jan's office had more boxes of tissue than Sepp had ever seen. There were pillows too. Lots and lots of pillows.

"Why don't you take the couch?" Dr. Jan sat in a chair and pointed to the couch.

Sepp sat down and took a deep breath. He was feeling shaky, like he might hurl, like how he felt when he first got dumped. Dr. Jan didn't look like she looked on TV. She didn't have much makeup on and looked older than she had a year ago, and she was wearing glasses—Sepp remembered one time Roxy made fun of some dude because he wore glasses—and on TV, Dr. Jan always wore suits, but here in her office she was wearing blue jeans and a cotton sweater.

Sepp had only had sessions with Dr. Jan on TV, so it was a little weird to be in her office. There was no camera or sound or anything. It was just the two of them.

There was no director to tell him what to do, and, for a few minutes, Sepp didn't know how he was supposed to start or what to say. But then Dr. Jan asked him why he was there and Sepp told her about his San Francisco sex-panic daydream. She made some notes on a pad and then looked at him.

"Are you afraid of women?"

"I like women."

"What is your relationship with your mother like?"

Sepp thought about his mother. He hardly saw her anymore. She had gotten remarried to a guy who owned a couple of drag racers and they were always traveling around in an RV going from race to race. Last time he talked to her was almost two months ago when they were getting ready for the Rebel Yell Funny Car Reunion in Marietta, Georgia.

"We get along pretty good. I mean, I love my mom. We're amigos."

"Why do you think this daydream caused a panic attack?"

"I was hoping you'd tell me."

Dr. Jan smiled. "I'd bet you have a pretty good idea."

Sepp realized that he was hugging one of the pillows. "Roxy." He sniffled. He wasn't crying or anything, but his nose was a little drippy like maybe he had allergies, so he reached for a tissue.

Dr. Jan nodded and leaned forward. "Look, Sepp, everyone gets their heart broken. It's part of life and in this case I don't think you should take it personally."

"Why not?

"Because she was a contestant on a TV show. So were you. It's not real."

"It seemed real."

...

How many times had Dr. Jan seen this? Twenty? Thirty? Maybe more. Dr. Jan didn't want to be unkind, but if she were being objective and honest, she would have to say that, generally speaking, the people who became contestants on reality TV shows had lower IQs than the general public. They were usually pageant queens and jocks, airheads and athletes. You didn't get a lot of doctors or other professionals on these shows. Usually the women were cosmetologists or bartenders or worked in some kind of marketing. The guys were almost always in sales. They were not the cream of the crop and there was a reason for that. A rational, intelligent person with the ability to think critically would not do half the ridiculous things the producers asked them to do. They wouldn't, for example, lie to each other and then hook up in the hot tub in full view of the person they'd just lied to. Which is not to say that smart people don't cheat, but that they don't do it so stupidly. Reality show contestants were cast because they weren't the brightest of the bunch and then they were plied with copious amounts of alcohol, innuendo, and misinformation.

When the tribe eventually spoke or the rose was given to someone else, they came down hard. One minute they're in a fantasy land of hotties and hunks without a care in the world, the next minute they're back home with a stack of bills to pay, an angry boyfriend or girlfriend, and a feeling of being completely disconnected from the ordinary world. They usually fell into depressed behavior, lying around watching TV, unable to go to work, or they'd swing wildly into partying too much and hooking up with strangers, trying to re-create the feeling they had on the show.

Celebrity, even the passing fifteen minutes of fame you get from being on these shows, is a powerful narcotic, it warps your sense of who you are and where you fit in the world. The camera may add ten pounds to your body, but it also completely distorts your self-perception. Dr. Jan had to counsel lots of deluded reality stars, men and women who thought they were just as talented as George Clooney or Amy Adams and there was no reason why they couldn't make it big. Those people now waited tables and tended bar at various restaurants in the Valley, although, to be fair, Dr. Jan had seen several working as hostesses.

Sepp was an unusual case. Because he'd been on two shows that were almost back-to-back he'd lived outside of ordinary reality for longer than most contestants. And even then, his day-to-day reality consisted of an almost reality TV–like schedule. In other words, he didn't do much. Had no real responsibilities. His brain might not notice the difference between being on a show and his routine existence.

Dr. Jan thought that there might be a book in this. A real in-depth study of perception and reality framed by the psychological damage reality TV could inflict on a normal psyche. After her appearance on *Love Express* a few agents had called, including a team from William Morris Endeavor, all wanting to sign her up for a daytime chat show like *Dr. Oz*. That didn't interest Dr. Jan. But a book deal? That had prestige written all over it.

She smiled at Sepp. "You just have to get back out there."

"I've been out there, Dr. Jan, and it ain't workin'." Sepp tried to hide the pain in his voice, but Dr. Jan could detect it.

She nodded and said, "They always say that there are lots of fish in the sea, and I know it sounds corny, but it's true. You just have to hang in there."

Sepp noticed that Dr. Jan nodded a lot. "It's just . . ." Sepp tried to think of the right word for what he wanted to say. He finally settled on "humiliating."

Dr. Jan was suddenly more interested. "You mean sexually?"

Sepp nodded as he blew his nose.

"How long has this been going on?"

"Since Roxy."

Dr. Jan looked surprised. "You're a young man. Have you seen a urologist?"

Sepp nodded. "I'm fine physically. Until I get with a girl. I mean, I can beat off and everything."

Dr. Jan stood up and went to her desk. She opened a drawer and pulled out some little packets.

"This issue sounds a little more complicated than anything I can help you with today, but here." She handed him a couple of packets.

"These are Clonazepam. Take one if you start to have another episode."

"Okay."

"But if you do, I want you to call me. Let me know what's going on."

Sepp nodded. She handed him another sample packet. "These are Viagra. Try one and see if it doesn't get you back into the game."

Sepp looked at the samples. "Can I take them at the same time?"

Dr. Jan smiled. "It's more fun that way."

17

Los Angeles

C urtis sat in the back of a taxi and stared at the massive melon of a head plopped atop the body of the cab driver. The driver's head was shaved, and rolls of fat undulated down his neck like soft-serve ice cream. As far as Curtis could tell the driver didn't speak any English and an unidentifiable flag hung from the rearview mirror, its blue, black, and white stripes signifying nothing to him.

He looked out the window and leered at Los Angeles. It was one gigantic nightmare, a hideous sprawlscape with generic buildings and traffic so ferocious that the streets were like parking lots; cars were reduced to idling hunks of metal baking in the blistering sun, reflecting glare into Curtis's eyes, searing his corneas. It was obscene; millions of cars, each one holding precisely one driver, spewing noxious fumes into the atmosphere. No wonder the planet was asphyxiating from greenhouse gases—this is where they were produced. This was all the proof Curtis needed that Los Angeles was destroying the world.

Curtis saw a giant drugstore—the boxy building large enough to hold all the drugstores in his neighborhood in Brooklyn—and a strip mall, a godforsaken L-shaped building that housed a Subway sandwich shop, a dry cleaner, a Chinese restaurant, and an optician. He asked the driver to stop. He had to get a pair of sunglasses or he'd need cataract surgery by the time he got to the hotel.

Curtis entered the optical shop and looked at the sunglasses on display. There were lots of stupid-looking hipster shades, sunglasses that were trying too hard. He'd brought his contacts with him. He didn't like wearing them in New York—too much grit in the air—but he was prepared to suffer the smog of Los Angeles for the chance to wear some cool shades.

It didn't take him long to find a pair of Ray-Bans that didn't look stupid. He put them on and looked at his reflection in the little mirror. They made him look cool, like a Brooklyn Steve McQueen, but weren't perfect. And he needed to look cool. He was going to be Roxy Sandoval's guest at a party later tonight, some trashy soiree at the Playboy Mansion, a full immersion in the kind of fucked-up faux-glamour universe of the grotesquely vacuous and self-absorbed. It was going to be awesome.

As a card-carrying member of the literati, Curtis knew that, on some level, partying at the Playboy Mansion should be beneath him; but he had to admit he felt a thrill, a certain frisson about going to the legendary home of Hef. Curtis had spent many hours of his youth—in between reading *Slaughterhouse-Five* and *Gravity's Rainbow*—staring at *Playboy* centerfolds and masturbating, a charter member of the Ham Slammers of America. He and his friends would cut out choice pictures from their fathers' magazines and hide them in the copy of *Stranger in a Strange Land* or whatever book it was they passed around at the time. Nothing was more fun than reading Philip K. Dick knowing that, any page now, a topless bunny was going to come leaping out of the book. So even though a part of him, a deeply rational voice buried somewhere in the recesses of his amygdala, told him that he should meet Roxy somewhere other than the Playboy Mansion—find neutral ground for their initial discussions—another part of him was excited. It would be kitsch, ironic, and cool to tell his Brooklyn pals that he'd been to the Playboy Mansion. It would give him some cred and, better, he might get to see some boobs.

Curtis adjusted his new, three-hundred-dollar Persols, paid the cab driver, careful to keep the receipt, and entered the hotel in Beverly Hills. As he waited for the receptionist to check him in, he saw three young women in bikinis out by the pool. They were unique specimens, unlike anything he'd seen before. They were simultaneously scrawny and voluptuous, with oxymoronically massive chests and teeny pinched waists. Their hair was molded into shape, their smooth skin bronzed and oiled and gleaming in the California sun, their breasts bulging out of microscopic triangles of fabric like hippopotami wearing tutus; they were absolutely repulsive, yet undeniably attractive.

The women were sitting together but they weren't talking to each other. Instead they were each focused on their smartphones.

Curtis had a flash of realization. An epiphany. He suddenly understood that he wasn't writing trash. Books like *Totally Reality* weren't pop-culture detritus or gossipy ephemera —these books were cultural anthropology, a cross-section slice of life as it was being lived in our culture right now. It wasn't that far removed from Margaret Mead or any of the serious scientists that studied the structure and mores of strange societies. These surgically enhanced skankazons were part of a subculture just as complex, ritualistic, and bizarre as any primitive tribe's. This was the world that Roxy Sandoval inhabited. These women were her. They just weren't on a reality TV show yet.

Sandy Panties could be an important book.

18

Century City

The offices of Forward, a talent agency, looked like they were designed by the same guy who did airport terminals in Japan. That's how it looked to Sepp anyway. There were signs with numbers and signs with colors and signs with colors and numbers and sometimes words and lots of empty white space so that your footsteps would echo when you walked around. Occasionally there would be some futuristic chairs clumped together. Sepp guessed you could sit in them, but he never did. He never had to wait. He was always ushered in like royalty. They would put him in a conference room with a fancy glass table and give him a filtered water or coffee or a Red Bull. They had cookies, too.

Everyone was young and well dressed and moving fast, like they were super busy doing super-important business. Everyone except his agent. She wasn't like them. That's why he liked her.

She'd spotted him in the first episode of *Sex Crib* and signed him. She'd gotten him endorsements—he always wore Adidas-brand shoes and workout clothes because they paid him to—and when *Sex Crib* was over she had put together the package—the producers and network—to make *Love Express* happen. It had been her idea to do the book and she found the book agent and the ghostwriter and everything. She was sharp and, even better, she was a cool person.

Sepp stood up when Marybeth entered the conference room.

"Hey!"

She have him a big hug—she smelled good—and then sat down in the chair next to him. He was always impressed how she looked like a total badass in her suits and stuff and, yet, she was naturally sexy. She flipped a strand of hair behind her ear, a sign that meant she was ready to get down to business.

"How's the publisher treating you?"

Sepp smiled. "I got no complaints. Everybody there is real nice."

"Well, take care of yourself. Book tours can be grueling. If you need something let me know and I'll get it handled."

"Thanks."

Sepp didn't know if Marybeth was the person he should talk to about his panic attacks, but then again, Dr. Jan had given him some pills so he thought he'd be okay. Sepp noticed that Marybeth was wearing a wedding ring, a simple gold band with some kind of writing on it.

"Did you get married?"

Marybeth smiled. "Yeah. We'd been together for a few years and it just seemed like time. Plus there were some visa issues."

"Your husband is a foreigner?"

Marybeth laughed. "Wife. She's Thai."

Sepp was surprised. Not that he cared that Marybeth was gay. Dude. Everybody knows that girl-on-girl action is hot.

He just figured that after all the time she'd been his agent, he would've known that about her.

"That's so awesome. I'm really happy for you."

Sepp leaned over and gave Marybeth a hug. "If I'd known I would've bought you a crock pot or something."

"It was a really small wedding."

"Crock pots are handy."

Marybeth laughed. "That I can't deny."

Sepp sat back down in his chair as an assistant, a young guy who looked like he was fourteen but was wearing a fancy suit, came in and put a cup of coffee in front of her.

"Thanks, Adam."

Adam sat down across the table from them and pulled out a notecard. Sepp waved at him.

"Hi, Adam."

Adam smiled. "Mr. Gregory."

Marybeth opened a folder and looked at it. "I'll be honest. There's not a lot of reality TV in the pipeline that's right for you. I've talked to the people at *The Bachelorette* and they're thinking of doing a show called *The Third Time* which you would be perfect for, but that's on hold right now."

"Third time's the charm?"

"Exactly."

"But I have some commercial offers." She flipped some pages around. "Fruit of the Loom is close to making an offer, but it'd just be print, billboards, that kind of thing."

Sepp felt a chill creep up his spine. "Me in my underwear? On a billboard?"

Marybeth shrugged. "Why not? Mark Wahlberg and David Beckham did it."

"What else?"

"Wasabi mayonnaise. That could be a good payday. Also Havaianas—you know, the flip-flops. They're sniffing around." She closed the folder. "But that's about it right now. I want to see how the book does and maybe get you something classier."

"I like wasabi."

"Yeah, but a national campaign for beer or a car company would be better for your brand than a condiment."

Marybeth always liked to tell Sepp that he was more than just a dude from San Diego, he was an international brand and they had to make smart choices to build his brand and keep it relevant. Like some reality stars just do all kinds of commercials, and dude, who could forget Roxy's stupid TV commercials for that all-day energy drink. Those didn't help her brand. But one of the problems with being a reality star is that, unless you're a star, you don't get paid. Contestants on these shows are just that, contestants. Sepp hadn't been paid anything but his travel expenses to be on *Sex Crib,* and most people, whether they're starving on a tropical island, trying to find true love, or racing around the world, don't get any money. You're not actors, you don't get royalties or residuals or anything. You're on and you get what you get and that's it. That's why *Love Express* was so good. Sepp was the star and associate producer and he got paid some serious money to bare his soul for America.

Sepp got a good payday with the book, but that money wouldn't last forever and he didn't want to end up doing night-club appearances like Cassandra from *First World Problems.*

"I think they all sound good."

Marybeth nodded. Adam made some notes.

"Okay. Let me make some calls. I should know something tonight when we go to the party."

Sepp blinked. "What party?"

Marybeth laughed. "You should read your schedule every now and then. After your reading we're going to the Playboy Mansion. Apparently Miss June is dying to meet you."

19

Los Angeles

While she waited for the rental-car clerk to finish processing her credit card and hand her the key to a super-economy car, Harriet typed a Twitter update on her iPhone and hit send. She had decided to microblog her trip to LA, driving a little traffic to her site by creating as much interest as possible in her search to find the ghostwriter. Even the mundane bus ride to the airport was already being retweeted and pingbacked and linked and Tumbled and favorited by hundreds of people.

Harriet was on to something. She could feel it. This was a big story. When she had initially planned this assault on cynical corporate profiteering at the expense of literature's soul, she had assumed that *Totally Reality* would be mediocre at best. She hadn't planned on the book being beautifully written. Now she faced a conundrum. Should the ghostwriter be praised for spinning shit into gold or excoriated for wasting his or her obvious talent? And whose fault was it really? The publisher? The agent? Or was it deeper than that? A civilization obsessed with celebrity is surely a dying culture.

She detailed her confusion, her sincere appreciation of the writing, and her deep anger at the pure sellout of it all in short bursts of text on Twitter.

@fatalinfluence *Totally Reality, entirely surprising? Enraging? Brilliant? A must read? A must never read? A supreme waste of real talent?*

It wasn't as if she read only literature. Harriet was a member of two different book groups, one that read the type of books commonly discussed on *The Millions* and in the pages of *The New York Times Book Review* and another one she went to with her friend Isabelle. That one was mostly women who did yoga together and read bestsellers and what the publishing industry called "commercial fiction." Evenings spent with Isabelle were equal parts fun—they usually ate well and drank bottles of wine—and exasperating. She'd given up trying to foist literary fiction on the group; they weren't interested in great writing, they wanted a story. Harriet began to look upon these meetings as cultural anthropology. Here was a tribe of bright, educated young women who could easily be discussing the finer points of any number of literary works but who, instead, yakked incessantly about their preternaturally gifted toddlers, real estate, and yoga vacations while guzzling glasses of good California chardonnay. Lately they'd been devouring hackneyed erotica as if they'd just discovered sex could be more than the missionary position and, to Harriet's shock and horror, they discussed these works as if they were legitimate literature. Harriet was usually quiet in these conversations, more an observer than active participant, and while she knew positively that these novels lacked literary merit, she did sometimes find herself, late at night, getting to certain scenes and reaching into her pants.

...

If she were a character in a novel, Harriet might be the loner who drifts in and out of people's lives offering scathing wisdom tinged with world-weary ennui, like Meursault in *The Stranger,* or maybe a forthright protofeminist heroine like Jane Eyre. She liked to think of herself, when she did think of herself, as someone who was a combination of the two: brutally honest and of superior intellect. Of course, her friends and family didn't see it that way. They looked at her life and thought she was lonely. What kind of young woman spends all her time at home with her nose in a book? Didn't she want a husband?

Of course, why anyone would want a husband was beyond Harriet. Unless it was a purely financial arrangement, why would any self-respecting woman limit herself like that? And men were historically unreliable. How many times had someone given themselves over to a partner only to be betrayed and discarded? Harriet had personal experience of that. Her college boyfriend, a graduate student writing his dissertation on British "Lake Poets" like Wordsworth and Coleridge, had gone to England to do some research and when he returned, presented Harriet with gonorrhea. He defended giving her the clap by reciting stanzas of romantic poetry about mariners and the lure of the sea.

While there were certain aspects of intimacy that she missed, Harriet was happy. At least she felt happy. She could find all the lovers and sex and adventure in the pages of a great book. She could be thrilled and transported and changed by art. She loved a good book more than she'd ever loved a person and there was nothing wrong with that. Wasn't it better than bragging about your kids or living vicariously through a husband? It was definitely better than getting the clap.

@fatalinfluence *We've arrived. Los Angeles, the birthplace of the In-N-Out Burger. Which we think is this city's only contribution to world culture.*

Harriet fiddled with the knobs on the dashboard of her rental car. She was trying to get the A/C to come on and cool the broiling car. Traffic was stopped, the 405 freeway a mindless pile of looping on-ramps and off-ramps apparently designed to constrict and coagulate the greatest number of cars as efficiently as possible. Harriet didn't need a dictionary of etymology to know that this section of oxymoronically named "freeway" would be more aptly called "clusterfuck." That was the perfect word for Los Angeles.

Harriet was planning to stay with an old college friend, a woman she barely knew anymore, but who was nice enough to say, via Facebook, that she had a guest room and Harriet was welcome to it. But that wasn't until later. First she had to negotiate the traffic and get to Sepp's signing.

She reached into the fast-food bag sitting on the passenger seat and pulled out an In-N-Out burger, specifically a double-double animal style. Her followers on Twitter had told her about In-N-Out's secret lexicon and hidden Bible references. None of that impressed her, but she had to admit, as she chewed a big, sloppy bite and felt a drip of sauce slip down her chin, that it was about as good as a fast-food burger could get.

@fatalinfluence *In-N-Out Double-Double Animal Style . . . it's everything you say it is.*

As she sat, sweat rolling off her head like she'd just been in a sauna, the car moving forward millimeter by millimeter, she decided she had become an instant Angeleno. She could eat and tweet and drive.

@fatalinfluence *Just discovered why people in LA shoot each other.*

20

West Hollywood

Curtis stood outside Book Soup, a bookstore on Sunset Boulevard right in the heart of the world-famous Sunset Strip, and glared at the giant photo of Sepp that was hanging in the window. He looked up at the marquee and saw Sepp's name spelled out next to the names of more illustrious authors. It annoyed Curtis that the bookstore obviously didn't have more than a couple letter *p*s. Underneath "Sepp Gregory" were the names "Chuck   alahniuk" and "Laura Li   man." Curtis would've given all his consonants to see his name up on that marquee.

He had several hours to kill before he was scheduled to meet Roxy Sandoval at the Playboy Mansion and couldn't contain his morbid curiosity. What were the crowds at a *Totally Reality* signing like? How was Sepp in front of an audience? Curtis admittedly had mixed emotions. When it first came out he didn't care if the book tanked, he had hated it, but now he desperately wanted it to succeed. Amy had been adamant about getting him a piece of the royalties, and although it was only a small percent, he'd need it for his new home, for the art he wanted to collect and the bitters he wanted to brew.

As he entered the bookstore he couldn't keep from smiling. The store wasn't big, only a couple modest rooms, but it was packed with books and laid out like a labyrinth. Books were piled on shelves, on tables, and in a couple of instances they were stacked up on the floor just like Curtis did at his house. The shelves muffled the noise from Sunset Boulevard and blocked out the glare of the sun. It was cozy and cavelike and Curtis felt like an explorer—a "spelunker." He'd always liked that word.

. . .

"I have something to confess. I was a big fan of *Love Express*. I didn't miss an episode. So for me, this is a real treat."

Sepp smiled at the bookstore manager, a cool-looking guy named Frazier, and shook his hand. Sepp noticed some gnarly tattoos peeking out from under his shirtsleeve like he was secretly wearing Japanese art under his skin. He was super friendly, giving off a vibe that was part badass, part funster, and Sepp liked him instantly. Frazier wasn't your typical bookstore employee. He was like a real dude, a bro, even. "Thanks man, thanks for having me in your store."

Kathryn had taken Sepp in through the back door of the bookstore and the three of them were now crowded into a tiny office filled with boxes. Frazier stuck his head out the door. "I'd welcome you to look around, but we've got a big crowd tonight. You're quite the draw with the ladies."

Sepp smiled. "Awesome."

Frazier smiled. "You mind just chillin' in here for a bit? I'm going to go see how we're doing."

"I'm cool."

Frazier nodded and slipped out of the room. Kathryn looked at Sepp. "You want anything? Some water or coffee?"

Sepp realized that he wasn't feeling that great. He wasn't sure if it was another panic attack or stage fright or something he'd eaten.

"There's an envelope with some pills in the car. Can you bring me one?"

"Just one pill?"

"Yeah. I don't want to carry the envelope around."

"I'll be right back."

Kathryn closed the door behind her. Sepp sat down in a chair, surrounded by books, books, and more books. Books were everywhere. What if an earthquake hit? Would he be buried under books? Is that how he would die? Drowning in book soup?

Sepp started wondering why he ever got mixed up in this book business in the first place. It wasn't like he had any books at his house. He couldn't remember the last time he read a book, although he did look at a guide to growing marijuana once. What if the books were mad at him? Like they wanted revenge because they knew he didn't write his book. Maybe the books were just waiting until he was alone with them and then they'd just all jump on him at once. Sepp looked up at the books and apologized. He hadn't meant to anger the book spirit. Was that why he couldn't get a boner? Had the Book Goddess put a curse on him?

By the time Kathryn got back with his medicine, his heart was pounding and he'd broken into a cold sweat.

...

It cost her ten bucks to park in a little lot tucked behind the Viper Room, but Harriet didn't let the high cost of parking in West Hollywood—the obvious law of supply and demand in effect—get her down for long. She was energized by her mission. The more she thought about it the more she found herself deeply curious about who the ghostwriter was. She was going to interrogate Sepp and find out. Then she was going to track the writer down and get to the bottom of this mystery. She had to know why. Why did they do it? The writing was so good she wouldn't have been surprised to learn that some down-on-her-luck Pulitzer Prize winner might've taken the job. Or worse, maybe they even liked Sepp's TV shows. Was Michael Chabon a reality TV junkie? It wasn't inconceivable.

Her lunch spun and settled in her stomach when she walked into the bookstore. Bad enough to see Sepp's name on the marquee and be greeted by a giant poster in the window— Sepp's leering grin making him look like a genuine Kentucky fried half-wit—but now, crowding in the famous bookstore was a huge crowd of people clutching copies of Sepp's book to their chests like it was the Holy Bible itself.

She turned away from the crush and headed back into the recesses of the stacks.

...

Curtis looked up and noticed that a lot of people were starting to arrive for the signing. A few collectors congregated near the back, an odd group of men with bulging sacks of books; a lanky guy with a mod haircut and carnation-colored shoes chatted with a ruddy-complexioned man in a Hawaiian shirt about first editions; a portly collector in a Harley-Davidson motorcycle T-shirt sat and encased his books in protective plastic sleeves.

Curtis felt conflicted. Why would someone want to collect a book about a reality star? Was the resale value that high? Or did they want to keep them? He was baffled and somewhat bemused and, at the same time, thrilled that there were people who thought something he wrote could be valuable, even if his name wasn't on it. This, he understood, was the ghostwriter's dilemma. He'd solve the problem with his next book. He'd make the Roxy Sandoval story even better than Sepp's book. He'd write the best celebrity novel ever. If *Totally Reality* had been his *Bartleby the Scrivener,* then *Sandy Panties* was going to be his *Moby-Dick.* Best of all, this one would have his name on it.

...

Harriet saw him out of the corner of her eye. He was her type, she could tell. Not so much because of his fancy leather shoes, or the Dickies pants, or the plain red T-shirt under a rumpled navy blazer; it was the book he was reading. He was standing in the store, his cool glasses slipping down his oddly deformed nose, perusing a copy of Steve Erickson's *Our Ecstatic Days.*

Harriet had often written about Steve Erickson; she loved writers who felt compelled to use language so rich and dense that the words became more important than the story. In a perfect book, the prose would be so resonant with meaning and metaphor that it would be infinitely dense; comprehension would require maximum mental concentration and a PhD in philosophy. The perfect book, in Harriet's opinion, would contain the universe.

Despite her ferociousness when it came to criticism, Harriet was somewhat timid when it came to members of the opposite sex. On the rare occasions when her friends set her up with someone or invited her to a dinner party only to sit her next to some single man, the conversation would invariably turn to their favorite books. This usually ended the date. Really, who claims the *7 Habits of Highly Effective People* as the best book they've ever read? She'd learned early on in the dating game that if a man says *Catcher in the Rye* is his favorite book, that just means he hasn't read any fiction since high school. And, honestly, she didn't know what to make of an adult male who claimed to admire *The Lord of the Rings*.

But there was something about this guy—he had the look, he had the book—that made Harriet say, "You read Erickson?"

The guy shoved his glasses back up his nose and turned to face her. "I read his last one."

Harriet smiled at him. "What'd you think?"

"It was challenging. I really enjoyed it."

The guy self-consciously smoothed his hair forward, so it fell across his forehead. "Are you here for the signing?"

Harriet found herself sputtering. "No. God no." She found that she couldn't control her left hand as it began to play with her hair. "I mean, yes, I am. But in a professional capacity."

"You're a journalist?"

Harriet nodded. "Yeah. And I have a blog."

"Which one?"

"*The Fatal Influence.*"

The guy's face changed. It suddenly bloomed in a mix of surprise and reverence. "You're Harriet Post?"

Harriet nodded. "That's me."

"I love your blog. I read it all the time."

Harriet extended her hand. "What's your name?"

The guy wiped his hand on his pants and then shook hers. "Curtis. I'm a fan."

His hand was warm.

...

Sepp still felt a little weird, but at least he had more energy. He stood off to the side, nodding and smiling as a woman from the store explained to the crowd that you had to buy a book if you wanted to get any memorabilia autographed and how the line was going to work. She looked hipster-nerdy in that way bookstore people always looked kinda cool. You know? Groovy eyeglasses, weird color in her hair, vintage clothes. Not sexy or trashy, just smart and proud of it. Like she had nothing to hide. She was the opposite of Roxy and Caitlin.

Sepp wondered what it would be like to get it on with a nerdy bookstore girl like the one introducing him. What if nerds were better between the sheets than hotties? OMG, dude. Wouldn't that blow your mind? What if Poindexter could give a girl multiple orgasms? Or like if Betty Bookworm could make your nuts dance in the sack? What if it was like some kind of secret that only the nerds knew and that's why you always saw nerds with other nerds? Like nerds were the hotties and hotties were really nerds and everything you thought you knew about the world was upside down and backwards?

Sepp felt his skin tingling, his face flushing. He didn't know why that was happening. He checked to make sure his zipper was pulled up.

...

Harriet couldn't see anything from the back of the mob. That's what it looked like to her. A rabble of reality show wannabes queueing to take sacrament from their savior. "Queueing" has five consecutive vowels. That's unusual.

@fatalinfluence *Queueing at Book Soup to see a slab o' abs.*

Harriet turned toward Curtis, but he'd drifted off, pushing his way deeper into the crowd until she couldn't see him. Harriet liked talking to him and wished he'd stayed to keep her company. But it was okay. She'd probably see him after the talk. Besides, she was on a mission.

...

"It is my distinct, and somewhat guilty pleasure, to introduce the man, the myth, your favorite hunk of reality, Sepp Gregory."

Sepp knew she was paying him a compliment, but he was kind of puzzled too. Why was he a guilty pleasure?

"So give him a big Book Soup welcome."

The audience—Sepp guessed about three hundred people—clapped as he stepped to the podium. He saw Kathryn, his media escort, standing in the back typing something on her smartphone. Marybeth was there too, looking at a big art book with nude ladies in it. Sepp looked out at the crowd. There were a lot of women there. He felt a hot trickle of sweat run down his side.

"Hey. Thanks. Um . . . I wrote this book to tell my story, but I wanted it to be a novel because novels are more fun to read. At least I hope you all think it's fun. And it kinda gives everyone a look at what happens behind the scenes and under the covers."

A couple of women in the audience whooped at that line. They always did.

"People always ask what inspired me. Why write this book?" Sepp's throat was dry, and he'd developed a strange tremor in his voice. He reached for a bottle of water on the podium and took a drink. "Well . . . there are a lot of reasons."

Sepp didn't tell them the truth. No one wanted him to say that it was easy money or admit that he hadn't really written it. He never mentioned the fact that he'd just bought a condo and wanted to have some money in the bank for a rainy day. They didn't want to know the truth about being a celebrity, especially not being a broke celebrity because after taxes, it's not that much and after a year or two, it's long gone. And he definitely didn't want to be one of those dudes like MC Hammer who lost everything and ended up being a preacher. That's so lame. He put his name on the book because they gave him an advance and now he was promoting the book to help make as much money as possible from it. But he didn't tell them that.

"I wanted to get my feelings across. You know, the real . . . raw stuff." Sepp realized his voice sounded shaky. He looked down at his hands and noticed they were trembling. His heart began to pound and he felt sweat roll down his face. "That you can only get into in a fictional novel . . ." He stopped midsentence and reached for the bottle of water. He gulped it down in long, desperate glugs, like he was dying of thirst.

"Sorry. Being on book tour is hard work. Harder than I thought, anyway."

And that's when he began to feel his penis grow. It was shuddering to life in pulsing spasms, like Frankenstein's monster rising off the table. He didn't know why that was happening or why he was suddenly experiencing a panic. It sucked having a panic attack in front of all these people. It made it so that he was panicking on top of a panic attack on top of a crazy boner. Maybe it was all starting to get to him, the morning DJs with their cowbells and their jokes, the TV news shows with the old dudes and the hot chicks who wanted him to strip, and the creeping feeling that he was the butt of some kind of cosmic joke. And now the bookstore woman who was kinda hot and seemed like a totally nice person was calling him a "guilty pleasure." What did that mean?

"I suppose you want me to take off my shirt."

Sepp whipped his T-shirt over his head. There was a burst of applause from the audience. Sepp flexed and there were a couple of gasps. Sepp grinned. "You know what's funny, or maybe it's not, but what I've discovered lately, is that the reality that I thought was real, you know the reality I was living, is not that same as the real reality that people really live. Like your reality is different than my reality and TV-show reality isn't like this reality or mine or yours."

He stared at the audience. "I know I'm probably not making any sense with this."

A young woman shouted from the back. "Your six-pack looks real!"

Sepp smiled and patted his washboard abs.

"Crunches. Lots and lots of crunches. Crunches are real. Even on TV. You crunch and work your abs and you know, eat a pretty lean diet and they'll look like this. They'll be real."

Sepp began to sweat harder. It was pooling under his hair like he was in the middle of a workout. He gripped the podium tightly to keep his hands from shaking, but he couldn't grip anything with his voice. He warbled and gasped, growing more panicked with each hitch and falter in his speech.

"I'm sorry. I don't normally get nervous like this."

He took another sip of water. He didn't know why he'd departed from his prepared speech, but he had and he wasn't sure how to get back to it. He was usually so relaxed. So cool. The kind of dude who could sit on his balcony naked and play the bongos on a Sunday afternoon and not have a care in the world. But here he was a guilty pleasure. A guy people made fun of. Why?

Sepp's knees buckled and he had to bear-hug the podium to keep from collapsing. He didn't know what was wrong with him. He realized he hadn't said anything for a long time.

"But, like, love is different than a sit-up. It's like you think you're in love, you have the feelings of being in love. And you see yourself on TV and that's you and you're with someone and it really looks like you're both in love. Like with each other. It's like looking at love how it's really supposed to look. Right?"

Sepp felt a strange gush of emotion, a bittersweet punch to his stomach, take the wind out of him and send liquid squirting out of his eyes.

"But, dude, the real reality is . . ."

Sepp choked on his words.

"The love isn't real love. It's something else. It's definitely not a crunch."

Sepp's voice caught again and, to the surprise of the audience, the bookstore employees, his agent, and the media escort, he stood, shirtless, at the podium and began to sob. "I'm sorry." He wiped the tears from his eyes and tried to continue. "It's really hot in here. Isn't it? I mean, I feel like my clothes are strangling me."

And with that, Sepp slid out of his pants and revealed his fully erect penis to the crowd.

. . .

It's an old saying that there's no such thing as bad publicity, and Marybeth reminded herself of that as she watched Sepp drop his pants. There was a collective gasp from the crowd, followed by the sound of hundreds of cell phones taking photos. How long before the first Instagram or Flickr hit the internet? A second? Ten seconds? They were probably already up on Twitter. Which meant that in the next ten minutes or so they'd be retweeted across the world and millions of people would get a good look at Sepp's penis. And then people would start photoshopping it. Taking Sepp's penis and making animated gifs and digital wallpaper. How long before the parodies started? Would she wake up in the morning and be able to find Sepp's penis singing Lionel Richie's "Hello" on YouTube?

The first thought that crossed her mind was that her client had lost it. He was having a nervous breakdown in public, which is, let's be honest, never a good thing. Her second thought was one of relief. If Sepp had exposed himself and revealed a normal-looking penis, well, then it's just kind of creepy, but his penis was majestic, a rigid pink shaft in full bloom. This would only enhance his brand appeal. She made a mental note to ask for more money for the underwear ad campaign.

...

"Are you okay?"

Marybeth stood there, taking in the scene. Sepp was sitting behind a counter, a towel draped across his lap, the fabric tented dramatically where his erection stood. Sepp nodded at her.

"Hey, Marybeth."

She turned and scanned the crowd. There was still a long line of fans waiting patiently to get their books signed. "You're sure you're okay?"

"It's all good. He's got my back."

Sepp nodded toward the tattooed hipster standing behind the counter. "Frazier's the best."

Frazier smiled at Marybeth. "Hey, Whatever makes him happy, you know? We're just going with it."

While Frazier handled the signing table, Kathryn walked down the line, taking names and writing them on Post-its so that Sepp didn't have to deal with all the variations of names like Debbie, Debbi, Devi, Debby, Dybbie, and whatever else their parents, desperate to be original, had come up with. Marybeth watched Sepp greet a fan and personalize her book. The girl looked at Sepp and said, "That was something I'll never forget. I hope you feel better, Sepp. "

Marybeth looked at the young woman. "Just don't put it on Facebook. Okay?"

The girl giggled. "No worries. They kick you off if you post any nudity."

Marybeth looked at Sepp and cocked an eyebrow. "Well, that's reassuring."

But as concerned about her client as she was—both his meticulously constructed brand and his apparently fragile psyche—she could tell that the fans were touched by what had happened and were being protective and gentle around Sepp.

"You want to put on some clothes?"

Sepp shook his head and began signing another book. "It's too hot."

"It's not that hot."

Sepp looked at her. "I thought I was taking a pill for, you know, stage fright. Anxiety."

Marybeth thought for a moment. "I can cancel the rest of your tour. It's not a problem."

"No. No. I'll be all right."

"Maybe you should see a doctor."

"I saw one today. I'm feeling better now."

He signed some more books. Marybeth looked over at Kathryn. "You couldn't do anything?"

Kathryn held up her hands. "It just happened."

Frazier smiled. "This is nothing. You should've seen Hunter Thompson when he was here."

...

Harriet had heard the commotion from the back of the crowd and tried to see what was going on. In desperation she stood on a chair and held her smartphone above her head, trying to get a photo. She succeeded. She had a very clear shot of the author known as Sepp Gregory standing next to the podium, a large erection jutting up into the air. It wasn't something she'd ever seen at a reading before and, if she was being totally honest, it wasn't something she'd seen anywhere in a long time. She wasn't sure what she could do with the picture. She didn't want to make her blog NSFW, but then it was too good a shot not to use. She was zooming in on Sepp's erection when a woman behind her said, "Wow. Good one. Will you email that to me?"

The crowd's reaction was strange. It unnerved Harriet. For a while it looked like the signing was going to be canceled, but no one wanted to leave. Normally Harriet would've mocked Sepp's incoherent presentation—it really sounded like he was having a nervous breakdown—and snarked about it online. With the photographic evidence she could've sold the piece to *Gawker* or *Vulture* or *TMZ*. So she was somewhat taken aback by the reaction of the crowd. They weren't angry or annoyed, they were actually worried about this charlatan's well-being. Harriet shook her head in amazement. People are so fucking stupid. And yet, she couldn't deny that there was a sweetness about Sepp that was compelling. Unless that was fake, too.

...

Sepp appreciated having a team of handlers to help him deal with his fans. He wasn't himself lately, not the self that was the winner of *Sex Crib*, not the person that these people had come to see, so it was important to have Marybeth, and the media escort, and a dude like Frazier there to back him up. Even the hot bookstore nerd who introduced him was on his side—although she did brush her hand against his boner a couple of times when she put the towel on his lap.

A stocky white guy with a trim mustache and baseball cap ambled up to Sepp. It was almost the end of the line and

RAW

the guy had waited patiently—humming an almost unrecognizable version of A-Ha's eighties classic "Take on Me"—for two hours. Sepp smiled. "Sorry it's taking so long."

The guy hoisted a large canvas bag onto the table. "It's worth it."

He pulled a dozen boxes of Girl Scout cookies out of the canvas bag. There were Samoas, Thin Mints, Tagalongs, and Trefoils. Sepp was confused. "Are you selling cookies?"

The guy chuckled. "No man, remember that episode of *Love Express* where you took that smokin' hot Mexican chick to the cookie factory in San Antonio?"

Sepp nodded. "Yeah."

"Remember how you an' her made out on a bed made out of gingersnaps?"

Sepp winced at the memory. That had been one of the producer's brainstorms and he and the young woman had spent the night in the Emergency Room getting cookie shrapnel picked out of their skin. They didn't show that part on TV.

"Don't try it at home, bro. That's my advice."

The guy slid the cookies in front of Sepp and, for a brief strange second, Sepp thought he was going to be asked to roll around in cookies with a stocky guy in a baseball cap.

"Would you mind signing these?"

"The cookies?"

"Pretty cool, huh?"

. . .

Harriet had waited at the end of the line, behind the guy with the Girl Scout cookies, and now had the A-Ha song stuck in her head. She thought about the guy she'd just met, the fan of

121

her blog who read Steve Erickson, and regretted not getting his number or asking him to meet for a drink while she was in town. But it wasn't a total failure; she'd told him to friend her on Facebook. Maybe he would.

She watched as Sepp shook hands with the eighties-rock cookie fetishist and then turned toward her. If he recognized her, he didn't show it.

"Hey. Good turnout."

Sepp nodded. "LA's great."

"So are you ready?"

He looked at her blankly.

"I'm here to interview you."

It was a gamble on her part. She hadn't made plans or cleared it with his publicist. But if the publicist knew it was her, after that late-night phone call, they'd never allow it. Harriet was pretty sure that Sepp wasn't the kind of author who checked his schedule that closely.

"It won't take long. I promise."

Harriet thought she detected a flash of disappointment in Sepp's eyes. "I'm supposed to go to this party."

"I can drop you there after we talk."

Sepp hedged. "Yeah, but I don't want to be out late."

Frazier interrupted them. "I got you something." He handed Sepp a book. It was a copy of *Being and Time* by Martin Heidegger. "It's about reality. It might help you sort things out."

"Cool. Thanks."

Harriet cleared her throat. Sepp turned back toward her. "Hey, why don't you just come to the party? You can interview me there."

21

Beverly Hills

Sepp liked the critic. She was kind of bossy, but he thought it showed she was spunky and he'd always liked what his dad called "feisty" women. It reminded him of some of the contestants on *Sex Crib,* the women who were there to have fun, who were up for anything. Chicks with game rule, bro.

Sepp couldn't help it, he started thinking about Roxy, comparing the critic to her. Is that why he was having a problem with women? He compared them all to Roxy? Roxy was a force of nature, a juggernaut with implants and a smile that launched a million boners. Add in her ruthless strategic genius, her mastery of mind games, and you've got all the essential qualities of a reality TV superstar. Most girls didn't stand a chance, but maybe a super-smart nerd could give Roxy a run for her money.

Marybeth drove, pointing out streets where famous actors and directors lived. Sepp heard Harriet clear her throat. "You want to do the interview now?"

Sepp turned and looked into the backseat. "Why not?"

He watched her click on a small digital recorder and then she began. "What happened back there at the bookstore?"

A sheepish smile flashed across Sepp's face and he blushed. "I took the wrong pill."

Marybeth interjected. "He had a bad reaction to some prescription medication his doctor gave him. But we really don't want to talk about it. His medical history is off limits."

Sepp looked at her. "It is?"

Marybeth turned and looked at him. "It is now."

Harriet remained upbeat. "No worries. I was just curious. It did make it one of the more interesting readings I've attended."

Marybeth cleared her throat in a threatening way and Harriet changed the subject. "So tell me, just so I can get some background about your process, how long did it take to write the book?"

Sepp pretended to thoughtfully consider the question by putting his hand on his chin. "About nine or ten months, I guess."

"What was your process like?"

Sepp blinked.

Marybeth looked at him. "She wants to know how you write. What your day is like."

Sepp nodded. He cocked his head to one side and looked out the window. "My process is pretty boring."

Harriet encouraged him. She wanted to get him talking. "People are fascinated by how writers come up with ideas."

Sepp nodded again. "I have a computer. That's a big help. And, you know, a lot of my best ideas come from when I'm at the beach."

"You get inspired at the beach?"

"Pretty much. Yeah. I really like the beach."

"What inspires you at the beach?"

Sepp scratched his head. "It's like, you know, the waves and the sand. That kind of thing."

"That pretty much describes a beach."

Sepp agreed. "Totally."

Harriet smiled. "I'm surprised because most celebrities, you know the really big stars, have professional writers helping them, but you wrote this yourself."

"I never said I didn't have help."

Harriet nodded. "You had a ghostwriter?"

"Well. I'm not the best when it comes to computers."

"So your publisher hired the best."

Marybeth interrupted. "I think this is getting off topic."

Harriet looked at her. "Is it? I was asking about his process. If he had someone help him, then that's part of his process."

Sepp nodded. "Yeah, this dude helped."

"Do you remember his name?"

Sepp shook his head. Harriet looked at him, surprised. "You don't remember his name?"

Sepp legitimately struggled to recall the name of the dorkatron who'd hung around for a couple days. "I'm pretty bad with names."

Before Harriet could say anything else, Marybeth interrupted. "Voilà. The Playboy Mansion."

Sepp looked up and saw the mansion.

"You sure that's it?"

Marybeth nodded. "What were you expecting?"

What he'd been expecting was some kind of magical kingdom with larger-than-life sculptures of naked women lining the drive and neon nudity flashing from every window. In his fantasy, buxom bunnies cavorted on the lawn and the mansion was like the illustration on the original poster for *The Little Mermaid* where some of the Disney Imagineers discreetly hid veiny erections amongst the gilded towers of Neptune's undersea palace; instead the Casa de Hef looked a lot like the mansion they'd used for *Sex Crib* or any of the episodes of *The Bachelor* and *Bachelorette*. It looked nice, but not the resplendent pleasuredome of his dreams.

...

Phony-breasted Playmates greeted them at the door like short-circuiting animatronic Barbie dolls; their haywire enthusiasm nearly knocked Sepp over. "Sepp Gregory! Oh my God! Let's see those abs!" The Playmates surrounded Sepp, yanked his shirt over his head, and began running their fingers up and down his washboard torso. A catalog of squeals erupted as they stroked him.

Harriet's eyes rolled so violently that she thought they might flip out of her skull and go spinning across the floor. Seeing *Playboy* Playmates in the flesh was bordering on a surreal experience, like seeing a leprechaun sitting on a pot of gold with a shillelagh in one hand and a Guinness in the other. She liked that word, "shillelagh." The truncheon or cudgel was named after the Irish town of Shillelagh, which was famous for the hardness of its oak trees. She also liked the words "truncheon" and "cudgel." "Baton," "nightstick," and "billyclub" were pretty good too. Why were all the good words used to describe something that you beat people with?

"Oh my God! These are, like, totally rock hard!"

The bunnies kept squealing.

"Awesome!"

Harriet couldn't believe that they looked the way they looked—it was so plastic, their heaving fake breasts holstered in bikini tops, pushing against the fabric that yoked them, like tethered blimps. Marybeth looked at Harriet and, as if reading her mind, said, "I'm going to find the bar."

Harriet was no prude and had, in fact, ranted and railed against PC lit crit as often as she could, but she'd also taken enough women's studies classes in college to know that there was something deeply wrong with these Playmates. Of course, if you thought about it, there was something wrong with calling grown women Playmates in the first place.

The Playmates surrounded Sepp in a huddle of manicured flesh. Their skin was pool-tanned and glowing, their hair processed and molded, their limbs thin, almost scrawny, the aforementioned breasts, bulbous and aggressive. They weren't women anymore, not really, they were more like genetically engineered breast displays, every part of their body designed to emphasize the heft and heave of their mammaries, their brains exhibiting all the gravity of meringues. Even their personalities were frothy. They pogo'd with jiggly excitement at the slightest comment from Sepp.

As more women ran to touch Sepp's body, Harriet stepped to the side, out of the way. She looked at the other guests. Apparently "Reality Night" at the Playboy Mansion meant that all the women were required to wear bikini tops and all the men were either shirtless hunks like Sepp or middle-aged players who hid their tubby guts under retro bowling shirts. There were a few women not in a state of near nudity, obvious professionals, publicists, agents, and journalists. Women like her. She saw Marybeth standing over a buffet table.

Harriet walked over and joined her at what turned out to be an improvised sushi bar where two Latino chefs cranked out specialty maki rolls for the occasion. The roll inspired by the hit show *Big Island Nudist Camp* was sushi rice wrapped around a sliver of cheesecake and a slice of ham, while the *Southern Roadkill Diner* roll was venison smeared with marshmallow fluff.

Marybeth turned to Harriet. "Get your interview?"

"I'm going to wait until they've finished adoring his abdomen."

Marybeth smiled wryly. "Better get a drink then. You're in for a long night."

Harriet looked at Marybeth. "What about you? Are you just going to hang around?"

Marybeth shrugged. "It's my job."

Harriet looked at the sushi. It didn't offer any reassurances. "I think I'll go exploring."

Marybeth stuck a piece of California roll in her mouth and said, "I'll be outside."

. . .

Sepp had been wandering through the mansion, looking for Marybeth or the critic. He walked outside and saw some topless women bouncing on a trampoline. He heard splashing in the pool and laughter coming from the famed Playboy Mansion grotto.

He continued down the path, past the flapping fabric of several tents that had been erected on the lawn, walking toward the pool. He stopped when he heard a voice ask, "Ever do it bunny-style?"

He turned and saw a woman in the flickering candle-light lying on a round mattress in a little Arabian-fantasy tent just off the path. He moved closer, ducking his head as he entered. He saw a brunette, topless, her long hair framing a face that would've looked pretty if it hadn't been for her strangely oversize front teeth.

"Can't say I ever have."

"Well, if you were ever considering it, this is the place."

She stretched out on the bed, her body sleek and long, more athletic than those of the other women in the house.

Sepp sat down, mostly to keep from crouching, and smiled at her. "What's happening out here?"

She lifted her long legs up, touching the roof of the tent while simultaneously giving Sepp a very clear look at her magnificently muscled ass. She noticed Sepp's stare.

"I played goalie on my college soccer team."

Sepp nodded, unsure of the significance of this new information.

"Cool."

"I was waiting for you."

"Me?"

"And here you are."

She reached out and stroked his abs. "I've wanted to touch your body since I first saw you on TV."

"I get that a lot."

She sat up, putting her face an inch from Sepp's.

"Let me get off on your abs."

"What?"

"Here. I'll show you what I mean."

She pushed him down on the mattress, yanked off her bikini bottoms, and straddled his belly. She leaned over him and he felt her breath, hot and minty, on his face as she whispered in his ear.

"I won't scratch you. I just shaved."

. . .

Harriet felt like a documentarian—Albert Maysles, maybe —roaming the world's most exclusive frat house. She saw middle-aged men swaggering and strutting, desperate to impress women half their age. The Playboy Mansion encouraged this behavior; it was a safe zone where they could, with apologies to Dylan Thomas, rage against the fading of their erections, and attempt to recapture the vigor of their youthful ejaculations. "Ejaculation." There was a good word. It was from the Latin *eiaculari,* meaning to "throw out or shoot out," and based on *iaculum,* the Roman word for "javelin." Harriet was certain there was some ejaculation going on in the mansion.

. . .

Curtis had looked everywhere for Roxy, searching the mansion, opening doors, sticking his head in where he'd really rather not. He'd found people doing dark and sticky business in every crevice, crack, and crawlspace of the mansion. He'd seen middle-aged, pot-bellied barons-of-some-kind-of-industry wielding their pharmaceutically afflicted hard-ons, their chemical boners, at fake blondes with overinflated tits; it was all like some exaggerated caricature, science gone off the rails, Norman Rockwell's domestic heterosexuality redrawn by Tom of Finland.

So far Roxy Sandoval had blown off his attempts to interview her. He'd find her lounging on a couch or squatting near a settee and just as they started to talk, she'd jump up to say hi to a friend, refill her cranberry and vodka, thank Hef for throwing the party, and, the last time, she'd confided to Curtis that she really needed to "go take a dump." Every time she flitted away she promised Curtis that she'd find him, that she would be back in a minute. Curtis got so annoyed with her that he threatened to call the publisher and resign—implying that this would cancel her advance too—so she finally agreed to meet him in the Mansion's library in "a half hour or so."

It was not the ideal way to start a working relationship, but Curtis didn't care. Roxy Sandoval wasn't Sophia Loren or Madonna or even Meryl Streep. She wasn't a star, she was a good-looking young woman who got famous for playing hot and slutty mind games in a stupid TV show. The sense of entitlement these people had surprised him. What had they done to earn it? Give a guy a hummer on network TV? Is that what makes someone a star nowadays?

Curtis didn't like the Playboy Mansion either. Not that he didn't enjoy seeing young and buxom women in various states of undress. That wasn't the problem. It was the fact that the women were flirting with every man in the place except him. He was ignored by hotties, shunned by bunnies. It flashed Curtis back to high school, of only getting to dance at the school parties with the weird girl who liked comic books, or the total humiliation of being picked last for sports, standing in a row of his peers watching as tubby spastics and stick-legged girls were chosen ahead of him.

This feeling of humiliation was compounded by the fact that now, with the flesh and pheromone dial cranked up to eleven, Curtis found himself incredibly aroused. He felt a surge rooted in his scrotum that caused his balls to tingle. He'd have liked nothing better than to drop his trousers and bury his dick into some mindless twenty-two-year-old's mouth, but that wasn't going to happen, even if all the men in the mansion, the reality studs and the aging geezers gobbling pills, suddenly dropped dead. Even if he were the last man standing, the bunnies would take one look at him and start making out with each other, which, now that he visualized it, wouldn't be such a bad thing.

But all things being real, reality being way more real than the reality portrayed on reality TV, he found himself doing what he always did, sitting in a library, typing on his laptop, trying not to think of the square footage of the mansion, the ratio of bathrooms to bedrooms, or the market value of prime Beverly Hills real estate.

...

Sepp had let the raven-haired soccer bunny rub her crotch up and down and back and forth against his torso. He'd helped her out by performing a series of rhythmic crunches to make his muscles pop out as she got more and more into it, lashing his face with her hair and moaning as she rode his rippling belly to a frantic climax.

She collapsed on top of him, panting for breath, her sweat dripping onto him, her body melting into a serotonin bliss. Sepp found himself, for the first time in quite a long time, in a state of arousal with a woman. Dude. Finally. He wasn't sure if the curse of Roxy was at long last broken or if it was a combination of the bunny's hotness and the residual

Viagra in his system, but he didn't care. He gave her a kiss and said, "My turn." She sat up abruptly and shook her head. "That would be nice, but I don't think my husband would approve."

Sepp blinked up at her. "You're married?"

"Yeah. He lets me have my fun as long as I don't do it."

"You just did it."

"Not it. I didn't do *it* it."

She turned and looked at his erect penis. "I'll watch you beat off if you want."

Sepp let his head drop back on the mattress. "No thanks."

She started to say something, but changed her mind and gave his torso a pat. "See ya."

And with that, she scooped up her clothes and padded out of the tent.

. . .

Sepp walked out to the pool. He felt the bunny's juices still wet and sticky on his body, the smell of sex wafting off him like the world's oldest cologne. His erection still throbbed in his pants. At first he'd been thrilled to get one, like maybe the curse was finally lifted, but now it felt like carrying a burden. He walked with a strange gait, slightly hunched over, like a primate with a waxed chest, following a trail of tiki torches until he came to the world-famous Playboy Mansion grotto.

Several men and women were skinny dipping, affecting a playful splashing foreplay, sipping cocktails, letting their legs mingle under the water.

It was dark and Sepp hoped that the pool might cool his erection, so he slipped out of his clothes and lowered himself in the water. His body glided through it, the chlorinated liquid cleaning his torso. It made him tingle. He felt his mind refresh, like the entire episode was some kind of dream for a new series.

He swam underwater, feeling like a dolphin, until he bumped into a pair of legs and surfaced, his face emerging from the water directly in front of a large pair of perfectly tan and medically symmetrical breasts—breasts that he immediately recognized—the magnificent pair of tits that belonged to Roxy Sandoval. Roxy noticed his boner.

"I guess you are happy to see me."

...

Harriet walked down a darkened hallway, past a young couple making out, their lips locked, the woman shoved up against the wall as the man ground his crotch into her. She found a door that was partially open and peeked in. What she saw astounded her. It was Hef's private library.

The fact that a room for books—and from the look of it there were real books collected here—existed in a world that seemed to be constructed to keep out any thought that wasn't about sex was surprising enough, but what was truly surprising, what made Harriet smile, was the sight of the attractive hipster—the guy she'd met and felt a connection to at Book Soup—sitting on an overstuffed leather couch, typing on his MacBook Air.

"Do they have wi-fi in the mansion?"

He looked up at her, and she could see he was simultaneously embarrassed—perhaps he didn't want to be caught at the Playboy Mansion—and excited to see her.

"I never expected to see you here."

"I could say the same thing. Curtis, right?"

Curtis nodded.

"Am I disturbing you?"

Curtis closed his laptop and put it on a backgammon board that doubled for a coffee table. "No. God no." Then he smiled. "Please. Join me."

Harriet entered the room and shut the door behind her, locking out the repetitive thud and boister of the hip-hop blaring throughout the mansion's sound system. She sighed. "It's like 'Night of the Living Brain-Dead' out there."

Curtis grinned. "Glad to see you didn't get bit by a zombie bunny or chupacabra or whatever they are in those outfits."

Harriet laughed and moved toward him. "I'm supposed to be doing an interview."

"Me too."

Harriet cocked an eyebrow at him. "Mind if I sit?"

"Please."

Curtis slipped his laptop back into his backpack and scooted over as Harriet sat down next to him on the fainting couch. In the two seconds it took for her to join him on the couch she decided not to ask about his work—that would only lead to him asking her, and she didn't want to talk about Sepp Gregory or his ghostwriter. Her mission could wait.

She pointed to the shelves of books. "I'm impressed. This is a real library."

"Yeah, but do you think he's read all of them?"

"I'd believe that before I'd believe he really has sex with his girlfriends." Harriet made air quotes around the word "girlfriends" and then immediately apologized. "I don't normally do air quotes." She couldn't believe how dorky she sounded. Why was she nervous around this guy?

Curtis laughed and shifted in his seat. "Yeah. It's a strange setup. But a nice house."

Harriet nodded. "'Mansion' seems a misnomer. It's more like a chalet." Harriet liked that word. She assumed it was the diminutive of the Old French word *chasel*, meaning "farmhouse."

"Twenty-nine rooms on five acres. A wine cellar. That's bigger than your average chalet. Let's call it a mansionette."

"I've never thought of 'chalet' as being particularly pejorative." Harriet turned toward him, letting her leg press against his leg. Curtis laughed.

"Have you heard about the Elvis Suite?"

"Like Elvis Presley?"

Curtis nodded. "Apparently he spent the night there with eight women."

"How very Scheherazade of him."

Curtis laughed, a little too loudly, Harriet thought, like he was nervous, but at least he got the joke. Curtis leaned in toward her and, for a brief moment, she thought he might try to kiss her, but instead he whispered.

"Can you imagine what something like this would cost in Manhattan?"

...

"We need to talk."

Sepp blinked the water out of his eyes and felt his erection quickly fading. He looked at Roxy. "Sure."

Roxy slicked her hair back. This action, the raising of her arms to squeegee the water out of her hair, lifted her breasts up. Sepp couldn't help it, he stared as the twin nipples pointed at him.

"So, like, what's happening?"

"Not here, numbnuts."

Sepp swallowed. He'd been dreading this showdown. He'd heard that Roxy, like Caitlin, wasn't happy with one of the characters in his book.

"Wherever you want to go, Roxy."

. . .

Curtis had finally summoned the courage to lean in and kiss Harriet Post, world-famous literary critic. He was surprised that she'd responded not by slapping him and saying something dismissive, but by kissing him back. In fact, every move he made—getting from first base to second as smooth as any of the professional playboys in the mansion—was met with equal ardor. It had been a while since Curtis had stuck his hand under a bra and felt someone's breast, but she'd let him do just that. She even unbuttoned her blouse to enhance the accessibility. His brain began an inventory of sensations, a sexual status report. He'd want to be able to recall the details later, when he was alone. So while his left hand gently caressed Harriet's breast—his thumb and forefinger taking a lazy spin around her erect nipple—his right hand fumbled with her bra strap, trying to unlock the complicated snarl of hooks and loops that kept him from being able to undress her. Maybe he was distracted by her tongue, which was shoved aggressively into his mouth, swishing and dancing with his tongue, exchanging spit for sensation.

Curtis tried to remember if he had ever met a woman and then been intimate with her on the same day. Maybe there's something to the Playboy Mansion after all. Maybe it really is a magical place, a kind of parallel universe where sex is as natural as breathing, where people feel free to take off their clothes and copulate, because before Curtis could solve the enigma of Harriet's bra, she reached back and deftly unhooked it, revealing a pair of beautifully proportioned breasts, dappled with freckles.

...

The crowd in the Great Hall, a mingled mass of bunnies and bozos freak-dancing to the ear-blistering thud perpetrated by the DJ, parted as Roxy plowed across the dance floor toward the stairs. She was like an icebreaker crushing through the polar caps or that dude in the Bible who spread the Red Sea as easy as long tan goalie legs.

Sepp followed in Roxy's wake, throwing a knowing nod at the dudes and players, all the while his eyes yo-yoing back and forth from the crowd to Roxy's tight ass and back again.

...

Curtis kissed Harriet again and their eyeglasses collided, causing both of them to be temporarily blinded as their optics went askew. But with his glasses off, he could look more deeply into Harriet's highly intelligent eyes. He thought he detected something in them, a spark, maybe a glimmer of emotion that looked like desire. Unless he was projecting, which was entirely possible; it wouldn't be the first time.

But what if her desire was real? When was the last time he'd seen anything like that? He felt his insides quiver as he dove back toward her, their lips meeting, tongues touching. He pressed his body close to hers, pushed her down on the couch, and, in his awkward way, mounted her.

Which is exactly what Roxy and Sepp saw when they entered the library.

. . .

Sepp stopped. He didn't want to walk in on a couple who were obviously in the middle of something, but Roxy didn't care. She strolled in like an actress taking center stage. At first Sepp thought that maybe she hadn't noticed—sometimes Roxy could be a little self-absorbed—but before he could say anything he saw her look down at the couple clinched on the couch.

"Break it up before I throw water on you."

Curtis and Harriet separated quickly, Harriet struggling to put on her bra. Sepp watched as she pulled her shirt closed. He couldn't help noticing her cute freckled breasts. And the way she covered herself was so natural, so innocent, that he felt a stir in his pants.

Sepp frowned. "Come on, Rox. Let's leave 'em alone."

"Fuck that. This isn't a whorehouse."

Harriet looked at Roxy, then at Sepp. "I'm not a whore. But then I wouldn't think that would need clarification."

Sepp had a thought, a glimmer of irony that flickered in his head, and he wanted to make a joke—he wanted to say something about the Playboy Mansion not being a whore-house because the girls gave it away, maybe, but then it was extra ironic because they didn't really give it away, they got paid to pose in the magazine so it was more like it was a job to them which is what it is for prostitutes. So, like, Roxy was wrong about it not being a whorehouse.

Roxy flopped down in a chair on the other side of the small room and went into her signature "now I'm gonna do us all a big fucking favor and tell it like it is" stance, a position that she'd used repeatedly during *Sex Crib*. She put one hand on her hip, cocked her head, and pointed a finger at Harriet's breasts.

"Those could be C cups easy with some implants."

Harriet reflexively covered herself even though she had her shirt on. "I like my breasts."

Roxy gave her a fake smile. "It's not about what *you* like."

Sepp shook his head. Dude. Roxy could be such a harsh bitch. There was nothing wrong with the book nerd's boobs.

Curtis stood up and extended his hand to Sepp. "Congrats on all the success."

Sepp shook hands with him and smiled. "Thanks, bro."

Sepp looked at Harriet and chided her good-naturedly. "So? Where have you been? I thought you were going to interview me."

Harriet blushed. "I looked for you."

Roxy snorted. "You find him in that dude's pants?"

Harriet stammered. Roxy gave Curtis a withering look. "And weren't we supposed to have a chat tonight?"

Curtis shrugged, attempting to play it off by being cool. "The night is young."

Sepp thought the dude with the glasses looked familiar. He'd met him before, he was sure of that, but, you know, he was bad with memory stuff.

Harriet looked at Sepp. "Close the door. Please."

Sepp realized he was still standing in the doorway. "Roxy. We should go."

Roxy scoffed. "Apparently everyone is interviewing everyone." Then she noticed Curtis's shoes. "Nice kicks. Custom?"

Curtis nodded. "A friend made them."

Roxy smiled. "I know footwear."

Sepp shut the door behind him. He leaned against it, partly to keep anyone from entering and partly because he didn't know what to do with himself. He was embarrassed for the nerds they'd caught in a lip-lock and embarrassed because of Roxy's behavior. Why had they barged in? There were other rooms in the mansion. Why did Roxy always act this way? Sepp knew that Roxy wasn't going to budge, she was stubborn, so he turned to Harriet. "I'm sorry about all this. We'll do the interview. I promise."

Roxy scoffed. "Men are always promising things to girls. Guys will say anything to pop a load in your mouth." She leaned toward Harriet and spoke softly. "Real gratitude sparkles."

Roxy twisted her arm up in the air so that everyone in the room could admire the bracelet on her wrist; dozens of diamonds blinged in the light. Sepp wondered how many blow jobs that bracelet represented. A dozen? A hundred? Or just one really good one?

Sepp cleared his throat. "Rox. C'mon. Let's go."

Roxy leaned back in her chair. "I like it here. Libraries are sexy." Roxy began to examine her French-manicured nails in earnest. "Let's just do all the interviewing here. It'll be like an interview orgy."

Curtis and Harriet exchanged a look. Curtis asked, "Who are you interviewing him for?"

"It's part of a bigger piece I'm working on. What are you doing?"

Curtis smiled a bit ruefully. "Assignment."

Roxy laughed. "Look at the nerds talking their nerd talk. They're so cute."

With that, Harriet stood up and looked at Sepp. "Let's just do this tomorrow."

Sepp nodded. "You can call my publicist and set it up."

Harriet nodded. "Great. I'll do that."

Harriet grabbed her shoes and left the room. Curtis looked at Roxy. "So is this gonna happen tonight or . . . not?" Roxy stuck her finger in her mouth and then held it up, as if testing for wind direction. She shook her head. "Doesn't look like it."

Curtis shrugged. "It's the publisher's dime." He collected his things and went into a small bathroom off the library. The door shut and Sepp turned to Roxy.

"How can you do that?"

"What?"

"Treat people that way."

Roxy stopped looking at her fingers and looked at Sepp. "You know what your problem is?"

"No."

"You let the help upset you."

"The what?"

"The help. The background. The little people who run around on the outskirts." She leaned in, emphasizing her words. "There are two kinds of people in this world, Seppy. The stars—people like you and me—and the help. Don't let the help upset you."

...

Harriet was in the hallway, bending over, tying her shoes, when she felt a hand glide up the back of her thigh, the fingers spreading, taking in her contours, gently caressing her flesh as it slid up and across her ass. She heard a man's voice.

"So very nice."

She jerked upright to confront the groper, but he just kept walking and she could only see him from the back, a dapper gentleman in burgundy pajamas and velour smoking jacket, a blond bunny attached to each arm.

22

Beverly Hills

Harriet sat in the back of a cab with Curtis. She let him lean his leg so that it touched hers. His warmth sent little quivers through her. She looked out the window and noticed the distinct lack of traffic. What had happened to all the cars? It wasn't late, maybe ten thirty, and yet for some reason the streets of Los Angeles were empty. Where did everybody go?

She saw Curtis's profile—as handsome as any hip young adjunct English professor—briefly illuminated in the street light. She felt a warm glow filling her body, like a teenager who'd just played spin the bottle for the first time. She was giddy. That was a funny word. If she remembered correctly it came from the Proto-Germanic word *gudig* and meant "to have a confused sensation."

Harriet was enjoying the ride, the contact with Curtis, feeling the fresh night air blow through the windows, reveling in sensation, trying to wrap her head around the idea that she had a physical self, a body that craved sensual experience. Her yoga teacher had told her she lived too much in her head and now she was starting to think maybe she was right. She heard Curtis clear his throat.

"Um. Want to get a drink? We can pick up your car and go to my hotel. It isn't far."

Before she could even consider what this invitation might mean or what consequences might unfold she said, "'That sounds perfect." Curtis turned and smiled at her. "I was hoping you'd say that."

The plan set in motion—and surely some kind of sexual encounter was forthcoming—Harriet began to overthink what was happening in earnest. Her default setting in these male/female scenarios was typically critical and anxious, parsing every word, thought, and feeling, and now she went into full catastrophic-thinking mode. She felt her pulse race. Why was she so nervous?

She remembered an insipid book that one of her friends gave her called something like *Get in the Game!*—with the hopeful subtitle *Find a Husband, Get a Life*. According to *Get in the Game!* she was supposed to be some kind of unique creature with confidence and attitude that proclaimed her fabulousity. Somehow she was supposed to "let her true colors show" by only emailing him back once for every three he sent and by not returning his calls over the weekend. How that was good advice or got you a husband or was anything more than infantile game playing, she couldn't say. Besides, the advice didn't apply to this situation; Curtis hadn't emailed at all. What was she supposed to do? Give him her email address and then wait a couple days? She knew that one-night stands were against the *Get in the Game!* code of conduct, but maybe it would be fun anyway. Or was that sleazy? Should she just get in her car and then agree to meet for breakfast? Or does brunch sound more noncommittal? What did she want? A husband? Some fun? And what would she do with a husband anyway?

Harriet realized that she could've gone for some hot animal sex in the library of the Playboy Mansion but now, the heat and pheromones drained away, she was left feeling apprehensive, anxious about everything.

She decided the only reasonable course of action was to do nothing, just sit back and enjoy the ride.

...

Sepp sat in an uncomfortable chair across from where Roxy was splayed out on the leather couch like some kind of over-sexed and barbiturated Cleopatra. Usually he would look at her, or, dude, all things being honest and such, he would look at a picture of her in a magazine or on TV, and he'd feel a twisting pain in his stomach and a dull ache in his nuts like he was being gutted, but now he looked at her and all he could feel was kinda blank. Roxy waved her hand in the air. "Is your book in here, Seppy?"

Sepp looked around the library. There were a lot of books. He shrugged. "I hope so."

"My book will be in here."

"That's cool."

A wicked smile danced across her face. "I didn't like your book. I'll be honest. It wasn't my cup of tea."

Sepp didn't really know what to say to that. He hadn't gotten much criticism for the book and, you know, since he didn't really write it, he didn't take it personally. "I didn't know you liked tea."

"Ha. Ha." She sat up and looked him in the eye. "I guess you needed your revenge."

It occurred to Sepp that maybe he ought to read the book he wrote. If he'd gotten revenge on Roxy, that might be pretty cool.

Roxy narrowed her eyes at him. "What did that slut from your other show think?"

"What slut?"

"You know. The dyke."

Sepp knew Roxy was talking about Caitlin. He just didn't think Roxy, of all people, should go around calling other people "sluts." But then it takes one to know one. "She knew it was a fictional novel. It didn't bother her."

Roxy smiled. "Good. Then it won't bother you when my fictional novel comes out." Roxy stood and glared at him. "And, trust me, you're not going to like how the real you turns out."

Roxy mussed his hair on her way out. "You're still cute though."

...

Curtis told the room service guy to set the champagne on the table on the balcony. It was nice out, the air perfumed with jasmine and stirring in balmy swirls, and the small balcony overlooked the pool. It was all so California. The water was inviting, relaxing; just the sound of it was sensual. Mellow soft rock—what his friends derisively called "yacht music"—drifted up from the poolside speakers, and pastel-colored lights illuminated the palm trees ringing the patio. It was the perfect night for drinking champagne and getting laid.

He'd been making out with Harriet, waiting for the drinks to arrive, and now that the champagne was chilling in the ice bucket and the Mexican waiter was setting out the stemware and unwrapping the plastic wrap off the fresh fruit platter, it was all becoming real. If the Playboy Mansion was reminiscent of a surreal and cheesy version of a painting by Brueghel—the Elder, not the Younger—now that they were alone in a hotel room, the scenario was suddenly intimate, charged with nervous energy, doubts and fears bubbling inside him. The ghosts of girlfriends past flickered through in his head, memories of failures, miscues, clumsiness, and premature ejaculations. Curtis felt a jolt of apprehension seep into his brain. But why was he so nervous? He really liked this woman. She seemed to like him. What was the problem? He decided to just relax, to enjoy the moment, to not crowd it out with memories or thoughts of the past, or his career, or Harriet's importance in the literary world. He reminded himself not to ask her to read anything. Tonight he just wanted to feel like a real playboy. If not James Bond, then at least Ian Fleming.

He saw Harriet jump when the champagne cork popped and it made him laugh. He couldn't believe his good luck. To have one of his literary heroes about to go to bed with him? Wow. That just doesn't happen every day.

...

Sepp sat in the front seat of Marybeth's car and looked out the window. He was tired. It had been a long day and tomorrow was a radio show and a late-night TV thing, then he'd be off to another city, more interviews, more autographing and then another, and another after that and then another. Sepp knew he should be happy, normally he was a happy dude, but all he felt was confused. He looked at the book that the nice dude at the bookstore had given him.

"What's that?"

Sepp looked over at Marybeth. "Oh, it's uh . . ." Sepp turned the book and read the cover. "It's *Being and Time* by a dude called Heidegger."

"I didn't know you liked philosophy."

Sepp opened the book and tried to read a few lines in the darkened car. "Is that what it is?"

Marybeth nodded. "I only know that because I used to work for a guy named Heidegger and he thought it was hilarious he had the same name as a philosopher."

"Why is that funny?"

Marybeth laughed. "Fuck if I know. I think it was his own inside joke."

Sepp looked out the window. "I think everybody in this town has an inside joke."

Marybeth nodded. "Remember that Hollywood isn't like the real world. It's got its own rules and its own way of doing things."

"What do you mean?"

Marybeth looked at Sepp. "When you're hot, for example right after *Sex Crib,* you can do anything. The entire world opens up to you. But if you don't move fast, it closes."

Sepp nodded. "When you're hot, you're hot."

"Exactly. But that's not real. Do you understand? That heat, the fact that everyone thinks you're great and can do no wrong, that's not who you really are. That's how they perceive you." She patted Sepp's shoulder. "And their perception can change in a second, while you are still the person you've always been. So it's important not to take it personally."

Sepp didn't say anything for a while. Marybeth looked over at him. "Does that make sense?"

"Kind of. Like you're saying that famous-people reality depends on what people think, not what's really reality, and that they can always change their mind depending on stuff."

Marybeth smiled. "In a lot of ways, it's all a big game. Your goal is to just keep being you and don't let any of this celebrity craziness mess with your head."

Sepp thought about what Marybeth was saying and it made him wish he could be more like Roxy. She knew how to play the game. Hell, dude, she owned the game. Even without any talent she had made herself a celebrity. Roxy may have practiced stripper moves in the mirror, but she was hardly a dancer, her singing sucked, and if those energy drink commercials were anything to go by, she couldn't act her way out of a paper bag. But like some kind of crazy magic trick she'd become famous. She was famous because she was famous which only made her even more famous. Dude. She didn't have to do anything but be a celebrity.

According to Roxy, part of being a famous person was using and abusing other people. That's how celebrities rolled. But Sepp couldn't do that. It just wasn't in his nature. Sure, he liked being famous, enjoyed the attention and the cash and the fact that he didn't have to work a regular job like most people. It was the fake stuff that he couldn't do. Acting like a douchebag so people would treat him like a star seemed, like, totally douchy. Besides, Dr. Jan had told him that he wouldn't be happy until he could just be the way he was and that's what he was trying to do.

They pulled into the hotel and Marybeth turned to him and gave him a hug.

"Keep your pants on in Arizona. The laws are different there."

...

@**fatalinfluence** *Los Angeles is magic.*

Harriet had read dozens of books on the craft of writing and they all said the same thing. *Conflict, character, conflict, character, repeat as necessary.* Conflict was like the Oreo filling of fiction. The sugary center that binds the chocolate cookies of character and plot together. Most readers will twist the cookies apart, skipping ahead, hungry to find the filling. It's the tasty part.

The main criticism Harriet heard from publishers when they passed on her book was that it lacked conflict. "An overbearing amount of description, excessively wordy, and much too long to sustain interest or enthusiasm for the protagonist's travails." "Windy, wordy, and stylistically pretentious." And Harriet's favorite rejection, "Nothing happens." *Yeah, well, nothing happens in Proust either.*

Harriet thought it was funny that her writing lacked conflict and here she was, conflicted. Internally debating the pros and cons of going all the way. She'd been conflicted when she accepted his invitation for a drink, she was conflicted when she drove back to his hotel, conflicted when they walked into the hotel lobby, past the modernist furniture and large glass windows that looked out onto the pool, and she was conflicted when they decided to have a drink in his room. She wondered what those publishers were talking about. Her writing was part of her life and her life was bursting with conflict.

Harriet wondered if Curtis had a condom, because she'd never carried a condom in her purse. Never ever once. Not even when she stopped taking birth control pills a couple of years ago. She just didn't see the point of it. Was that part of some sort of internal conflict? The good girl versus the floozie? "Floozie." That was a good word. She wondered where it came from.

Curtis had set his laptop on the table outside and put on some old-school jazz, anything to drown out the soft rock Muzak coming from the pool. She watched him pour a couple glasses of champagne. He'd made a big show of tipping the waiter twenty dollars, like it was the first time a writer anywhere had ever done something like that. He brought her the champagne and she took it with a smile, miraculously suppressing her internal doubts.

"Cheers."

She held up her glass and smiled at him. "Cheers."

They chinged glasses. Harriet was turned on. But she didn't want to show it. In fact, she didn't really know what it meant. What do you do once you're aroused? Harriet wanted to play it cool and thought about the cliché "cool as a cucumber." Where had that expression come from? It might make an interesting book, trying to figure out the history of axioms. Harriet made a mental note to look into it.

She took a sip of the bubbly wine. It was delicious, and before she knew it, she'd finished half the glass.

"This is yummy."

Curtis moved to refill her glass. "Shall we sit outside?"

There were a couple of outdoor chairs next to the table on the balcony. Harriet settled in and looked down at the pool. They were up on the third floor and a light breeze caressed her skin, causing goosebumps to erupt along her arm. Curtis gave her a concerned look. "Are you cold?"

She shook her head. "I like it."

The idea of making love on the balcony, no, the idea of fucking on the balcony, so everyone could see them, flashed through her head. She knew she didn't have the courage to go wild like that, but the champagne tasted good, the bubbles prickled her nose and swirled through her mouth and, as the alcohol worked its way through her body, she started to feel a little rock 'n' roll. In other words, she felt good. Really fucking good. And then here was Curtis pushing a strawberry into her mouth with his plump fingers.

. . .

Sepp said good night to Marybeth but knew he wasn't going to be able to sleep. Not yet anyway. It'd been a strange day and he was feeling wired. He walked through the hotel lobby, past the space age furniture, and stopped to look out the large windows at the darkened patio with its dramatic mood lighting and groovy pool.

Sepp didn't drink alcohol very often. If you want to be an elite athlete or just keep your abs looking cut, it's not a good idea. Normally when he was stressed out he'd go to the beach with a nice fatty and blaze on the sand. But he didn't have anything like that with him, so he walked into the bar.

The bartender, an intelligent-looking young woman who was sexy in a way that would never make the pages of *Playboy*, turned her attention from the bottles lined up on the bar back.

"What're we drinking tonight?"

Sepp didn't know.

"What do you recommend?"

The bartender recognized him—he could tell from her expression—and smiled. "Saw your picture online."

Sepp nodded. "How'd I look?"

"Like you could use a drink."

Sepp laughed.

"Well, what's your pleasure?"

Sepp blinked. The bartender continued, "What would you like to drink?"

Sepp was confused. "I don't know. What do people drink in Los Angeles?"

The bartender crossed her arms and looked at him. She was surprisingly serious about her work. "Well, there's so many different cultures in LA. In one part of town, Koreatown for example, you could be drinking soju or Mekong whiskey, in another part it might be pisco, or you could have a classic cocktail with rye whiskey, maybe a nice hot sake."

It was too confusing. If he was home in San Diego he'd just have a beer.

"What do you think?"

"I'd say the margarita is the endemic LA cocktail."

Sepp felt suddenly relieved. A margarita was something he'd had before. "Then I'll have a margarita."

Sepp wanted some air, not the conditioned air that a compressor chugged into the bar, but fresh night air, or at least, as fresh as you could get in Los Angeles. He took his margarita and walked out to sit by the pool.

It was quiet out on the patio. There wasn't anyone else around, so Sepp settled into a soft chaise lounge in a dark, secluded area. He could hear the low hum of traffic on the streets outside the building, the rustle of palm fronds in the breeze. It was soothing. He took a sip of his cocktail, letting the warmth of the tequila melt the stress right off his bones.

The restful sounds of the band Coldplay drifted out over the poolside patio. Sepp took off his T-shirt and lay back in the chaise. He stroked his abs absentmindedly, as rippled and firm as terra-cotta tiles. He hoped the cocktail would give him a good night's sleep. That was what he needed more than anything else. A solid eight hours of snooze. Then he'd wake up refreshed, eat a bowl of oatmeal, maybe hit the gym and give his abs a real workout, then get the show on the road. Sepp looked up at the stars. Did they really shine for him? Was that possible? Maybe, but he wouldn't know for sure because he could hardly see them through the haze and light pollution.

Sepp drank some more of the cocktail and felt his eyelids droop. The music murmured on and his body began to feel light, like it was rising, like he was in an elevator.

Sepp began to snore.

. . .

@fatalinfluence *We've come to the conclusion that champagne is underrated.*

Harriet had heard the expression "don't drink and tweet" but had never really thought about it until now. It might be good advice, but how could she resist? Even with Curtis feeding her berries and stroking her ass with his hand as they kissed, she wanted to make it real, not that it wasn't really happening in real life, but by commenting on it, putting the experience online, that somehow made it really real. It wasn't just real to her, it was real to the world. Her fans loved little glimpses into her personal life and her writing process and she didn't need fancy metrics to figure it out; every time she put something personal online she would get dozens of "likes" and retweets and favorites and +1s. In fact, she felt like writing more than a little chirp about how she was feeling. She felt like writing an extended essay on the health benefits of copious champagne consumption. She'd never felt stronger or more energized or more confident. Or more daring.

"Do you always have to be connected?"

Harriet looked up at Curtis. He was refilling their glasses with more bubbly wine. She smiled at him.

"It's an addiction. Sorry."

...

As Harriet was typing furiously into her iPhone, Curtis stood and looked out at the pool. A lone figure sprawled out on a chaise lounge below but otherwise it was empty. It's really true what they say about Los Angeles, they roll up the sidewalks after ten. A fantasy popped into Curtis's head, a kind of heroic daydream porn star scenario featuring him and Harriet engaged in wild monkey sex on the balcony. Oh yeah. LA may be asleep, but this is how Brooklyn rolls.

He wished he'd had the nerve to stop and buy some condoms but, at the time, he didn't know that the evening would progress so swimmingly. If he was going to have sex tonight, it would be unprotected. That didn't really bother him. There was no way he was going to say no if she offered; a starving man doesn't leave a banquet because he can't find a fork. Besides, Harriet was an intellectual, and smart people didn't pass STDs to each other, Curtis was sure of that.

. . .

Harriet put her iPhone on the table and looked up at Curtis. "Sorry. Sorry. I get carried away."

"Welcome back."

He handed her a freshly topped glass of champagne. Harriet took a sip and decided to make small talk before he started shoving more fruit in her mouth.

"So why were you interviewing that sea witch?"

"You mean Roxy Sandoval?"

He shrugged and sat down, reaching a hand out and stroking her leg. "I'm under contract to ghost a book for her."

"What?"

"I'm a novelist. But I'm unpublished."

Harriet interrupted. "Prepublished." She preferred to use the more hopeful expression, however ridiculous it sounded.

Curtis just shook his head. "Whatever. This is how I pay my bills. I ghostwrite. In fact one of the books I ghosted is on the bestseller list."

Harriet froze. "You what?"

"It's hack work, I know. Terrible. But I was broke."

The happy buzz of the champagne and pheromones and fresh fruit was instantly replaced by a chill that raced up her spine and made her skin crawl. Harriet spoke very slowly. "Which book is it?"

Curtis leaned back, his expression a mix of embarrassment and pride.

"*Totally Reality*. The Sepp Gregory book."

Harriet was in shock. Here was the man she wanted to interview, the ghostwriter who could shame Sepp Gregory and his publisher, the extraordinary prose stylist who spun schlock into beauty and beauty into schlock. Here was a brilliant writer who chose to make his living shitting on the altar of literature. He was also the man she had been making out with, someone who, until a few seconds ago, she had been planning on having sex with. She didn't know what to say.

Finally some words emerged from her mouth. "You're fucking kidding me."

Curtis looked at her and appeared to not notice that she was upset. "No joke. I'm a big-time famous author that nobody's every heard of."

Harriet put her glass of champagne on the table. The champagne which had been so delicious moments ago now tasted saccharine and bilious. The cool breeze that had felt so sensual now gave her a shiver. The jazz that had been so seductive was grating, the speakers on the Mac Air turning the sultry saxophone into a rasping sound that hurt her ears.

"You should be ashamed of yourself."

She hadn't meant to sound so harsh, but there it was.

...

It slowly dawned on Curtis that maybe he'd just blown his opportunity for sex. From the look on her face, he was going to be spending the night imagining what sex with her would be like while he beat off on the fancy hotel sheets. But while that realization was slowly dawning on him, another thought, a steady counterpoint of resentment, began to percolate in his head. What right did this chick have to judge him? Who does she think she is? She's no James Wood. Not that he'd try to go to bed with James Wood. She was a critic, a self-proclaimed authority. And while Curtis had, in the past, respected her demanding aesthetic judgements about other people's work, it was an altogether different experience to stare down her twin barrels of judgment and pretension about his own work.

Now that he thought about it, why did people respect her opinion? What had she done to earn it? Where were her credentials? She was like a quack who hung a shingle and proclaimed herself a doctor. But then he caught himself. He didn't want to be mad at her. She was, in almost every way, his dream girl. In addition to her braininess, she was also the hottest potential piece of ass that had come his way in a long time. Well, if he was being honest she was the *only* potential piece of ass that had come his way in a long time.

"Why?"

"*Why?*"

Curtis became animated. "Yeah. Why should I be ashamed of myself? Writers have been doing stuff like this for hundreds of years. Kingsley Amis, Larry McMurtry, H. P. Lovecraft. There are lots of great writers who have worked ghosting. For chrissakes, Dickens wrote newspaper ads."

"Yeah, but . . . a reality star?"

Curtis sat down and took a drink.

"I spent a long time writing a novel that nobody wanted. I was broke."

Harriet glared at him, her eyes fierce. "You should have some dignity."

Curtis flashed with anger. "Oh, look who's talking."

"What's that supposed to mean?"

Curtis could tell from the edge in her voice that he definitely wasn't going to get laid tonight. "Nothing. I'm sorry."

"No. Expound. Please. I'm all ears."

Curtis shook his head. "It's nothing."

Harriet laughed. "The funny thing is, I was looking for you. I wanted to find Sepp Gregory's ghostwriter. And I did."

Curtis raised an eyebrow. "Why were you looking for me?"

"I'm working on an exposé of the publishing business. I was going to focus on your opus, but now I see you're a veritable factory of cheap celebrity novels."

Her tone annoyed Curtis. He wasn't even going to think about her or her freckled breasts while he masturbated tonight. Maybe he'd think about Roxy Sandoval or any one of the dozens of Playmates he'd seen at the mansion.

"I may be a whore, but I'm not cheap. I'm getting two hundred grand for the Roxy Sandoval story."

Harriet sighed.

"That's even more disappointing."

She stood and looked off into the distance, not saying anything for what seemed like a long time.

Curtis stood too. He was unsure what was about to happen. Was she leaving? Going to the bathroom?

"We can't all teach at Yale or get fellowships at Yaddo or NEA grants. Some of us have to earn our money by doing what we can."

Harriet tossed back the rest of her glass. She was leaving. He could tell.

"You're a brilliant writer. Really. You don't deserve your talent if you're going to squander it."

Curtis put his champagne down and narrowed his gaze, staring at her. Harriet noticed he was clenching and unclenching his fists. Finally he just shook his head.

"Do you think I like this? I would rather be writing my own work but, you know, I have to eat. This is the real world and not some literary la-la fantasy land."

Harriet felt the champagne stick in her throat. She whipped her head around and glared at him.

"Fuck you."

Curtis was nodding, letting the anger take control of his tongue.

"Nice. You just sit on your throne and render judgment. What qualifies you? I always wondered. And why do you use the royal 'we' on your blog? What's that about? Are you the queen of some realm?"

Harriet glared at him, her body trembling. "*We* are sorry *we* ever met you."

Curtis's eyes stung. Was he about to cry? "That's right. You failed at writing fiction, so you just *criticize*."

There was something about the way he said it.

Harriet scooped his Mac Air off the table, slammed the lid, and threw it off the balcony, sending it spinning like a Frisbee out into the sky. Her sudden movement coupled with the shock of seeing his new computer fluttering toward the swimming pool caused Curtis to react instinctively. His movement was awkward, impaired by alcohol and the fact that he was not particularly coordinated, but he launched himself in a heaving, spastic lunge, his hands pawing the air in the hopes of catching his laptop. He missed the computer but managed to trip over one of the chairs. He lost his balance, lurching and stumbling. And, as he tried to get some traction on the tile floor, he realized that the cool handmade shoes Pete had made for him were not sufficiently broken in to prevent him from slipping and skidding toward the railing, where—in a freakish move—he somersaulted over the bars and fell three floors down, landing on the concrete patio with a wet slap that, for some reason, made Harriet think of a sack of pork.

...

Sepp sat up in his chaise, groggy and unfocused from sleep, and saw Curtis lying on the concrete. Curtis's eyes were open, but his head was bent at an unnatural angle, his neck snapped by the impact. Sepp knew instantly that something was wrong.

"Dude? Are you okay?"

...

Harriet stood on the balcony, stunned. One second Curtis was here, insulting her and smirking, the next he was gone, *vanished into thin air.* Harriet thought about that one. It was from Shakespeare, *The Tempest.* She was pretty sure about that.

She heard a voice from below.

"Hello?"

She looked over the edge of the balcony and saw Sepp Gregory staring up at her. Even though it was dark by the pool, she could see from the angle of Curtis's head that he was dead. Sepp gave her a wave.

"I think this dude is hurt."

Harriet's brain spun. She tried to think. If Curtis was dead, had she murdered him? Manslaughtered him? She hated being so self-centered but, well, was she in trouble? It's not like she pushed him off the balcony, but then again it's not like her actions didn't cause him to fall. If she hadn't thrown his laptop, they'd still be arguing on the balcony. That made her responsible for his death. But where did she stand relative to the laws of the State of California? She was pretty sure she'd murdered Curtis. Even if it was accidental. Negligent homicide or involuntary manslaughter or stupid accidental homicide or something like that. A depraved indifference, a wanton disregard. A crime of passion. The cops would call it whatever they could to make her responsible.

Fuck.

She'd go to jail for depraved indifference to a wafer-thin laptop. She hadn't meant to do the crime but she really didn't want to do the time. She looked over the edge at Sepp. He was the only witness. She needed time to think and she needed to do something fast. She focused her champagne-impaired brain and concentrated.

"Stay there. I'll be right down."

. . .

Sepp bent down close to Curtis's face.

"Hey man? Can you hear me?"

Sepp listened for a moment and thought he heard a gurgled response but then he realized it was the pool's automatic filter system swirling the water around. He turned when Harriet came running out. She stopped next to him, her hand reflexively going to her mouth.

"Oh my God."

She turned to Sepp and grabbed his arm.

"Will you help me? We need to get him to a hospital."

"Shouldn't we call an ambulance?"

Harriet shook her head. "He doesn't have insurance."

...

Sepp stood outside the hotel's back door, propping Curtis up. It reminded him of helping drunk people, how their bodies go all floppy and they piss themselves. He didn't have time to put on a shirt, so he stood there in khakis and flip-flops feeling the warmth of Curtis's body in his arms and the tingle of the night air on his back. The only thing that looked weird was Curtis's head. It kept lolling, rolling, drooping, and dropping from side to side. Sepp tried to bolster it with his shoulder, raising his elbow, but then the head would tilt and spin, owl-like, in a random direction. It reminded Sepp of that game with the marble where you twisted knobs and tried to roll the ball through a little labyrinth, avoiding the pitfalls and dead ends. He used to be pretty good at that when he was a kid.

It took her a while, Sepp had no idea how long he'd been standing there, but Harriet finally pulled up to the entrance in a very small car.

Harriet jumped out and opened the door.

"Let me help."

She took Curtis's legs while Sepp held his shoulders and they gently slid him into the backseat. Curtis's head spun again, unnaturally, like the devil girl in that scary movie whose head did a three-sixty and then she puked green vomit everywhere. Sepp hoped that didn't happen. That would be gross.

Sepp bolstered Curtis's head as best he could against the door. He looked at Harriet.

"He looks kinda dead."

"Well, he just fell off a fucking balcony, how do you think he's supposed to look?"

Before Sepp could answer she snapped, "Get in the car."

...

Harriet headed east. She didn't know what, exactly, she was going to do. In fact, she was beginning to wonder what had possessed her to bundle Curtis into the car and take off with a reality TV star in the passenger seat. Had she just lost her mind? Was this what they meant by temporary insanity? Did she seriously think she could get away with it? And what was the "it" she was trying to get away with? Why not just tell the cops the truth? They'd been drinking, Curtis fell off the balcony. That *is* what happened. She'd never broken the law before, had no history of violent behavior or domestic abuse. So what was she worried about? Somewhere around La Brea Avenue she almost turned around, almost went to look for a hospital, but then she realized there was no way she could explain this and come out of it looking innocent. He was dead because of her, and this driving around like a crazy person wasn't going to provide the verisimilitude her story needed. Harriet imagined herself sitting on a chair in the police station sobbing into a paper towel as she confessed, admitting how she'd unintentionally killed an innocent man. There would be a trial. Publicity. It would cost her a fortune in legal fees and, in the end, they'd send her away for a few years.

But was Curtis really innocent? He was a fucking ghostwriter. Maybe he got what he deserved—karma and all that.

Harriet had always been a good student. She got straight As for most of her life. Maybe she hadn't been the most social butterfly in high school or college, but she'd applied herself. She'd read a lot of literature. She'd graduated *cum laude* from Mills, an all-women's college, with a degree in English. She tried to think. What would Elizabeth do if she'd accidentally caused Mr. Darcy to fall off his horse and break his neck? What would George Sand do if she accidentally dropped a piano on Chopin? Harriet wished she was more familiar with the oeuvre of Raymond Chandler or Dashiell Hammett. Then she'd know what to do. She made a mental note to add some genre books to her reading list.

None of what was happening seemed like a conscious decision to her. It was like she was on some kind of maniac-on-the-lam autopilot bubbling up from her subconscious from all the bad TV shows she'd watched as a teen. She drove east, because if she'd driven west they'd hit the ocean and then there's nowhere to go, but east of Los Angeles was nothing but miles of road and the open desert. She needed to figure out what to do and going to the desert to look for answers was a pretty common trope in literature.

...

It was midnight when Sepp realized that they weren't driving to any hospital. He turned and looked at Curtis in the backseat. The dude was looking pale. Sepp looked at Harriet. She was driving, concentrating on the road with a savage intensity. She looked kind of pale too. Maybe it was just the light. Or maybe something was going on.

"I think you passed the hospital."

Harriet kept her eyes on the road. "He's dead."

Sepp twisted in his seat and looked at Curtis again. He'd never seen a dead person before. Well, technically that wasn't true because once he'd seen a surfer get clobbered by a board and then wash up an hour later but he didn't get a good look at him because there were so many people standing around, so he wasn't sure what a dead person looked like. But now that he looked, the dude wasn't breathing and Sepp was pretty sure that breathing was a big part of being alive.

"You sure?"

"Pretty sure."

Sepp settled back into the passenger seat. He didn't know what was going on. Here they were, a dead guy in the backseat, and they were just driving. Brenda and Marybeth were going to be pissed off if he screwed up his book tour.

"I'm supposed to do a couple of TV shows."

"Now?"

"Tomorrow. Then I've got a signing in Phoenix the day after."

Harriet stared off into the distance.

"You'll have to reschedule the TV shows. We're going to Phoenix."

23

Mojave

Sepp remembered this stretch of road. The narrator of *Love Express* had said, "Interstate 10 runs in a relatively straight line along the sunny bottom of the United States, linking the earthquake-ravaged blight of Los Angeles to the hurricane-blasted sprawl of Jacksonville. Will this lonesome desert highway be where Sepp Gregory finds 'The One'?"

Sepp remembered a date with a woman who called herself a "desert rat" and wore gold sneakers and cargo pants that were filled with odd rocks, loose tobacco, and a lizard skull. She was sweet, with a nice smile and wind-damaged hair, but she had a tendency to laugh out loud at nothing, which, dude, kinda freaked everyone out. Still, he'd enjoyed spending time with her, unlike the tennis pro from Indian Wells. That woman was certifiable. Even Dr. Jan said so.

Sepp looked at Harriet. Something freaky was going on. He didn't know what exactly, but whatever was happening was totally not normal and he didn't need to be a Dr. Jan to figure that out. He was beginning to think that he might be in some kind of danger. Was Harriet certifiable? She seemed a lot nicer than the tennis pro, but then there was a dead guy in the backseat and even the tennis pro didn't have that.

Harriet swung her head and glared at Sepp. "Stop staring at me."

Sepp looked out the front window. "So, like, did you kill him?"

Harriet turned to look at him. "What?"

"I mean, like, how'd he die?"

"He fell off the balcony. You saw him land."

"Actually I didn't see anything. The sound of it woke me up."

"The sound of what?"

"When he hit."

"The splat?"

"It was crunchier than a splat."

Sepp watched Harriet's face for a clue, but all she did was look off into the dark freeway. He didn't know what to think. She hadn't exactly answered his question.

"So, how come we're going to Phoenix?"

. . .

Harriet didn't answer. She just drove. A sign announced they were passing through the city of Colton. Harriet had never heard of Colton. She didn't know that it was one of the busiest railway crossings in the country, a major linkage point between transcontinental rail lines. She'd never heard of the city's namesake, Civil War General David Colton. She didn't know that Morgan and Virgil Earp settled there after surviving the shootout at the O.K. Corral. Harriet wasn't sure it was even a real city. It looked like part of the never-ending suburban sprawl. Strip malls and car dealerships next to monstrous rectangles called "big box stores," next to fast-food restaurants that stood in front of strip malls and car dealerships next to monstrous rectangles, all of it a kind of Möbius strip of the rise of capitalism and the fall of Western civilization.

Harriet wondered what it would be like to live in Colton. Maybe she could hide out there. Would she be bored? Or was it cozy? Maybe the town just off the freeway was really cute and she could get a lot of reading done. She could disappear. Start over. Get away with murder.

As they headed out toward the Mojave Desert, like a tiny skiff entering uncharted waters, passing dark windmills, strange guardians of the desert spinning against the night sky, it began to dawn on Harriet the exact degree of how fucked she was.

"I don't know what to do."

She looked at Sepp.

"What would you do?"

"What would I do what?"

Harriet bit her lip. She didn't know why she did it. Maybe somewhere deep in her DNA she had a damsel-in-distress nervous tic that would make her look vulnerable and sexy and bring a prince to her rescue. Of course that was nonsense; she was a postfeminist feminist, she didn't believe in that bullshit for a second.

"What would you do if you had a dead guy in the backseat?"

"It's not an if. There *is* a dead guy in the backseat."

"Right. So what should we do about it?"

She watched Sepp think about it, hoping that the "we" might throw him, like he might accept some culpability. After all it was his fault. If he hadn't been a celebrity and needed a ghostwriter for his stupid book she wouldn't have come to LA and tried to expose their scam. In a lot of ways he was more culpable for Curtis's death than she was.

At first she took his thoughtful stare for some kind of deep and profound thought, but when she followed his gaze she realized that he was staring at the exact spot on her blouse where her cleavage was exposed. Harriet shifted in her seat, twisting her torso so that her breasts' hypnotic powers could work on Sepp's reptile brain.

"I don't watch a lot of movies, but they do things like this in movies, don't they?"

Sepp nodded. "I love movies."

"So what would they do in a movie?"

"Depends on the movie."

Harriet sighed. "Say it was a Scorsese movie."

Sepp scratched his head. "Chop the body up. Or bury it somewhere. That's what they usually do. Sometimes they make it look like a suicide or an accident, you know. Leave it in a hotel room."

"This doesn't look like a suicide."

Sepp twisted and looked back at Curtis. "He coulda slipped in the shower."

. . .

They stopped at a gas station just outside of Palm Springs. While Sepp watched the numbers spin on the pump—he couldn't remember ever seeing them spin so fast—Harriet went inside and asked about motels in the area. Sepp wondered if she was going to rob the gas station. Maybe she'd kill the cashier and clean out the till. Isn't that what happens in movies? Isn't that what people do when they're on a rampage? Sepp wasn't sure exactly what was going on. They were on the lam, obviously, he wasn't a moron. But it didn't feel real. He kept waiting for the assistant director to say, "Okay. Lunch." But there was no camera, no crew, and no catering truck. Sepp didn't know how to be on the lam, but he did know how to be in a reality show. You just sit back and let events unfold. Your job is to play your part and stay in the moment. That was the key to being a star in a reality show. Stay in the moment. Even if there are evil schemes swirling all around you, someone wants you to vote someone out of the house and really they know and you know that they're lying to you, that they'll vote a totally different way and you just have to sit there and nod and not call them on their lie because that's the way reality on television works, no matter what kind of scandalous nonsense is being perpetrated, you have to act like it's totally normal when the cameras are there.

Sepp looked at Curtis in the backseat. He wasn't looking so good, but maybe that was the mercury vapor lights. Gas stations have notoriously bad lighting. Sepp had learned that from *Love Express*. He could see the lights of Palm Springs twinkling in the distance. He considered running off, escaping, fleeing into the black night of the Coachella Valley. But where would that get him? He did have a book signing in Phoenix. What was he going to do, walk there? He couldn't just split, he had responsibilities. And he left his stuff at the hotel. He'd call Brenda or Marybeth in the morning and they'd take care of things. That was their job.

...

The Pioneertown Motel is tucked down a dirt driveway behind a honky-tonk roadhouse called Pappy & Harriet's Pioneertown Palace. It is completely isolated: off the side road, off the bypass, off the highway, off the charts. In fact it is about as far out of the way as you can get without driving into the Mojave Desert. It is the perfect spot for drunken weekends, stargazing acid trips, survivalist reunions, and spontaneous cremations of dead rock stars.

Harriet drove the rental past the roadhouse, surprised that any bar anywhere in the world would have the same name as her. Sepp noticed it too.

"Hey. Harriet. How cool is that?"

Harriet had always thought of her name as perfect for a stodgy librarian type: a prude and a know-it-all. But now here it was, flashing and gleaming in colored neon, promising cold beer, barbecued ribs, loud music, and rockin' good times. It was strangely reassuring.

She resisted an urge to update her Twitter account with a call for her readers to make a pilgrimage to the roadhouse. It could be a travel piece or something she mentioned on her blog. First she had to get them a room. Then they had to do something about Curtis.

. . .

Pioneertown was built in the 1940s as a set for movie westerns—the Cisco Kid films *The Valiant Hombre, The Gay Amigo,* and *The Daring Caballero,* as well as episodes of *The Gene Autry Show,* and even more recent films like *The Life and Times of Judge Roy Bean* had all been filmed there. The motel was erected to house the movie stars and directors who came to work on the films and was made to look like some kind of 1870s Wild West way station, a hardscrabble burg carved out of the sun-blasted desert and populated by rattlesnakes, roadrunners, and their human equivalents.

Harriet learned all this from the brochure while she waited for the manager. Eventually she noticed a box by the office door that informed her that check-ins after midnight just needed to drop a credit card in the slot and to take a room key. Harriet went back to the car, fished Curtis's corporate credit card out of his wallet, and took a room on the back side of the motel. People in the desert, she realized, were different.

...

Harriet told him to duck down in the car and so Sepp ducked down. She thought it would be better if no one saw him and that sounded good to him. He wasn't a celebrity like Ryan Seacrest, but still, people might recognize him. So he didn't mind lying low. Besides, slumped in the seat he could relax and look up at the stars. Out here you could actually see them. He cracked his window, and his nose caught a lingering smell of barbecue smoke from the roadhouse that caused his stomach to gurgle. He hadn't realized how hungry he was.

Harriet got back in the car and drove around to the other side of the motel. She parked between two dusty pickup trucks. The trucks had dirt bikes strapped to their beds and it occurred to Sepp that riding a motorcycle out into the desert might be a fun thing to do. Dirt bikes are cool.

...

While Harriet scampered out and opened the door to the motel room, Sepp pulled Curtis out of the back of the car. Curtis's corpse wasn't nearly as pliable as he had been before. His legs stuck out in stiff scarecrow angles, and Sepp had to yank and jerk a few times to get him out of the small car.

Harriet came around and grabbed Curtis's legs. "Quietly and quickly."

They hustled Curtis into the room and gently set him down on the floor. Harriet closed the door and locked it.

They both stood there staring down at Curtis's lifeless form. He didn't look good, not at all. His face was white, his lips blue, as if he'd been stuck in a freezer, and dark bruisy splotches were beginning to form on parts of his body as gravity forced the blood to settle.

Sepp looked up at her. "I'm hungry."

"You're hungry?"

Sepp nodded. "I think the bar is open until two. We could just make it."

Harriet glared at him. "What we need to do, right now, is put this guy in the shower and then hit the road. We need as much distance between this place and us as we can get."

Sepp thought about it. "What if I just got something to go?"

Harriet shook her head in disbelief. "I'm not a pro at doing this, okay, but I'm pretty sure it's important that nobody sees us." She looked at Sepp and her eyes filled with tears. "This is stressing me out."

She sat on the bed and began to cry. Sepp felt bad. He'd seen a lot of women cry on TV shows but this seemed realer than that.

"I'm sorry. I'm just . . . I don't know why I'm here."

Harriet wiped her nose on her sleeve. "I'm sorry I got you mixed up in this. I don't know what the fuck I'm doing. I don't know why I'm doing this."

"You freaked out. It happens."

Harriet nodded and blew her nose on some tissues. She looked up at Sepp. "Just help me out here, okay? I can't do this on my own. Just help me and then I'll take you to Phoenix and then I'll be out of your life and we'll never talk about this again to anyone. Okay?"

Sepp nodded. "What do you want me to do?"

. . .

Harriet's plan was simple. Make it look like Curtis had slipped in the shower, cracked his head on something hard, and died. It wasn't an airtight, foolproof, Sherlock-Holmes-will-never-solve-this plan, but she was hoping it would work.

"Help me with his clothes."

Harriet knelt over Curtis's body and untied his shoes. They were, she noticed, exceptionally nice shoes, nicer than any shoes she could afford, and it made her wonder what kind of man wears such fancy shoes. Is that why he was a sellout? So he could wear fancy shoes?

Sepp looked at the shoes.

"Those are cool."

Harriet didn't say anything. She put the shoes by the bed and then unfastened his brown leather belt, unbuttoned his pants, and yanked them off his body while Sepp fumbled with the buttons on Curtis's shirt.

Harriet reached under Curtis's ass and pulled his white briefs off, exposing genitals which, if things had gone better, she might be pleasuring right now.

"Do you have to do that?"

Harriet looked at Sepp.

"Do you take a shower in your underwear?"

"Well, I could."

"Yeah, but you don't."

"Right."

Harriet helped him get Curtis's shirt and T-shirt off. The fact that his arms had gone rigid made it difficult. This, Harriet realized, is why they call dead people "stiffs." She saw the tattoo on his bicep.

Sepp read it out loud. "Fail better?"

Harriet nodded. "It's a quote from Beckett."

From Sepp's expression she could tell he didn't know what she was talking about.

"It's so you're not afraid to try something. Okay. Let's try to get him into the shower."

Sepp looked at her. "How're we going to do that?"

"You're going to hold him up under the water."

"My shorts will get wet."

Harriet snorted. "Take 'em off."

"You want me to get naked in the shower with a dead guy."

Harriet nodded. "I'll help."

Now was not the time for modesty so Harriet pulled off her shirt and removed her bra—her freckly breasts bouncing into view—and slipped out of her pants and underwear.

Still Sepp hesitated. Harriet smiled at him. She wanted to be reassuring.

"The idea is to make this look as normal as possible."

...

Sepp unfastened his shorts and let them drop to the floor. He didn't wear underwear, preferring to go commando, and, miraculously, once brought into the light, his penis began to rise, telescoping in length, swelling in girth, until it stood straight up. Why hadn't that happened with any of the other women he'd tried to be with in the past year? Why was it happening now?

Harriet put her hands on her hips. "Oh my."

Sepp felt himself blushing, a pulse of heat flashing across his face. He was feeling distinctly mixed emotions. On the one hand he was delighted to have an erection with a woman and, on the other, he was mortified that he was waving his woody in front of a dead guy. But he could tell it wasn't the dead guy that turned him on, it was Harriet, there was something about her.

Harriet looked at Sepp.

"One thing at a time."

...

Sepp had really hoped his erection would go down, that it would show some patience, bide its time until the appropriate moment, but no, it stayed hard as he lifted Curtis's body up under the shower and held him there, locked in a variation of the life-saving embrace he learned when he was a lifeguard on the beach one summer. His dick actually got harder as he watched Harriet soap Curtis's body down—in her quest for credibility she didn't care where she ran the washcloth—and his cock stayed that way even when Harriet instructed him to let Curtis topple backwards and Sepp heard, for a second time that night, the sickening thwack of human head hitting a hard surface.

...

Harriet adjusted the water so a modest stream sprayed down on Curtis's corpse. She felt bad about wasting water in the desert, knew it wasn't the most ecological option, but she didn't know what else to do.

She grabbed a towel and went into the bedroom. Sepp was standing there, drying himself off, his body lean and strong, his abs rippling, and his penis bigger and pinker than any she'd ever seen. To think only a few hours ago she'd been so close to having sex with Curtis, to letting physical sensations take her out of her head. Maybe she was out of her head. What was she doing? Covering up an accidental death? It was so random. So bizarre. Completely out of character for her. She could blame it on the champagne, or on the fact that she hadn't had sex in a couple of years. But would a jury care? Would anyone care?

Harriet felt that she was doing the right thing. She was sorry Curtis was dead, but then he'd written that book and was planning to write another. They kept paying him hundreds of thousands of dollars and he'd write more of them and before you'd know it, the world would be drowning in fake celebrity novels while real novelists worked at Starbucks or taught freshman comp.

Harriet dried herself and saw that Sepp was looking at her in a way no man had looked at her before. There was an animal hunger, an undisguised desire in his eyes. She felt a trickle of moisture running down her thigh. It wasn't from the shower.

Harriet walked over to Sepp and, without saying a word, pushed him down on the bed. She then straddled him, grabbing his cock with her right hand, and inserted him inside her.

24

Arizona

The eastern sky began to lighten as they drove past Blythe, crossed the Colorado River, and entered the great state of Arizona. The early morning sun backlit the mountains on either side of the freeway, causing sharp and craggy silhouettes to loom forward like an old-fashioned 3-D effect, the Dome Rock Mountains becoming creepy and predatory in her peripheral vision. It felt to Harriet like the world was ready to pounce, just waiting for the perfect opportunity to crush her.

She wasn't normally paranoid or afraid of shadows and wondered if it might be her guilty conscience affecting her psyche. Why hadn't she just called an ambulance and told the hotel that Curtis had fallen off the balcony? That's what a normal person would do. He was drunk. Goofing around. All she had to do was omit the fact that she'd touched his computer.

Harriet had always considered herself smarter than most people, but now she considered that perhaps she was like everyone else. Was she really doing this? Or was it like some cheap sci-fi story where you're replaced by the android pod person who looks exactly like you but isn't? And if she was replaced by an android, how could she think that she was replaced by an android? Wouldn't they replace her mind too? Or erase her memory or something? Maybe she was in a sci-fi novel and had entered a parallel universe where everything was the same only slightly different because now she was a nymphomaniacal killer. She remembered reading Stewart O'Nan's novel *The Speed Queen,* which was about a drug-fueled killing spree in the desert, but she wasn't really planning to kill anyone or spree—which is a funny word, now that she thought of it—and her flight wasn't fueled by anything but a weird sense of guilt and panic.

She prided herself on taking responsibility for things. She'd often railed about it in her essays. *Why don't people clean up their own messes? Own up? What's wrong with the world?* But now here she was, avoiding responsibility for Curtis's death, acting like everybody else. It occurred to Harriet that she might've had a case against the hotel. Low railings and a slippery balcony? They're begging for a lawsuit.

And why hadn't she felt any remorse? She hadn't shed a tear for Curtis. She had cried in frustration, in fear, but she hadn't cried because Curtis was dead. He was, after all, a talented writer, even if he did sell his talent to the highest bidder like a little keyboard whore. She'd been attracted to him and they'd been swapping saliva only a few hours ago and now he was dead and she couldn't even get misty-eyed. What was wrong with her? And what did these mountains want from her?

She looked over at Sepp. He was asleep, his head against the window, his mouth hanging open. He still didn't have a shirt on and she couldn't help but admire his torso. In fact she admired everything about Sepp's body. He was a stud. Even she could say that. Normally she hated that word. It was Old English for a "pillar or post" and then, because language was controlled by men and so is, by nature, phallocentric, it was used to mean a "horse for breeding" and then, later, to mean a man of "significant sexual prowess." Linguistically a stud was just a big hard dick. That's what Sepp had. And he wasn't shy about using it either.

She thought they'd done a pretty good job of covering their tracks at the Pioneertown Motel. After getting fucked like she never even knew possible, an experience that gave her an entirely new and comprehensive appreciation for the word "fuck," after having an orgasm that caused her entire body to spasm from the inside out, building from her core until it rippled across her skin in the form of goosebumps, sending tingly bolts of pleasure cannonballing from her fingers to her toes—literally the force of her climax caused her to gasp—and after feeling Sepp roll her over, throw her legs up on his shoulders, and ride her deep while she sucked on her fingers and continued to have orgasmic aftershocks; after all that, they'd cleaned up the room, wiped fingerprints off every surface they could think of, and left as covertly as possible. They even rolled the car down the dirt driveway about thirty yards before starting the engine.

But now what?

Was she just going to drop Sepp off in Phoenix, return the rental, and fly back to San Francisco? Was that it? Mission accomplished?

Harriet wondered if she could trust Sepp. Would he keep his mouth shut? Would he tell the authorities? Could she trust him or did she need to make sure he never said a word? Isn't that the killer's protocol? Cover your tracks? Rub out the witnesses? Tie up all the loose ends?

It would be easy to do. She could unhook his seat belt, lean over, open the door, and give him a shove. He'd be roadkill in a matter of seconds and she could go see the Grand Canyon.

Harriet worried that she was becoming a sociopath.

25

Arizona

Sepp tried to decipher the graffiti scrawled in marker on the wall of the bathroom stall. *Trip when you ball, deformed babies are amusing.* He had no idea what it meant. Was it some kind of sports reference? To the right of that, the words "TUCSON LOVES PUSSY" were scratched into the paint underneath a crude drawing of a giant cock blasting spunk and a pair of cartoonishly hairy balls. That was easier to understand. The city of Tucson, Arizona, loves pussy. Clearly. And, dude, why wouldn't they? Because here in this freeway rest area bathroom stall Sepp was loving some pussy himself. He was standing behind Harriet, sliding his cock into her, reaching around and stroking her clitoris, as she bent forward and braced herself against the graffitied wall. Sepp felt good. He was back, like back from the dead back, he was back in the game, back in the saddle, and back at it. Harriet had saved him from a life of erectile failure, she was like that mad scientist who reanimates dead things and while maybe it didn't work on the dude who fell off the balcony, it totally worked on Sepp's dick. In fact, dude, it was working too good. The sex they'd had in the motel had been awesome and now all Sepp wanted to do was have awesome sex again and again. Cooler still, she wanted to do it again too. That's why they'd pulled over to the rest area. Sepp couldn't help it, he had pulled his dick out in the car and she'd taken one look at it and, you know how these things go, they just had to get it on immediately.

Despite all his travels and his *Love Express* road trip experience, he'd never had sex in a freeway rest area bathroom stall before. I mean, he'd had sex in bathroom stalls, duh, but not at a rest area. It was different, like new and hot, but also there was something more different going on here as he pumped in and out, grinding in tight circles, making her shudder and gasp and moan. He realized that he'd never felt this way about anyone before. She wasn't a phony actress fame-whore like Roxy or Caitlin. She wasn't all up in herself; she was passionate about ideas and smart things. She cared about stuff. Maybe it was wrong to help her with the dead guy and all, maybe he'd get in trouble for doing it. But he owed her. She'd saved him. She'd given his penis life again. How could he rat on her now? What if he dropped a dime on her and then he never got it up again? No way that would be worth it. Sepp knew it was wrong to put a price on a human life, but what price can you put on your sex life? It was, like, too much math.

Their thrusting built up speed, his fingers attaining a slippery velocity, moving gently over her swollen clitoris as he pushed deep into her. He felt her muscles clench, her pussy constricting around his cock as she let out a screech and a groan and a shudder and slapped the walls with her hands and shouted "Fuck yes" over and over.

Sepp felt a dull energy shiver through his body, building in intensity, traveling up to the head of his penis which was buzzing, like it was on fire.

Sepp looked up at the graffiti drawing of the ejaculating cock as he came. TUCSON LOVES PUSSY.

26

New York City

Being a book publicist is not an easy job. Every month
you're assigned four or five titles to promote. It's usually a mixed bag: fiction, nonfiction, self-help, diet
books, even celebrity autobiographies. That translates to long
hours sitting at a desk answering emails and yakking on the
phone, begging reviewers, newspaper editors, bloggers, bookstores, radio producers, and TV shows to take one of your
authors and give them a little press; you do, basically, anything
and everything you can to get someone, somewhere to pay
attention to one of your books.

The stress and monotony of this is broken by editors
demanding special attention for their titles and authors calling in a cold rage demanding to know why they weren't a
book club pick or on NPR or in *The New York Times* or on a
fake-news comedy show.

And then, occasionally, an author disappears. In this case
leaving a trail of nude photos plastered on every corner of the
internet. Even mainstream media outlets showed the photos,
but gave Sepp a pixilated penis because the raw stuff was NSFW.

The first sign Brenda got that something was wrong was
when she turned on her computer and saw that she had over

two hundred emails in her in-box. Then she got the first of several angry phone calls. This one from a producer from an LA rock radio station complaining that Sepp hadn't phoned in that morning for a live chat with the DJs. The producer was especially miffed because Sepp had talked to their competition the day before. Brenda promised to reschedule. The second call came later. Sepp was supposed to go do a morning TV show at the local Fox affiliate and then be a guest on *Ellen*.

It wasn't that unusual for a celebrity to blow off small things like phoners with rock stations, but a major TV show? Even more worrisome was that she'd arranged for Kathryn the media escort to pick Sepp up and take him to these interviews. Kathryn was waiting at the hotel and had no idea what had happened to Sepp since his agent had taken him back to the hotel after the Playboy Mansion party.

Brenda tried his cell phone but kept getting routed to voice mail. Marybeth confirmed she'd left Sepp at the hotel.

Brenda was struck by the sudden fear that Sepp might've taken a bunch of different drugs at the party, gone back to the hotel, and promptly OD'd. Or maybe he'd killed himself. From what she'd heard from the bookstore, he'd acted totally bizarre at the signing yesterday. Taking off his clothes? Crying? Maybe he cracked and jumped off a bridge or something. It'd be a tragedy, of course. Very sad for his family. But it'd be great for the book. She could get all kinds of publicity for that. Once before, one of Brenda's authors committed suicide and the book stayed on the bestseller list for thirty-four weeks.

27

Arizona

@fatalinfluence Just had the best. breakfast. ever. Scrambled eggs with cactus and chorizo. Fear and loathing on Interstate 10.

. . .

"What are you doing?"

"I'm updating my Twitter."

Sepp was confused. "But if you tell everyone where we are . . . I mean, aren't we supposed to be on the lam?"

Harriet shook her head. "No. I'm writing a piece on you. I'm joining you on your book tour."

Sepp grinned. "Are you going to write about last night?"

Harriet felt herself blush. They couldn't pass a rest area without pulling over and fucking each other's brains out. "Maybe. It's part of the story."

As Harriet hit send, the waitress, a young woman suffering from an overexposure to fried foods, came to their table and refilled their coffees.

"Still working on that?"

Harriet looked up at the waitress, then down at the plate. The plate was completely cleaned of food.

"There's not much left to work on."

She looked up at the waitress for a reaction. But she wasn't looking at Harriet, she was squinting at Sepp, her peeling, trans fat–enhanced cheeks scrunching up to get a good look at him. Harriet watched as recognition erupted on her features. It was as if her face had been run through one of those digital morphing machines; one second she was a sunburned frump with a pot of coffee and then the next she was an excited young woman, her face alive with the joy that comes from recognizing a TV star.

"Oh my God. Sepp Gregory. It's really you, isn't it?"

Sepp nodded. "It is really me."

The waitress put the coffee pot down on their table. "You know I tried out for *Love Express*."

"You did?"

She hung her head at the memory of her lost opportunity to be on a reality TV show. "I guess I didn't make the cut."

Sepp reached out and patted her arm. "The producers missed a good one. I can tell."

Harriet watched the waitress's face flush crimson. A bell sounded from the kitchen and the waitress turned and hesitated. "Wait. Okay? Don't go anywhere."

Sepp smiled. "I'm not going anywhere."

The waitress scampered off, moving surprisingly fast considering how slow the service was in the diner. Harriet shook her head.

"It's amazing."

"What?"

"The effect you have on women."

Harriet took a sip of her coffee. It was scalding and tasted like boiled burned tires.

"It's not me. It's the fame."

Harriet thought about that. "Why do people like reality shows? They're so stupid."

Sepp smiled. "That's what I like about you."

Harriet looked at him. "That's not really an answer."

The waitress came rushing back with a dog-eared copy of *Totally Reality* clutched in her hand.

"Will you sign it for me?"

Harriet stood up. "Excuse me."

...

Sepp absentmindedly signed the waitress's book as he watched Harriet walk off to the bathroom. He felt life stirring in his pants again as he eyed her ass moving underneath her skirt. He handed the book back to the waitress.

"Enjoy."

The waitress grabbed the book and pressed it to her breasts as she squealed.

"Thanks so much! I can't believe I got to meet you."

"It is totally my pleasure."

There was an awkward pause and then the bell rang in the kitchen. She rolled her eyes and bobbed her head in a spastic curtsey.

"Oh well, back to work."

The waitress retrieved the pot of coffee and skipped off.

Sepp caught his reflection in the window of the diner. He'd bought an Arizona State University T-shirt at the truck stop gift store and was admiring the mischievous little devil on the logo. He poured a blob of cream into his coffee and watched the white and brown liquids swirl together. He figured he should call Brenda and tell her what was going on. Also, he needed his stuff from the hotel in Beverly Hills. Then he wanted to call Dr. Jan and tell her that he was being authentic. At least he thought he was. I mean, how do you know you're authentically authentic? What if you're just bullshitting yourself again? But then the feelings he had for Harriet seemed real, more authentic than anything he'd felt before. It wasn't like on the TV shows. There was no strategy involved, no alliances to be formed, no challenges to win. Dude. This was the real deal. At least, he thought maybe it was.

But what was the next step? Should they do a show together? Race around the world as a team? Should they get married? Host some kind of beach-wedding spectacular? That could be amazing. He'd invite a bunch of ex–reality stars and she'd invite all her famous author friends and literature professors. It'd be like *Hotties vs. Nerds* only better. They'd argue, come together, argue some more as their families and friends duked it out over seating arrangements and the menu in a series of fun challenges. Then they'd be united in holy matrimony and everything would be beautiful. Love conquers all. And then, when they had kids, they could bring in the *Nanny 911* experts to teach them how to be good parents. As his producers would say, it's a home run.

Sepp pulled out his phone and remembered that he'd turned off the ringer while they were doing it on the hood of the car when they'd pulled into a scenic overlook. That was cool. The sun was coming up and some truck drivers drove past and blew their horns. Sepp checked his phone and saw that Brenda had called six times.

. . .

Harriet squatted over the little paper toilet seat liner and micturated. Now there was a funny word. It was from the Latin *micturire,* "to desire to urinate." Not many people used the word anymore and whenever she saw it in a book she thought the author was trying too hard, doing a lexiconical cartwheel, grandstanding with the vocabulary.

She wiped herself, stood, and pulled her panties up. The rank but not unpleasant smell of spent sex wafted from between her legs. She wished she could take a shower. Or brush her teeth. She made a mental note to buy some condoms from the truck stop gift store. Maybe some lubricant to go with it. She wasn't sure.

She splashed cool water on her face and studied her reflection in the mirror. She knew it was a cliché. Wasn't this trope in every single crime movie ever made? If she was following the script, this was the moment when she was supposed to reflect. Look in the mirror and contemplate the choices you've made that led you to this moment in time. It was a completely heavy-handed, ham-fisted metaphor. And yet, for Harriet, it worked. *So this is what it looks like.* She was part of a couple on the lam. Like Bonnie and Clyde or Charles Starkweather and Caril Fugate. Not that she looked like a killer. Neither did Sepp. He was too handsome for that kind of thing. Maybe they were more like Warren Beatty and Faye Dunaway or Martin Sheen and Sissy Spacek than the actual killers. Harriet smiled. She might not be able to pull off Faye Dunaway, but she was a perfectly respectable Sissy Spacek. In the mirror, an attractive young woman with a couple of hickeys on her neck stared back. She looked worn out, a little "ridden hard and put away wet" as her Uncle Norman might've said, but it wasn't necessarily a bad thing. She had a glow. Maybe it was her aura, maybe it was an adrenalized sex energy racing through her. She might end up with psychic scars from this experience, but physically, she'd never felt better in her whole entire life.

...

Sepp and Harriet stood in the parking lot by the rental car. Harriet was checking something on her phone. She did that a lot. He watched as her mouth screwed up in a grimace.

"Your book is still on the bestseller list."

Sepp grinned. "Awesome."

Harriet looked at Sepp.

"'Awesome' is from an Old Norse word meaning fright or fear. When something is awesome it should inspire fear and dread."

Harriet gave him a stern look. "A burrito cannot be awesome."

Sepp shook his head. "So you say." He wasn't going to let it bother him. It was awesome, totally, that his book was on the list. But he could tell that Harriet was upset about it and since he was her partner now—her boyfriend, even though they'd never really said anything to each other about it—he wanted to make her feel better because that is what boyfriends do. The good ones anyway.

"You'll get on that list, someday. I'm sure of it."

Harriet sighed and unlocked the car doors. "I don't care about the list. I'd just like to get my book published."

Sepp looked at her and got an idea. Inspiration is a funny thing. Like you never know when the muse is going to whisper in your ear and give you a million-dollar idea. For Sepp, it had never really happened before. Not like in a genius way, not like where you actually invent something cool. Sure, he'd had some radical ideas in his day, like when he auditioned for *Sex Crib*. But everything was usually someone else's idea. Some producer thought of *Love Express*, and it was his agent's idea to do the book. But now, it was his turn to have a great idea. The force was with him. The little twenty-five-watt bulb inside his Easy-Bake Oven head blinked to life.

"I have a plan."

28

Mojave

On nice days, when the sky was clear, the early morning light peeked through a crack in the trailer, a little seam that ran just below the roof, and shot across the length of the mobile home. The beam of light would hit the stained glass mobile that spun over the sink, giving the little glass angels and their haloes an otherworldly glow. It was like the silver Christmas tree at Walmart when they put the blue-colored lights on it and it made the tree look all cold and shivery.

Sally Francher thought that it was God giving her a message. The Universe was making the angels glow. It was saying, "You may live in a single-wide, but it's a real nice one, a Fleetwood Festival, and you are blessed."

Sally sat up and stretched. Her joints popped and cracked as she performed a kind of stay-in-bed slacker yoga. Then she stood and walked into the kitchen, the mobile home shuddering with her steps. She wasn't a coffee person and it was too hot in the desert for something like tea, so she dumped yesterday's water out of her bong, refilled it, and sat down at the kitchen table for a little wake 'n' bake.

She exhaled and felt her brain relax. It was like her brain was an overfilled volleyball and the weed let a little air out, just taking some of the pressure off, softening it up for the day ahead. Her volleyball brain would still bounce; she could spike it over the net if she had to.

Sally poured herself a big bowl of Frosted Flakes and drowned them in skim milk. It was sweet and crunchy, two of her favorite things.

She put the bowl in the sink, blazed another nugget in the bong, and then got ready for work. She decided the Eagles of Death Metal T-shirt she'd gone to bed in, the one that said "Death By Sexy" across the front, was still perfectly clean enough to wear to work, so she slid on her blue jeans, banged her sneakers against the door to knock out any scorpions, and then hopped out of the mobile home and into the old Toyota pickup her husband had bought for her before he'd gone off to Afghanistan with his Marine Corps buddies.

It was the slow season, Sally was thankful for that, so she'd only have to clean half of the rooms at the motel. Scrubbing toilets, making beds, and picking used condoms off the floor were not the kind of things she normally liked to do— she could hardly be bothered to change the sheets on her own bed—but it's not like there are a lot of job opportunities in the desert. Her husband's military salary barely covered the necessities. For him that meant the mortgage payment on the trailer, insurance, the satellite TV bill, and dumb stuff like that. For Sally, necessities meant cold beer, a healthy stash of OG Kush, and the occasional night out at a bar so she could drink and dance. She liked dancing to cowboy music. It wasn't country and western, it was more what she liked to call "shit-kicker rock." But to do it right, to really kick some shit, you needed boots and a hat and money for beer. So she showed up at the Pioneertown Motel every morning to tidy up the rooms, disinfect the toilets, and change the sheets and towels.

She'd finished cleaning all but one room. It was an hour past check-out time and the little clipboard that the manager gave her said they were supposed to have checked out, but hadn't, so she had to roust them. Sally went up and banged on the door. She got no answer, so she unlocked it, opened the door a crack, and said the magic word.

"Housekeeping."

29

New York City

Brenda was annoyed. *What am I? A fucking concierge service?* Sepp had finally checked in, apologized for missing the phoner—he'd left his schedule behind in the room—and explained that he'd decided to drive to Phoenix with a friend but had somehow neglected to pack and bring his things. He promised he'd make it up to Ellen somehow. Maybe give her a personalized ab workout or do a dance or something. And would she mind having someone send his stuff to Phoenix? *Would she mind?* As a matter of fact she did mind. But that didn't mean she wasn't going to do it. She had to do it. *Totally Reality* was her big book this season and she was going to do whatever she could to keep it on the bestseller list, and if that meant flying out to LA and picking his dirty underwear off the floor, she'd do it. Hopefully it wouldn't come to that.

30

Pioneertown

The sheriff walked out of the motel room and looked at Sally. She sat on a rustic wood bench in the shade, underneath a little overhang, sipping a Fanta that the manager had pulled out of his minifridge.

"Where'd you get that soda?"

"Manager's office."

The sheriff nodded. He lifted his hat and wiped the sweat off his forehead. He was a good cop. Thoughtful, meticulous, logical, a real by-the-book kind of guy. He didn't really like leaving his air-conditioned office or his air-conditioned patrol car; he figured if it was too hot for law enforcement it oughta be too hot to commit a crime. But that was the thing about criminals, they weren't logical. Not that this looked like a crime. In the world of homicide, the bathtub was the most dangerous serial killer in history. How many slip 'n' fall corpses had he seen in his career? A dozen? A baker's dozen? Two dozen?

He felt bad for the motel. Some lawyer was probably getting ready to sue them right now. A man's dead. A motel gets shut down. All because nobody bothered to put those little nonskid daisies on the shower floor.

He put his hat back on his head and looked at Sally. She was a nice-looking filly. Especially since she wasn't wearing a bra under that "Death By Sexy" T-shirt. He wondered if her husband was going to make it back from Afghanistan. He hated to think about it, but if he didn't, well, someone would have to console her. Show her that life goes on.

"So you opened the door. Found the fella in the shower."

Sally nodded.

"Was the water running?"

"Yeah."

"Did you turn it off?"

"Was that wrong?"

The sheriff shrugged. "Not with this drought."

The sheriff watched the condensation building up on the outside of the soda bottle; icy drops of moisture gaining weight and then gravity sending them sliding down the side of the bottle. It made him feel like jumping into a pool. But that'd have to wait until after the coroner got there and looked at the body. He smiled at her. "I'm gonna go get me a soda. You want another?"

Sally shook her head. "I'm good."

31

Arizona

Harriet drove. Sepp yakked on the phone with his TV producers about his new idea. He was going to make Harriet a reality TV star and then she'd get her book published. It had worked for him. It would work for her.

Harriet found herself feeling simultaneously repulsed and attracted by the idea. If it succeeded, well, then she'd be a real author. But she'd also be a reality person, just like Sepp, just like what she'd spent her life fighting against. Although she could reclaim the high ground by writing a tell-all autobiography about becoming a reality TV star and expose the hypocrisy of the media that only paid attention to books by celebrities. And wasn't that her plan in the first place? She could bring the whole fucking machine down and the machine would pay her for the privilege. Think of all the struggling authors she'd be helping.

Harriet realized that this helped explain why she was with him and what she was doing. If the shit hit the fan with Curtis, she'd need a reasonable explanation, if not an alibi. She'd already written about her mission on her blog, so there was that, only now she was going deeper into the story. She was going to destroy the beast from the inside.

Sepp rattled on to the producers about his vision for the show. Harriet tried to tune it out, and normally she would've been able to, but this plan involved her getting married to Sepp. It was just an unbelievably weird idea. Married? To the dude with the abs?

She looked out at the red dirt extending off into the distance. *There's a lot of hot fucking nothing out here in Arizona.* Although it was kind of pretty. If you like unending vistas of dirt. Harriet wondered what she would tell her friends. Her family. That the man whose book is dumbing down our culture is so awesome—she couldn't believe that she'd just thought that word—so carnally adept in the sack that she put all her ideals and scruples aside to hump him raw. She had to admit that the sex was transcendent and while her intellectual friends might think she'd gone bonkers they would be jealous of his physique. They'd send her text messages wanting to know what it was like. She'd tell them, too. Fuck yeah.

But what about her intellectual side? Could she discuss William Vollman's ouevre with Sepp? What would he make of David Mitchell or Zadie Smith's books? Harriet knew what Sepp would do with the books. He'd make her put them under her ass to raise her up, change the angle, and then he'd mount her.

She could see it happening to her and the image made her clitoris throb and swell. She felt herself get moist. Who knew that getting fucked on a stack of literature would be a fantasy? She'd stop at a bookstore and buy a couple of books to take back to the hotel with them tonight. She squirmed in the seat, letting her underwear put subtle pressure on her crotch. She thought about what books would be good. Philip

Roth? Or was that too on the nose? Harriet briefly considered something raunchy and contemporary, but those books seemed too lightweight. She wanted something with a little gravitas, but also thick enough to lift her ass into a good position. *Infinite Jest? Gravity's Rainbow?* Or was that too collegiate? What about the entire Booker Prize shortlist?

Harriet realized she was finally thinking outside her head. Sure, she was still being intellectual, but now she'd integrated her body and was becoming some kind of well-read sex animal. She reached over and grabbed Sepp's crotch, giving it a healthy squeeze. Sepp turned to her. Harriet smiled.

"How far to the next rest area?"

...

The producers were being a pain. They weren't seeing the show the way Sepp saw it. There would be no eliminations, no rose ceremonies, and no tribal councils. That stuff was old, played out. This was simple. Sepp had found "the one" and the twist is, she's really super smart. The bod and the brain, together at last. It would be more like *Khloé & Lamar,* the *Keeping Up with the Kardashians* spinoff that followed a couple around and watched them eat dinner and argue about what kind of curtains to put in the master suite. There were all kinds of shows like this: *Cracker Barrel,* where a family of moonshiners from Georgia tried to run their liquor business and send their seemingly gay son to a special musical-theater program in Atlanta, or *Praise the Lard,* which followed an obese pastor and his wife as they tried and failed to lose weight. These shows were all huge hits, so why not *The Six-Pack and the Brainiac?* But the producers weren't so sure. People loved Sepp, but the book-critic angle, the intellectual part of it, was a hard sell. They told Sepp they wanted to be in business with him, but it had to be the right project. Viewers might want to watch a show about a hairdresser or realtor or a personal trainer—especially if they worked with celebrities, were gay, or better, worked with gay celebrities—but Sepp didn't have a job. He needed to bring something fresh to the table.

Sepp wasn't prepared to take no for an answer. His brain was like a salmon, swimming upstream against the odds, avoiding grizzly bears, rocks, fallen trees, crab monsters, and other stuff. The salmon didn't stop, he swam no matter what until he reached the top. Then he spawned and died. But that was the salmon. Sepp might spawn, but he didn't think it would kill him.

So as the producer was doing what producers do, that is, thinking of ways to say no, Sepp's salmon brain kept pushing against the current. He zigged, he zagged, and when it finally looked like the grizzly bear was going to make him into Alaskan sashimi, the dude pulled out a game changer.

"What if we were on the lam? For murder? For real. Do you think the network would be interested? Yeah, like Bonnie and Clyde."

Sepp was surprised when Harriet yanked the cell phone out of his hands and tossed it out the window.

32

Pioneertown

S ally sat on the little wooden bench, the same bench she'd been sitting on since the motel manager called the sheriff. She watched as a string of ants climbed up the side of the empty Fanta bottle and did whatever it is that ants do. Take sugar-water back to their queen or something. She'd waited there while the coroner arrived, followed by an ambulance. The pudgy little guy had taken some pictures, complained about the heat, and agreed with the sheriff that the dead fella had slipped in the shower and died from whacking his head on the shower floor.

It was hot and Sally was usually done with her work and on her way home by now. She wished she had a bump of something to break the boredom. A little crystal or another bong rip would make sitting on a bench a lot more enjoyable. The coroner stood next to her, trying to stay in the shade, and gnawed on a sandwich from Subway. It made Sally hungry. Maybe she'd stop and get a sandwich on her way home.

The sheriff came over and took off his hat. He mopped sweat off his head with a bandana and looked at the coroner. "You sure?"

The coroner nodded and swallowed a bite of his sandwich. He mumbled. "Pretty sure."

Sally noticed that the sheriff's official sheriff hat had a salty ring around the base of it from his sweat. The sheriff put his hat back on his head. "You gonna do an autopsy?"

The coroner shrugged. "Not much point in it."

"What about his car?"

The coroner swallowed and wiped his mouth on his sleeve. "You sure he had a car? Anybody see him drive in?"

The sheriff shook his head.

"My guess is he had too much to drink at the bar over there and got a room to sleep it off."

The sheriff nodded. "He walk to the bar?"

The coroner pointed into the room with his sandwich. "Not in those shoes." He took a bite of his sub. A strand of lettuce hung out the side of his mouth and danced in the air as he chewed. He looked at the sheriff. "You suggesting foul play?"

The sheriff scratched his neck.

"Shit. I'm not suggesting nothing."

The sheriff turned to Sally.

"You can go ahead and clean the room. We're all done here."

33

Arizona

Harriet glared at Sepp. She had pulled the car off to the shoulder, ramming on the brakes and sending a huge cloud of red dust up in the air like they'd just hit a roadside bomb. She sat behind the wheel, her hands shaking with barely controlled rage. She really wished she had her bite guard with her—her jaw was starting to ache.

Sepp looked at her with a confused expression, like a dog that had crapped on the floor but didn't see why that should cause a problem.

"I thought we were gonna stop at the next rest area."

Harriet shook her head. "What are you doing? You can't tell people that we're on the run from a murder."

Sepp held out his hands, trying to calm her. "Whoa. Relax. They're cool."

Harriet shook her head in disbelief. She remembered that old expression, "get a grip." She didn't know where, exactly, the expression came from, but she knew what it meant. She took a deep breath, exhaled, and looked at Sepp.

"They're cool?"

"Yeah. They won't tell."

Harriet momentarily lost her cool. "They won't tell until they make a fucking TV show about it. Then how're they going to not tell? It'll be on TV. How cool will they be when I'm in jail?"

Sepp reached out and patted her shoulder. "I'm trying to make you famous. I thought that's what you wanted."

Harriet tried to calibrate what to say to Sepp. She couldn't believe how quickly things had changed. One minute she's got her alibi in place and she's dreaming of being boned on top of a first edition of Don DeLillo's *Underworld,* the next thing she knows, Sepp's unintentionally turning her in for homicide. How had her life run off the rails? Now there was a cliché she could get behind. "To run off the rails" is to behave strangely, to veer from the path of society, to leave the straight and narrow. Or maybe it was worse. To derail, to become completely unconnected to the norms of the world. She'd seen pictures of train disasters, the cars accordioned on their sides. *Off the rails.* She didn't want to end up like that.

"I did it because I'm in love with you."

Harriet blinked. "You what?"

Sepp reached out and took her hand. "I'm in love with you."

Her first thought was that she had to end this thing with Sepp. She would drop him at his hotel in Phoenix and get the next flight back to San Francisco. A couple yoga classes, some reading, an hour browsing in City Lights, maybe a glass of wine at Zuni and everything would be back to normal. She'd get back on the rails. She'd put this experience behind her, this aberration, this little excursus into the land of Playboy mansions and unintentional homicide and roadside sex.

But then what? She'd just be a lonely bookworm writing snarky blog posts. Is that who she really was? Is that who she wanted to be? She would be the first to admit it was ironic.

She came to destroy Sepp Gregory, to expose him as a fraud, and somehow he'd managed to turn it all around on her. How come she felt like a fraud? It was a lesson, Harriet realized, that might work for the protagonist in her book. One of Harriet's writing teachers had told her that she needed to leave the library and get out into the world; he said that experience was more valuable than imagination. She'd always doubted that, thought the professor was just an old horndog trying to wheedle his way into her pants. But now she wasn't so sure. The emotions she'd been feeling in the last twenty-four hours—the connection to Curtis, the anger at his betrayal, the numb horror of his death, the guilt at dumping his corpse in a motel, followed by the wild heat of coupling with Sepp—it all made her feel like a different person. Someone who wanted more out of life than a cozy chair and a cup of tea.

She couldn't help herself. When she looked at Sepp, she felt a pang of—something. Maybe love? Could she be falling in love? She had thought the craving for him was purely physical but now that he'd proclaimed his love she wasn't so sure. She leaned over and kissed him tenderly on the cheek.

"Let's not worry about being famous. Okay? Let's take this a step at a time. Let's go to your signing, then we'll figure out what to do. How's that sound?"

Sepp grinned. "Sounds hot."

Harriet smiled. "Good. So no more telling anyone about anything, right? All anyone needs to know is that I gave you a ride."

Sepp frowned. "What about being in love?"

"What about it?"

"Can I tell them that?"

Harriet smiled and put her hand against his crotch. "Yes. You can tell them that."

34

Studio City

Damon DeKalb adjusted the belt of his silk bathrobe as he waited for his coffee to steep in the French press he'd bought on his last trip to Paris. He looked out the window and watched the pool boy sweep the long plastic pole across the surface of the pool, the net on the end catching the pale pink petals that were floating on the clear blue water. The blooms were from the massive silk floss tree—*Ceiba speciosa*—that dominated his garden. It was a messy tree, no doubt about it, but Damon loved the vividness of it, the bright green trunk covered in thorns like some kind of prehistoric lizard, the pink blooms that popped against the blue California sky like a Warhol print. The garden had been designed to look like a wild Balinese forest and Damon spent several hundred dollars a week having it manicured to maintain the appropriately natural look.

The pool boy bent over to pick something out of the water and Damon admired his ass, the muscles smooth and young and firm. He considered inviting him in for a cold glass of lemonade. Damon's housekeeper made it fresh every day from lemons plucked off the tree in the yard. It was refreshing, both the lemonade and the pool boy, but Damon thought better of it. The last time he'd had one of the staff in for a drink it had cost him a half-million dollars in a sexual harassment settlement. Besides, he needed to make a decision about Sepp Gregory's strange pitch.

Damon DeKalb had made a lot of money off his relationship with Sepp. Ratings for *Sex Crib* had skyrocketed once the affair between Sepp and Roxy heated up. Then Sepp became America's sweetheart and *Love Express* was one of the most watched reality shows of all time. Damon had been responsible for a string of reality shows including the hits *My Mom Is Hotter Than Your Mom*, *Senior Sex Crib*, *Wildlife Dorm*, and *Afternoon Delight*. Those shows had made him a millionaire a couple of times over. But it was *Love Express* that earned the People's Choice and CableACE awards.

Damon pressed on the plunger and slowly pushed the grounds of Burundi Kayanza—a microlot coffee grown at almost seventeen hundred meters above sea level—to the bottom of the press. He poured himself a cup and added a dollop of cream. He gave it a stir with a tiny designer spoon from Italy. He had a couple of thoughts about what Sepp had said on the phone, and although it was somewhat incoherent, it was intriguing, and the nude photos circulating on the internet hadn't hurt. Sepp had never been a hotter commodity. One phone call and he could get a cameraman on the ground in Phoenix in a couple of hours. They could shoot some footage of Sepp on his book tour and, at the very least, he could use it in the special *Love Express* reunion show he was planning. People would want to see Sepp happy and in love. Wasn't that the point of all these shows? To see that love was possible, that you really could find happiness in this world? And didn't he say something about a murder?

Damon smiled at the idea of Sepp becoming an amateur sleuth. All he'd need was some new footage to cut together a sizzle reel—a taste of what the series would look like—to present to the networks.

The pool boy stripped off his shirt and stretched. Damon had never seen him without his shirt on and was intrigued by the large tattoo on the pool boy's back. It looked very intricate, indeed. Like a koi pond or something inspired by Japanese manga. Damon took a sip of his coffee and decided to ask the pool boy if he wanted some lemonade. It looked awfully hot outside. Besides, if he could get a new show going with Sepp, it would more than cover any lawsuits he might have to settle.

35

Arizona

Sepp sat in the passenger seat and watched as Harriet drove the car. She hadn't said anything since she lost her temper on the side of the road, but he could hear her teeth grinding.

"That's bad for your molars."

She didn't look at him. She just tensed her jaw and kept crunching her teeth. It sounded like she was chewing clam shells.

Sepp turned his head and looked out the window. Rolling hills of dirt passed by. Sepp saw a ratty, weather-beaten cactus standing alone in a gully of rocks. He felt sorry for the cactus. There were no cactus friends around, no cactuses to play with. Sepp felt a pang of compassion for the lonely cactus, and then after a moment he felt sorry for himself.

He'd told her he loved her, and he really felt like he did. But she hadn't said anything back, and you know what that means.

Sepp heaved a sigh. What do women want? He'd pondered this question before. He'd tried to give Roxy and Caitlin and all the girls he'd dated before he was on TV what he thought they wanted and he was always wrong somehow.

He thought he knew how to make them happy, but then it turned out he didn't know at all. He was clueless. That's what Roxy said. You'd think he would've learned something from Lauren or Rachel or Esther or Jackie or Shahar. He had a whole string of exes. Although, he had to admit, in fairness, he broke up with some of them because, well, he didn't know what he wanted. But, dude, what does anybody want? He'd tried to find out, he'd even asked sometimes. He did the open and honest communication thing like he'd seen on those daytime TV shows where they tell you how to talk to people, what to eat, and what books to read. He listened to Dr. Jan. All that advice was super helpful to lots of people, but it never seemed to work for him. It always came down to the same thing. It was always some version of how they really just wanted to be friends.

Harriet was different. She really didn't seem like she wanted to be his friend.

"Are you mad?"

"No."

"Do you want to talk about it?"

Harriet didn't answer. Instead she turned on the radio and a country and western song came on, interrupted by bursts of static. Sepp recognized the song right away. It was "Celebrity" by Brad Paisley. The song made fun of reality TV stars. The singer was saying how people on reality shows were talentless and lucky. Sepp didn't like the song much. He knew lots of reality stars and you would be surprised how talented they are when you got to know them. They had hidden talents. Like the little midget guy who was always pissing people off; turns out he's a great singer. A soul singer. And he plays the piano too. Not many people knew that. Caitlin had been a good artist. She drew funny pictures all the time. Sepp didn't particularly like the song. Well, actually the song was good, it was catchy and all, he just didn't like the message. He wasn't a jackass or a millionaire and he totally never threw a fit when his latte wasn't just how he liked it. Although, really, why shouldn't you get the drink you ordered? You paid for it.

Sepp turned the radio down. "I just want you to be happy."

Harriet looked at him. Sepp could see that her eyes were red and starting to get watery. "I appreciate that." Tears began to roll down Harriet's cheeks and she snorted what sounded like a big wad of snot up in her nose. Sepp put a hand on her shoulder.

"Let's stop at a motel and get some rest."

36

Phoenix

His real name was Wesley but people in the business called him "the Ninja." He was one of the forerunners, some would say inventors, of the down-and-dirty, run-and-gun style of documentary videography that was now the standard for reality television.

As a young man just out of film school the Ninja had gotten the job following teams of athletes on *Global Sprint 2000.* He crawled through swamps in Borneo, dragged himself over the Himalayas, stumbled down giant sand dunes in the Sahara, and swatted mosquitos the size of sparrows all while keeping the performers in frame and in focus. He could run a marathon and had a wiry physique that made him adept at scrambling up trees, scaling buildings, hanging from rafters or whatever natural formation was handy; anything to get the shot. In fact he'd pretty much single-handedly turned herky-jerky handheld cinematography into an art form. He didn't need a crane or a dolly or a Steadicam and, let's be serious for a moment, there's no way you can jam a three-person camera crew on a zip line or the back of a Jet Ski, so he'd figured out a way to shoot with one hand and one eye while driving snowmobiles down glaciers during an avalanche or rappelling down skyscrapers.

But most importantly, he had an innate ability to disappear. Even though he would be inches away, filming a couple having an argument or having sex, no one ever seemed to notice him. He could vanish, merge with the surroundings like a shadow warrior.

He'd been busy. Shooting a show called *What a Rush,* another race-around-the-globe meets extreme-sports-and-BASE-jumping show, and several editions of *Coeds vs. Great Whites,* a show that involved filming eighteen-year-old girls drinking enough tequila shots to feel sufficiently moved to toss off their bikinis tops and jump into a shark cage off the Australian coast.

It was nice work if you could get it.

He popped the last bit of his Whataburger with cheese, no pickles, in his mouth and reached into the bag for a handful of oil-slick french fries as he steered the RV toward downtown Phoenix. It was all coming together. He'd been on his way to the airport in Austin after shooting another fleshy coed exposé —this one called *Longhorn Gals!*—when he got Damon's call. He'd caught a flight to Phoenix in less than an hour.

The Ninja had been lead camera on *Love Express* and liked working with Sepp. Sepp was a reality television natural. He just did his thing, never looked at the camera, and let it all hang out. He kept it real, even as the producers were pulling strings off camera. Nothing was better than complete and utter cluelessness for compelling TV.

And the rented RV was a peach. A top-of-the-line custom from 4-Wheel Vantasy Custom Vans in Scottsdale. It had a water bed and small bathroom, a sofa and hospitality bar. There was even a temperature-controlled wine storage area and a pop-out patio with built-in hibachi grill and sunshade. Best of all, there were sunroofs all across the top. They'd give plenty of light for shooting. The Ninja was impressed. Damon had spared no expense. Now all he had to do was rig up some cameras and microphones and he'd be ready to get the show on the road.

37

Phoenix

Harriet felt better. They'd spent the night in a cheap motel, eaten crappy fast food in bed, and then Sepp had gone down on her. Harriet was amazed at what a little cunnilingus could do to cheer a gal up. It gave her a fresh perspective and she began to think that maybe she'd been holding herself back. Was it possible that she was her own worst enemy? Did her über-intellectualism keep her writing from having an emotional core, some feelings that readers needed to connect with?

She sat behind the wheel and watched Sepp come out of a restaurant with a couple of coffees and a breakfast sandwich for her. He had told her he didn't eat fried foods of any kind, and especially not fatty cheesy bacon and egg things, because he had to watch his body fat percentages. She had laughed at the time, thinking Sepp's obsession with his abdomen was neurotic, as obsessive as an anorexic teen's, but now that she thought about it, those abs were his livelihood. Why shouldn't he take care of them?

Sepp got into the car and Harriet started the engine. He handed her a coffee and said, "I hope my clothes get here soon. I can't go to the signing looking like a bum."

Harriet took a sip of coffee. It was scalding. Why did fast-food joints always make the coffee so fucking hot?

"They just ask you to take 'em off anyway. Cut to the chase. Give the people what they want."

She watched as Sepp thought about it. The wheels in his brain parsing the information, thinking of, well, something. "Yeah. I should do some crunches at some point."

"What time's your interview?"

"Not till five. Brenda's sending a copy of my schedule to the hotel."

"What time's the signing?"

"Seven."

...

Sepp watched Harriet look at the clock on the dashboard and run some calculations through her head. Usually the women he knew made scrunchy faces or stuck out their tongues when they tried to do addition or figure out something with numbers, but Harriet looked really pretty when she concentrated. She had the same look on her face right before she came. He wondered if there was any connection between having an orgasm and doing a math problem. Was that the secret? Is that why the nerds spend so much time hunched over calculators and graph paper?

...

The rock radio station in Phoenix was unbearable. It had all the smarm of the Playboy Mansion with none of the kitschy charm. Harriet stood scrunched against the wall, trying to make herself invisible in the claustrophobic control booth. She felt like an observer, watching an encounter between Sepp and a strange race of aliens whose teeth gleamed like bleached bone and whose skin glowed with a chemical-orange tan. The women had a uniform of brassy dyed hair and breasts that looked like medieval weaponry, while a pudgy-fingered middle-aged DJ with spiky bouquets of hair sprouting out of his ears cavorted with them. Everybody was ecstatic, jumping right out of their sports bras, to have Sepp in the room.

Cheesy innuendo flowed from the DJ's mouth like a Velveeta fountain while the women blurbled and bubbled as if their brains and not their boobs had been replaced by silicone-filled baggies. And in the middle of this whirling cyclone of bullshit, Sepp nodded and laughed and pulled up his T-shirt to expose his rippling torso.

@fatalinfluence *I am in Arizona. Witnessing the end times.*

There had been days when Harriet was alone in her apartment, sitting in her reading chair, immersed in a novel, sipping a cup of herbal tea, when she had sat up and wondered if she was missing something. She'd become so removed from mainstream America, so caught up in her highbrow pursuits, that she wondered if life was passing her by. She would be the first to admit that her worldview was parochial. Even her quest to confront Sepp and expose his book as fallacious was, she had to admit, narrowcasting of the most specific kind. But now, watching Phoenix's number-one afternoon drive DJ purr banalities into a microphone—something about someone named Sammy Hagar—while his coven of senescent cheerleaders urged him on, now Harriet realized that the problem was bigger than just a reality star and his phony book. The world was ruled by half-wits, imbeciles, boobs, and money. It made her want to go to Tibet and live in a cave.

But that's not confronting the problem. That's running away. What was the right thing to do? If the culture becomes idiotic, what should a sane person do? Ignore it? Join it? Or was it the responsibility of every single educated person to stand up and say something? To make it stop?

It was a topic, she realized, that she could write about for months to come. But would it matter? Wasn't the internet just an echo chamber? Weren't the literary blogs just a loop of self-aggrandizement? Writers writing about writing and writers so that someone would notice and give them a book deal to write for other writers. She'd seen it happen.

She turned and watched the DJ yammer away at Sepp.

"You must like Van Halen? Right? You and Diamond Dave have a lot in common."

"We do?"

"Yeah, man. He can do a flying kung fu kick."

"Really?"

"Oh my God! Where have you been living? Under a rock?"

Sepp shrugged. "Dude. I've been busy. They don't listen to much rock on the set. It's all hip-hop."

"Then let's cue up some rock 'n' roll! Name your favorite band."

Sepp grinned. "You can't go wrong with No Doubt."

As the DJ looked around for some No Doubt, Harriet noticed a cameraman standing off to the side, slowly creeping in close to Sepp, moving between the bimbos. He moved in slow motion, like he was in a different reality or something. It was unnerving. Harriet wondered how long he'd been there. She hadn't seen him when they arrived and hadn't noticed anyone enter after them.

As she watched him work, a thought suddenly occurred to her, filling her with a strange mix of emotions, part horror and part pleasure, fear and vanity blooming together in her cerebellum. She wondered if he'd been filming her.

38

New York City

Amy hung up the phone. At first she'd ignored the calls from someone claiming to be Curtis Berman's mother. She'd let her assistant take the message and then promptly deleted it from her call sheet. Curtis had never mentioned his parents and for all Amy knew he was an orphan. Besides it's not like a literary agent isn't deluged with a weekly quota of crackpots and weirdos sending manuscripts and leaving messages. What was the average? Sixty? Seventy-five? A hundred? More? People were desperate. Desperate, and desperately untalented. It was a sad fact of life in her business.

The fourth time Mrs. Berman called, her assistant decided that maybe she was for real and patched her through. It was bad news. Tragic news, really. Curtis had slipped and fallen in a bathroom in some godforsaken motel deep in the sand dunes of the Mojave and now he was dead. Dead as in no longer breathing, no longer speaking, and most importantly, no longer finishing the Roxy Sandoval autobiography that he'd contracted to do.

According to Curtis's mother, slip-and-fall accidents in the bathroom account for over twenty thousand deaths a year. Almost fifty-five a day. Second only to automobile accidents.

The Bermans were looking into litigation. Apparently the bathtub in the motel lacked nonslip daisies on the shower floor.

It was a tragedy. For sure. She'd have her assistant send flowers and then write up something nice and send it to *Publishers Weekly, Publishers Marketplace, GalleyCat,* and *Shelf Awareness.* It should be something glowing, albeit short. After all, they were contractually obligated not to mention his ghostwriting of *Totally Reality.* Other than that, what had he done? Maybe there wouldn't be an obituary after all. Scratch the write-up. Maybe his parents could put something in their local paper.

Amy wondered how many people died like that, never really realizing their dreams, and then slipping in the bathroom. She made a mental note to buy some nonslip daisies for the tile floor in her shower.

Curtis's mother wanted to know about all the money in Curtis's bank account. Where did it come from? Even Curtis's mom didn't believe he'd been successful. Amy told her that he'd signed a contract to write a book and that they'd probably have to give the money back. She'd have to give her commission back, that was for sure, but maybe she could sell his novel now. A posthumous book by an undiscovered genius. Of course it would've been better if Curtis killed himself. Suicides are always so dramatic. People love them. You can be an interesting author of experimental fiction and then, once you kill yourself, you become a beloved genius. It gave Amy an idea. Curtis's death was mysterious. In the desert. Who can say for sure what happened? Suicide? Murder? Mexican cartel? Mojave death cult? Anything's possible. A posthumous book could turn that godforsaken motel into a literary tourist shrine.

Amy picked up the phone and dialed an editor she knew.

39

Tempe

Sepp fell back on the bed and heard the distinct slap of water. He looked up at the Ninja. "Dude. Are you fucking shitting me? A water bed? This is totally outrageous."

Harriet swiveled in the passenger seat of the RV to face him. "What's outrageous?"

"A water bed in an RV."

Sepp smacked the bed and a sloshing sound filled the RV. "Come on, you won't believe it."

"I believe it."

Sepp grinned at her. "You've never been on a water bed before, have you?"

Harriet looked at the Ninja, then back at Sepp. "I get seasick."

Sepp winked. "I got the cure for that."

Sepp pulled a couple of pillows under his head and lay back on the bed. He felt the RV turn left, the water in the bed slowly leaning one way, then rocking him back as the RV straightened. It felt good, like swinging softly in a hammock. He saw Harriet staring at him. She looked beautiful. "Try it, you'll like it."

Harriet hesitated. "I need to return the rental. I can't just leave it here."

She watched Sepp bobbing on the water bed. It looked inviting. She felt a pang in her crotch that urged her to join him. How many orgasms had she had in the last twenty-four hours? Six? Seven? Was there a limit? Now that they were clear of the body and the car and Sepp had rejoined his book tour she was feeling tired. It had been an exceptionally stressful all-nighter.

The Ninja looked at her. "I can call the rental company and get it taken care of. The producer will even cover the bill. No sweat. Just give me the key."

Harriet handed him the key to the rental. The Ninja took it and said, "If you want to check your email there's a new MacBook on the couch. The whole RV is wired for wi-fi."

...

Sepp could see that Harriet was worried about something. He wondered if she was considering going back to California. People standing at the doorway of fame sometimes get cold feet. It happens. But you need to be strong, to have some faith and take the plunge. He didn't want to see her throw this chance at fame out the window. She had told him it was her lifelong dream to be an author, to have a book on the shelves, and he wanted to make it happen for her. This is how he realized that he was in love with her.

Sepp pulled his T-shirt off, over his head.

"Come here, Harriet. Let's talk."

Harriet moved to the back of the RV and sat on the water bed. She landed harder then she meant to, causing a micro-tsunami to slosh against the other side of the bed, raising Sepp up and back down. Harriet looked slightly stricken—maybe she did get seasick—as the wave ricocheted around the bed.

"Whoa. Splashdown!"

Sepp saw a smile creep across Harriet's face. He reached over and put his arms around her, pulling her close.

"How're you feeling?"

Dr. Jan had taught him to ask this question. Women want their feelings to be taken seriously. That's what Dr. Jan had told him and, wouldn't you know it, they really do. Sometimes feelings are even more important than reality.

Harriet propped her head up on her arm. "What do you mean?"

"It looks like you're worried about something."

Harriet narrowed her eyes. "No shit I'm worried. Do you think getting away with what we did is easy? There's so many loose ends to tie up and then you've got to think one step ahead of the law. It's exhausting."

Sepp nodded. "Oh. I thought you were worried about us?"

Harriet laughed. "Have you watched too many relationship shows? I'm not worried about us. There are bigger fish to fry." Now there was a good idiom.

"Well. Just know that I love you and that I'm here for you."

Sepp kissed her forehead and stroked her tangled hair.

Harriet sighed. "Thanks."

Sepp pulled her in a little closer. He felt his penis start to swell, a nice healthy rush of blood to his cock, his brain alerting it that there might be some action here.

"The thing about being a celebrity is that people don't really care what you did to become famous. Once you're famous, you're famous. You kill someone, you hide their body in the desert, they pretty much overlook all that."

Sepp gave her a hug and rolled his body so that his crotch pressed against her thigh. He gave her a gentle, reassuring pelvic thrust. She pushed back, but he could tell that she wasn't happy.

"But that's not how it should be. Why should famous people get a free ride? Why not smart people? Why do Americans make fun of smart people? They don't do that in other countries."

Sepp let her vent her frustration. It was good to get it out.

"Take France, for example, or hell, Holland. Intellectuals are rewarded for being smart. People want to hear what they have to say. They're the ones writing books and being interviewed on TV. Not hotel heiresses and random offspring of celebrities."

He gently stroked her nipples through her shirt. He felt them contract and harden.

"It's stupefying."

Sepp nodded. "Americans like to have fun."

He felt her body relax, as if giving up the fight temporarily, giving in to him. Sepp felt like his cock was about to explode. It was such a change from just a day ago when he couldn't even get it up. Now, because of Harriet, he was all authentic and real and hard as a rock. Sepp wondered why. Did he have to be in love to get a boner? Was that what was wrong with him?

He watched as she closed her eyes and seemed to drift off for a moment. She put her face next to his and whispered, "I want to live in a meritocracy."

Sepp kissed her face, tasting the salty sweet moisture of her skin, and gently slipped his hand under her panties.

She smiled at him. "You don't know what that means, do you?"

The RV rocked as the Ninja climbed back on.

"All set. Let's get the show on the road."

...

The Ninja had only driven a few blocks when he heard a muffled moan coming from the back of the RV. He looked in the rearview mirror and saw Sepp pull the curtain across the bed, giving them a cloak of privacy. He'd have to drive around for a while, circling a park or something. The Ninja stopped at a light and looked at his iPod. He didn't really want to hear them having sex—the microphones embedded in the wall just above the bed would pick up everything he'd need for the edit—so he spun the dial until he found something appropriate. He jacked his headphones into the iPod and hit play. The Ninja wished he had some classical music; Ravel's "Bolero" would be appropriate and also ironic. But he didn't have it so he selected the next best thing. His ears soon began to ring with the chunk and glimmer of Bob Marley's greatest hits.

Mounted in a compartment in the RV, braced by a metal alloy frame and floating on a platform of shock-absorbing rubber, a large hard drive spun in what's called an embedded DVR or digital video recorder. This one was specially built for military use and could record for days. The drive was capturing the images recorded by the tiny lenses of the digital cameras discreetly mounted around the water bed. The camera captured color images during the day, but automatically switched to black and white in low-light situations. With infra-red sensors, it could film in almost total darkness.

The Ninja had a little monitor in the front seat and was able to watch the action. He was a stickler for quality and wanted to make sure the cameras had the best angle and were in focus. He had to give it up for Sepp. The dude somehow knew to position his body so that he never blocked Harriet's breasts or face. Nobody wants to watch some dude's back no matter how muscular or tan, and Sepp instinctively played to the camera, even a camera that he didn't know was there.

As the RV idled at a red light the Ninja watched as Sepp worked his magic on Harriet. She began with a somewhat distracted look on her face, like she just wasn't that into it. But as Sepp began to kiss her underarms, working his way around her body, running his tongue along her rib cage while his hands found her nipples and crushed them tenderly between his finger and thumb, as he nibbled on her inner thighs, slowly moving toward her pussy, her expression began to change. And when he finally brought his warm mouth to her clitoris, sucking gently and swirling his tongue around this swollen nub of nerve endings, her mouth dropped open and she gasped, arching her back in an iconic image of pleasure.

A car honked behind the RV and the Ninja saw that the light had changed. He gently pressed on the gas and moved forward, heading toward the bookstore and Sepp's event.

. . .

The Ninja knew that Sepp was popular with the ladies, but he had no idea the extent and fervor of the female public's obsession until he saw the line waiting outside the bookstore. He figured there were at least three hundred women breathlessly clutching copies of Sepp's book, waiting for their chance to get close to him. Even though the women were all ages, all shapes and sizes, there was a striking uniformity to them. Perhaps it was an Arizona thing. Maybe they were all descendants of some kind of ancient, desert-dwelling tribe, marked by streaky blond hair, chunks of turquoise dangling from their necks and arms, and sun-blasted hides that had turned crinkly, like butterscotch pudding left too long in the fridge.

They were showing a lot of cleavage. Eager to impress the reality TV heartthrob, they dressed in their sluttiest clothes. The Ninja regretted not bringing an extra cameraman on this trip, someone to walk the line and get interviews with the fans. There were a lot of hotties in the line and nothing is better on TV than an excited woman and her breasts.

...

They entered the bookstore and were greeted by the manager, an intelligent-looking young woman who, if you asked the Ninja, was just a haircut and some makeup away from looking really good on TV.

"Mr. Gregory?"

"Call me Sepp. I know it's a funny name but . . . I'm stuck with it."

"Sepp. Can I ask you a favor?"

"Sure."

The Ninja zoomed in tight on the manager's face. He could see that she was slightly embarrassed, uncomfortable to be caught on camera scanning Sepp's body with obvious animal desire. It was like watching a librarian slowly turn into a stripper. That kind of internal conflict was great for television.

"Some of our customers are asking if you might, well, I feel really uncool asking . . ."

Sepp smiled, as if to reassure her. The Ninja adjusted his angle, zoomed out to get them in a two-shot.

"You want me to lose the shirt?"

She nodded. "Would you mind? I'll give you a Changing Hands Bookstore T-shirt in exchange."

Sepp flashed a smile. "I'd love that."

Harriet looked at the manager. "Can I get one, too?"

The manager smiled. "Sure."

Sepp yanked his T-shirt over his head and the women in line burst into applause and began squealing like schoolgirls. The Ninja was amazed. He hadn't seen a reaction like that since *Celebrity Super Stunts* when he'd filmed David Hasselhoff riding a zip line across Gendarmenmarkt in Berlin wearing only a Speedo.

The Ninja panned the camera to display the squealing mob of women, his lens greeted by a barrage of popping flashes from cell phones and digital cameras. It was like looking into a disco ball.

Damon was right. This show could be huge.

@fatalinfluence *Crazy 24 hours. I could write a book about it.*

Harriet sat in a coffee shop next to the bookstore catching up on her email, trying to decide what to write on her blog. She borrowed the MacBook from the RV and was happy to be back online after what seemed like a year. But what could she say about her mission now? She wasn't going to humiliate Sepp or knock his book off the bestseller list. It was too easy. And it would hurt him. Not that she felt overly protective of him. All she really felt was a little twinge in her crotch whenever she thought of him. How was she going to blog about that? What would she say?

> Traditionally we don't discuss our carnal appetites, but we do have to confess a sweet tooth for one Sepp Gregory. Not only did he write a novel that is evocative, emotional, and profound, but from the narrative dazzle of the story to the liveliness of the sentences, he has produced an important work of fiction that is almost as delightful and satisfying as the length and hardness of his cock; which we have put in our mouth and enjoyed in a variety of positions. Perhaps you've seen photos of his turgid member online.

She hit delete. Her readers would think she'd lost her mind or been hacked. Maybe she *had* lost her mind. Was she caught in some kind of bizarre delusion? Had someone at the Playboy Mansion slipped her some kind of experimental drug? Or was she experiencing an erotic obsession? Or had she lost her mind but discovered her body? Was she Constance Chatterley and Sepp the earthy gamekeeper?

@fatalinfluence *I feel like rereading D. H. Lawrence.*

She considered writing a tweet about how she needed a shower, but now, after a lifetime of compulsive hygiene and fastidiousness—she'd begun using antibacterial soap way before it was popular—now she didn't want to bathe. She enjoyed feeling like she'd spent an entire day wallowing in a sty of sex juice. She didn't mind that her armpits were starting to stink and a ripe, gamy scent was wafting off her body like some kind of porn-set perfume. In fact, she liked it. But she wasn't so sure about the people around her. *Love stinks. Yeah, yeah.* Wasn't that a song she'd heard in high school?

Harriet looked around the coffee shop. There were people staring intently at their laptop screens, a few reading books and newspapers. Mostly they were alone, like her. She sipped her latte and wondered if any of them were in love. Would she be able to smell them if they were?

Sepp had told her that he loved her. She could count on one hand, and not use her thumb, index, or pinky finger, how many men had said that to her. She wondered if Sepp only loved her for her body. That made her smile. That'd be a first.

She clicked through a couple of websites that she normally read, a few of her fellow lit bloggers, and then to *Publishers Marketplace* for publishing industry news. It was there that she saw a very brief mention of Curtis Berman's accidental death and realized that she'd gotten away with it.

. . .

Like the professional he was, Sepp worked the line. He signed books, he posed for photos, he nodded his head and smiled as people told him how much they loved him, how they never missed his shows, how they adored his book. They felt his pain at loves labored over and lost, they shared the dream of falling for the perfect person and felt the stab of heartbreak when he realized that the person wasn't so perfect after all. They laughed with him. They cried with him. He was an inspiration. He gave them hope.

Sepp found himself moved by these people. Everyone he'd met on the book tour, actually. The woolly-sweater women in Seattle who smelled like fresh rain, the fashionistas in San Francisco, the compassionate people who'd taken care of him when he had his breakdown in LA, the bookstore dude who'd given him the book about reality—they made him feel loved. And now, here in Tempe, he was hearing it again. He wasn't a talentless reality star. He mattered. Maybe being a guilty pleasure was something he shouldn't feel guilty about.

...

"Did you really hook up with Roxy Sandoval?"

Sepp was about to give his standard answer and prepared to receive a high five, but the voice behind the question sent an icy shiver through his body. He felt the hairs on his neck rise up like he was wearing a static-electric halo. He looked up and saw her in all her glory.

"Roxy? What are you doing here?"

"Didn't Damon tell you?"

Sepp shook his head. His brain was scrambling to process what was going on. "No."

Roxy grinned her wicked grin, the grin that had made her famous for breaking hearts and betraying friends, her mouth twitching up in a snidely asymmetrical smile, making one of her canine teeth protrude just enough to be vaguely threatening and sexy. It was a look that was uniquely Roxy's, part pout, part sneer; it was designed to make you feel unworthy and vile, small and annoying, like a wet clingy turd, and yet at the same time it made you want to fuck her like you never fucked anyone before. Roxy licked her lips and her smile grew even more sneerific.

"They said you needed an antagonist."

. . .

The Ninja zoomed in on Roxy's sneer. He wanted to capture it in all its magnificence. He backed up a little, intuitively avoiding a large cardboard display of the latest teenage-vampire-meets-pubescent-virgin bestseller, and let the camera do a slow pan down, revealing Roxy's hot-pink bikini top and the sarong that was casually tied around her waist. That was the power of Roxy Sandoval. She looked more attractive, more wood-poundingly humpable, in a bikini than she did buck naked. He'd seen her naked, everyone had, in that *Playboy* "Reality Girls" special edition. It had been somewhat anticlimactic.

The Ninja panned over for a reaction shot and, sure enough, Sepp was reacting. He looked like he'd been poleaxed, his eyes spinning, his jaw hanging open like a broken gate on a pickup truck. "What?"

"Check your voice mail. I'm sure he called."

The Ninja zoomed out for a wide shot. He hoped this would cut together, but he wasn't sure. He'd need to get some inserts of Sepp signing or something.

"I don't have my phone with me."

Roxy shook her head. "I guess you're surprised then. That would explain the dumbass look on your face."

Sepp swallowed, thought about it for a second, then looked up at Roxy. "Would you like me to personalize your book?"

...

The line wasn't as big as it had been an hour ago, but there were still fifty or sixty fans waiting to get Sepp's autograph, and now they were captivated. A reality show had just come to life right in front of them. Minds were being blown in the bookstore.

"Haven't you hurt him enough?"

Roxy turned her head and glared at a middle-aged woman in a bright yellow dress with bricks of turquoise jewelry dangling off her neck. "Do you know who I am?"

The woman nodded. She wasn't impressed by Roxy. "We all know who you are, honey."

There was something in the way the woman said "honey" that made it seem like a threat. Roxy swiveled on her heels to face the woman.

With the camera rolling Sepp knew that Roxy would turn this into an opportunity for a catfight. Those screechy, hair-flipping, head-snapping, finger-pointing, chest-thumping, out-of-control arguments were a mainstay of reality TV, but Sepp didn't want one here, not now. This was about his fans and the book.

"Roxy, please. Not now."

Roxy raised an eyebrow and snapped her head back toward Sepp.

"You don't want to go there, baby, not with me."

Sepp held up his hands. "Dude. She's been waiting. Let me sign her book."

Roxy turned back to Sepp, her lips leaping into her trademark snark. "Did you just call me 'dude'?"

Sepp knew she hated being called a dude, but he wanted to stop her from going off on one of his fans.

"Do I look like a dude?"

Sepp tried a little joke. "You have been working out."

Some of the women in line appreciated his sense of humor and giggled. That only annoyed Roxy more.

"You used to be all about this." She waved her hands up and down her body. "You couldn't get enough of this."

Roxy squeezed her breasts together and pointed them accusingly at Sepp. "If I'm a 'dude,' what's that make you?"

Sepp knew what was coming. It was like he was watching a replay of one of the thousands of squabbles they'd had during their torturous affair on *Sex Crib*. He knew what she was going to say as if he'd written the script himself. Roxy put her hands on her hips and cranked her eyes wide open. "If I'm a 'dude,' that must make you my bitch."

And there it was.

Roxy punctuated this exclamation with some kind of gang-related finger flapping that she'd obviously copied off a rap video.

There was a gasp from some of the women in line. Sepp shook his head and the Ninja smiled as he moved in for a close-up. Sepp knew that Roxy was just warming up, that this outburst was just the opening act to the freak-show emotional volcano that was about to take the stage. Honestly, it bummed him out. Things were going so well. Why did Roxy have to come? What was Damon thinking?

Sepp looked at the line of women waiting to get their books signed. "I'm really sorry about all this."

Roxy reared back, about to attack again, when Harriet showed up. She looked at Sepp, then at Roxy, then at the camera.

"What's going on?"

Roxy smirked. "Girlfriend, you aren't near as smart as you think you are. You're never supposed to look at the camera."

Harriet turned to Sepp. "What's she doing here?"

Sepp shrugged. "She's the antagonist."

Roxy squared up to Harriet. She poked her chest out and flipped her hands around in the air like she was trying to dry her nails and had a nervous condition.

"I'm gonna keep it real. You know what I'm sayin'? I'm here to see if he really loves you, or if he still loves me. It's a true-love throwdown."

40

Arizona

They left right after the event. The Ninja had brought along a couple of black beauties, enough to keep him alert—on the road and rolling camera—until they got to Denver. He was annoyed that Damon hadn't sprung for an assistant cameraman or an associate producer to help with the driving, but then he knew from experience that the fewer people involved, the more intense and intimate the material. As the amphetamines massaged his brain, he began to think that maybe it was time to move up to producer role, earn a little profit-participation. If this sizzle reel turned out as good as he thought it would, it could be just the thing to lift him to the next level—profit-participation—and he could start earning some real money.

...

Harriet sat on the couch and looked out the window as the RV headed north, up Interstate 17, toward Flagstaff. From there they'd turn east on the I-40 until they hooked up with the I-25 in Albuquerque and then head up to Denver, where Sepp had an event at a bookstore called the Tattered Cover.

She'd never driven through the Southwest before and was struck by the expanse of the land: miles and miles of gorgeous, moonlit, and ultimately tedious landscape.

Harriet turned from the window to catch Roxy glaring at her. She tried hard not to blink; she didn't want to give Roxy an inch, didn't want to capitulate in any way. Although she was unsure what they were actually fighting over and seriously didn't want to stoop to Roxy's level of discourse, Harriet was prepared to knock that smirk off Roxy's face if she had to. She wasn't going to let a blood-red set of press-on nails intimidate her.

Roxy turned to Sepp and flipped her hair in disgust. It was a move designed to disrespect, to get all up in Harriet's grill, but all it really did was make Roxy look like a spastic. Roxy pointed at Harriet's chest.

"They're not even C cups."

Sepp opened his mouth to say something but Harriet beat him to it. "You said that before. Is that all you got?"

"Your tits are an insult."

Harriet smirked at that. "Really? How big were yours, you know, before the accident?"

Roxy slapped her hands over her breasts.

"Ain't nothin' accidental about these. I told 'em to make 'em as big as they could without causing an explosion."

Roxy shot a sideways glance at Sepp. "He never complained about 'em."

"I've got no complaints about hers."

Roxy leaned forward. "Oh yeah?"

"I think Harriet's breasts are beautiful."

Harriet smiled. No one had ever said that before. Roxy flashed a totally insincere smile, as if she'd heard it all now. "Oh wow. Really?"

She turned toward Harriet. "Can I see them?"

Harriet didn't want to squirm—she knew that was the reaction Roxy wanted—but she couldn't help it. She squirmed.

"I'll keep them to myself, thanks."

Roxy laughed. "You didn't have a problem sharing them at the Mansion the other night."

It annoyed Harriet that she was so easily riled by Roxy's remarks. After all, the squirming, the self-conscious hesitation, the defensiveness and lapses of self-esteem were exactly what Roxy was trying to provoke. Why is it so natural for smart, grown-up people to fall back into juvenile fears? Is that our natural, human default setting? Do we socialize and educate ourselves out of that behavior until someone makes fun of our breast size and then it's all we can do to keep from yanking their weave out of their head? Harriet didn't know what bothered her more—that she let Roxy antagonize her or that she took the bait and sniped right back. Either way, she wasn't going to take her shirt off.

"Sepp, honey, we need to have a talk."

Harriet couldn't believe she called him "honey." She only used that word to describe a sticky substance made by bees, something that she'd liked to put in tea before she discovered agave nectar, but she'd never used it to refer to a human being before.

Harriet got up and went toward the back, to where the water bed sloshed behind the curtain.

. . .

Sepp looked at Roxy.

"Why do you always have to start stuff?"

She snapped her head at him and flipped her hair.

"Because if I didn't, we'd just be sitting here doing nothing."

Sepp got up and stooped as he moved to the back of the RV. He pulled the curtain open and found Harriet sitting on the water bed with the laptop.

Harriet looked up at him. "Close the curtain. I want you to see something."

Sepp pulled the curtain closed and then sat down next to her on the water bed. The water rippled and sloshed, causing them both to bob up and down gently. He couldn't help himself, he gave her a kiss on the cheek, then turned and looked at the screen.

"What is it?"

"It's your ghostwriter's obituary."

Sepp leaned forward and read the article. "Wow."

Harriet nodded. "They bought the whole slipping-in-the-shower thing."

Sepp looked at her. "So you, like, got away with murder."

"I didn't murder him."

"So you got away with accidentally pushing him off your balcony so he fell to his death."

Harriet grabbed his face with her hands. She was gentle, but Sepp could tell that she didn't want him to look away, so he focused on her eyes. They looked so smart behind her glasses.

"I need you to pay attention. Okay?"

Sepp nodded. She spoke slowly and clearly, like you might speak to a Labrador retriever. "We can never mention this again. Not to anyone. Not to each other. Curtis is dead. He slipped in a shower. The end."

Sepp didn't quite catch her drift. "But we're doing a show."

"What show?"

"Well, technically it's a proposal for a show, we call it a sizzle reel. We're doing it right now."

Sepp saw Harriet's face change. She looked at him, all concerned like, as if he was really out of it, like that time he was swimming and got run over by some surfer and saw stars and mermaids and stuff. But he wasn't out of it. No way. If he knew one thing, it was how to keep it real on reality TV.

"What do you mean?"

"This is the show. We're doing the show right now."

Harriet smiled at him. "Look, sweetie, I know you're trying to help me get a book deal and everything. But I don't think this is the right way to do it. It's too risky and I don't want to go to jail. I really don't."

Before Sepp could say anything, the curtain was ripped open and Roxy entered holding a giant purple penis made out of some kind of semitranslucent plastic. "Dildo." Where did that word come from?

Harriet couldn't help herself, her brow furrowed and she narrowed her eyes at Roxy. She glowered. "Glower." That's another good word. Allegedly Scandinavian in origin but most likely from *glowan,* meaning to glow.

"We're trying to have a private conversation."

Roxy tossed the giant purple dildo onto Harriet's lap. "Tag. You're it."

Harriet looked at the giant purple dildo.

"What are you talking about?"

Roxy shook her head. "That's the time totem. When I give you that, it means I get one hour of private time with Sepp."

"What?"

"That's the rule."

Harriet looked at Sepp. "Since when do we have rules?"

Sepp shrugged. "There's always rules on a show."

"We're not doing a show. I just told you that."

Roxy laughed at Harriet. "I don't know where you think you are, but this is the show. This is for real."

Harriet nudged the giant purple dildo with her foot. "Right. It's real. So fuck off. I'm not playing."

That set Roxy off. She leaned over, putting her face inches from Harriet's face, and started screaming.

"Who do you think you are? Huh? Miss Intelligentsia? Yeah? You so much better than everybody else? Is that what you think? You're the only one who knows anything. Is that it?"

Harriet noticed a string of spittle dangling from Roxy's over-glossed lips, as if threads of her cerebellum had flown out of her mouth and the more she screeched the stupider she became.

Sepp tried to be reasonable. "Harriet. C'mon. Just go sit out there. Nothing's gonna happen."

Roxy jumped on that. "You afraid I'll take your man? Is that it?"

More spittle.

"You don't think you're all that, do you now?"

Some hair flipping and head snapping.

"You can't handle the truth? Is that it? You afraid I'll steal his ass away from you?"

Finger jabbing. Hair flip. Head snap. Spittle.

"If you love him, you gotta trust him. That's what I'm talking about. You want to keep it real? Do you? Well, that's the real motherfucking reality."

Harriet felt some of Roxy's saliva hit her cheek. She snapped the laptop shut and stood up. "Whatever."

Roxy handed her the giant purple dildo.

"What am I supposed to do with it?"

Roxy smiled as if she'd been waiting for this moment her whole life. "I suggest you go fuck yourself."

...

Harriet sat in the front passenger seat and stared out at the scenery. What the fuck was happening? Sepp had told her that the networks wanted some background footage of his book tour for a reunion show, which was fine, that sounded normal, but now he and Roxy were babbling about being on a show. And what's with the rules? Was she witnessing some group delusion? Like those people who all dressed in black and kept their tennis shoes under their beds for when the aliens on the asteroids were going to come get them? Is that was this was?

Harriet chewed her thumbnail as a couple of fast-food restaurants flashed by on the side of the freeway, their parking lots glowing, sodium-vapor ghosts in the night. The Ninja looked over from behind the steering wheel.

"Nice dildo."

Harriet looked at the giant purple dildo resting in her lap. "Dildo." Perhaps from the Italian *deletto,* meaning "delight"?

"She called it the time totem."

The Ninja nodded. "She can't spell."

Harriet was confused. "What?"

The Ninja laughed. "She thought it was a clock."

Harriet didn't laugh. She wasn't sure she got the joke.

"You know. Instead of cock. She added the *l*."

Harriet nodded. "Good one."

Hanging out with denizens of the reality TV world made her feel a strange sense of dislocation. The natural order of things was backwards, the cosmos turned on its head. Normally she was the intelligent one. But even though these people had barely finished high school, among them she felt like the stupid one, the dork, the dweeb. They were all in on a joke that she didn't get. It was as if they were tuned to a whole different wavelength.

They drove in silence for a while. Harriet put the giant purple dildo on the dashboard. She didn't know what else to do with it.

She turned to the Ninja. "Can I ask you a question?"

"Sure."

"How come there's no one filming them, but they keep saying that we're on the show?"

The Ninja smiled. "Because we're on the show, babe. I mean, I'll be edited out, but this is the show."

Again it was like that thing that she couldn't comprehend.

"How can we be on the show?"

The Ninja tried to explain. "Did you ever see *Six Teens in a Van?*"

Harriet shook her head. "No."

"*Love Express?*"

"No."

"*No Gas, No Ass, No Free Ride?*"

"Never heard of it."

"*The Amazing Race?*"

"I've heard of that one." She felt apologetic. "But I don't really watch much TV."

The Ninja turned and looked at her, then turned his attention back to the highway.

"You seem like a smart person, but somehow you've missed the biggest cultural event in the history of our civilization."

Harriet looked at him. "You're joking."

The Ninja laughed. "Numbers don't lie. Millions and millions of people watch reality TV. More than go to movies or read books or do just about anything. It's the new, I dunno, the New Testament."

Harriet could tell he was serious. Worse, he might be right.

"Okay. Fine. But back to my original question, I know we're on the show when you're filming us, but how are we on the show when there's no one filming us?"

The Ninja smiled and waved his hand around the RV as he spoke.

"This is like a rolling TV studio. There are cameras and mikes everywhere. All digitally recorded to a server. When I get to Denver I just uplink it back to the producer."

Harriet realized her jaw had dropped. "So everything I say or do is on tape? Without my permission?"

The Ninja nodded.

"That's how we roll."

. . .

Sepp lay on the water bed and looked over at Roxy. A couple of RV sconces gave the bedroom a soft glow. The lighting was meant to be moody, the mood being romantic, but it didn't flatter Roxy's features, it only made her look sharp and bitchy. He couldn't believe that he had once been madly in love with her. Right now he couldn't even imagine that he'd ever been attracted to her, that he'd kissed her and stuck his penis inside her. Dude, that's totally repulsive. With her teased-out hair and weird fingernails and pounds of makeup and her brightly veneered teeth and her lame-ass tattoos, she looked like a swamp-thing Kardashian. Compared to Harriet, who didn't even wear makeup, Roxy was some kind of android; and who wants to bone a droid when you can have the real thing? That's what Dr. Jan would say. You never saw Princess Leia or Luke Skywalker sneaking off with C-3PO.

Roxy snaked her French-tipped claw toward his crotch and reached for his zipper.

"Roxy. Stop."

Her lips jumped into a practiced pout that was supposed to show that she knew she was being naughty, but didn't want to be denied. Sepp had seen it before. The world had seen it.

"What's wrong? The Seppster not in the mood?"

"Something like that."

"I know you've still got a thing for me."

Sepp looked at her. He really didn't have a thing for her. Not anymore. "Then you are trippin'."

She pushed the pout out, making it more noticeable.

"Remember when we used to do the nasty?"

"Of course I remember."

She slid a reptilian hand up his thigh. "Wouldn't you like to go back to the good old days? A little trip in my hot, wet time machine?"

Sepp gently picked up her hand, like it was a half-gnawed turkey leg, and set it on the bed.

"I don't know what you're talking about."

Roxy laughed. "A blow job, stupid."

"I don't want a blow job."

Roxy flipped her hair and scrunched up her face. "Are you gay?"

Sepp shook his head. "If I was gay I'd want a blow job."

Her head snapped. She wasn't used to rejection. "Not from me."

"Whatever." He didn't want to tell her that she looked like one of the drag queens he used to see in a club in San Diego's Gaslamp Quarter.

Roxy regrouped. She sat up next to him, letting her cleavage droop in his face.

"What about the show?"

"What about it?"

"We should do it for the show. Spice things up. Get our picture on the cover of *Us Weekly* again."

Sepp shook his head. "This is a different show."

Roxy flipped her hair and made a face. "Are you really that into little Miss Brainiac?"

Sepp nodded. Roxy whistled.

"Man. I never took you for a guy who'd get hot for teacher. Don't you think she's a little out of your league?"

"What do you mean?"

"She's smart, dude. And you're not. That's what I mean."

Sepp knew that Harriet was smart, and yet that was one of the things he loved about her.

"That's what's cool about her."

"Yeah, till she dumps your dumb ass."

. . .

The Ninja had gone on to explain to Harriet how the confessional worked. He'd rigged the bathroom to have a camera you could turn off and on. Just flip the switch next to the mirror, sit on the toilet, and spill your guts. Sepp had already done that—in fact there was almost an hour and a half of the dude yapping and philosophizing about his life, his loves, and anything else he could think of. Harriet had thought he'd just eaten something that disagreed with his digestive tract.

She went into the bathroom to check it out. The facility was what you'd expect, a prefab plastic coffin with tacky extruded-vinyl detailing in a vaguely Southwestern style with teal cacti and salmon-colored cow skulls patterned against a deep beige.

She looked at the mirror, then right below it, and, sure enough, peeking out of the wall, was the small unblinking lens of a camera. She found the switch, the microphone, everything. Sepp hadn't lied. He wasn't delusional or insane. Technology had turned their reality into a reality TV show.

Harriet had to sit down on the toilet and consider what it all meant. It was like an epistemological nightmare. There was the reality of her and Sepp in the van. There was the reality inside her head, her consciousness. But then there was another, parallel, reality acting as a kind of, well, she didn't know what. But that reality had been captured on a hard drive somewhere in the van and could definitely have an impact on her other reality. All this time he'd been in here "confessing" while she'd just assumed he needed more fiber in his diet. She had to admire him, he didn't need Heidegger or Wittgenstein or even Bertrand Russell to understand what reality was. He possessed an intuitive philosophical relativism. Sure, sometimes he sounded confused, but he was able to go with the flow, to just accept the reality of the moment and inhabit it, whereas she was starting to freak out.

She wondered if she had the legal rights to keep them from airing any of it. Surely they would need her permission. Then again, maybe by coming on the tour she'd given them implicit permission. It was Sepp's tour and Sepp's show and the show had gotten on the road whether she liked it or not. Everything she'd said—a virtual confession to murder, an admission they would broadcast on cable television for the whole world to see—was recorded and saved on a hard drive somewhere in the RV. The first thing she needed to do was find it and destroy it. That was keeping it real.

. . .

Harriet handed the giant plastic dildo back to Roxy.

"You'll need this."

Roxy glared and snapped her head. "Ooh. You're scary."

Harriet frowned. "Out."

Sepp shrugged. "You oughta know the rule, Roxy, you made it up."

Roxy rolled off the water bed and tugged at her tank top, holstering her silicone orbs, and stood up. She turned to Harriet. "He's a lousy lay, anyway. Not that you'd know the difference."

Roxy walked out of the bedroom with an exaggerated waddle, swinging her hips so that her ass cheeks rose and fell in a way that Harriet assumed men found appealing; to her, it looked like Roxy needed physical therapy.

Harriet turned toward Sepp. "Can I ask you a question?"

"I didn't mess around with her. Honest."

"I'm not doubting that."

Harriet sat down on the water bed, suddenly aware that she was being filmed. "So, Sepp, baby, when you were in the confession booth, what did you say?"

"I dunno. You just kinda talk."

"Did you mention the hotel and Curtis and why we're here?"

"You mean the murder?"

Harriet stared at him wide-eyed. Her look reminded Sepp that they were supposed to be discreet. "I mean the accidental death that we covered up."

Harriet felt her stomach lurch. "You said all that to the bathroom?"

"It's called the confessional."

"You said all that?"

Sepp nodded. "I told the whole story. That's what you're supposed to do."

Harriet felt her body sag as if her muscles just suddenly stopped holding her up. It was hard to breathe. She sat back on the water bed, feeling it roll with her weight, and hugged her knees to her chest.

Sepp must've sensed she was upset. "But they'll edit all that stuff out." He reached over and stroked her leg. "I also said I was in love with you."

Harriet thought about that. It was sweet, really. Touching. This is what happens when you get involved with a dimwit. Sure, a smart guy would've kept his mouth shut, but then he would've had neuroses and needs and problems with intimacy and commitment. Harriet realized she needed to take control of the situation.

"We've got to erase that hard drive."

Sepp looked worried.

"I don't think we can do that."

"We have to."

Sepp looked at her, his face registering an expression that Harriet could only assume meant that he didn't get it, he didn't have a clue why she would want to erase anything. Would erasing the reality of the show mean erasing the reality of the world? What was Sepp so afraid of?

"Don't you want to be an author?"

It was a good question. Harriet did want to be an author, more than anything else she wanted to get her second novel published—a bestseller would just be the cherry on top—but she didn't want to be a murderess and she definitely didn't want to go to jail. She realized that the reality TV show didn't care; it was just filming on, recording her panic and concern, and it would, eventually, shit out some version of what was happening. That's what they did. They were like some weird kind of psychoactive drug that manipulated events to create an alternate narrative. It occurred to Harriet that reality TV had a lot in common with a Haruki Murakami novel. But then it's a lot different outside the narrative watching the show and inside the narrative having your life turned upside down. Harriet had to do something and the one thing she wasn't going to do was sit there and let some TV show define her reality. She was going to create her own reality.

For Harriet it was an epiphany. "Epiphany." That comes from the manifestation of Christ.

41

New Mexico

They had passed through Santa Fe before the sun came up, following the edge of the Sangre de Cristo mountains, stopping off for huevos rancheros at a twenty-four-hour truck stop diner. They'd been driving for hours. Harriet and Sepp fell asleep, tangled in each other's arms on the water bed, while Roxy sat on the couch and texted her thumbs raw sending messages to her friends and intermittently snorting lines of coke with the Ninja.

As the sun blinked over the horizon and started to beam into the RV, the Ninja felt the speed and coke and caffeine beginning to fade. His jaw muscles hurt from the amphetamine clench they'd been locked in and his stomach gurgled from the chilies he'd eaten. He popped curiously strong peppermints like a chain-smoker as he fought to counter an onslaught of gastric acid–laced repeater burps. He knew he'd need to stop soon. Shoot some filler interviews and maybe catch a couple hours of sleep before popping another pill and hitting the road to Denver.

He checked his maps and remembered that they weren't far from a place where he'd filmed an ultramarathon early in his career. It was the perfect spot to chill out and grab some new footage with a dramatic backdrop. He flicked the turn signal and exited the I-25, just before Raton, New Mexico, onto Highway 64, turning east, driving directly into the rising sun. It felt good to put his sunglasses back on.

The Ninja drove about twenty miles down the road until he spotted a scenic overlook and pulled into it. He parked the RV at the edge of a gravel lot overlooking the Capulin Volcano National Monument. It would be the perfect place to get some reaction footage of Roxy. The Ninja could tell she was in rare form, coked out, angry, frustrated, waving the giant purple dildo around like a nutjob, ready to unleash a torrent of foul-mouthed outrage and scorn. The dormant volcano in the background would add a nice subliminal touch. Would Roxy erupt? Stay tuned.

The Ninja ground his teeth and smiled as he set the parking brake and turned off the engine. He was good at his job.

He rewarded himself with a small paper cup filled with bourbon. Just the thing to smooth out the morning. He climbed out of the RV and walked to the edge of the scenic overlook. He rested his bourbon on a rickety wooden fence, obviously erected to keep numbskulls from falling over, and peered at the canyon floor below. It was a good two hundred feet down. Maybe Roxy would freak out and do a Wile E. Coyote and crater on the canyon floor. That'd look good on TV.

The Ninja unzipped his fly, tugged his dick out of his pants, and let a stream of urine arc over the edge. As his piss rained into the abyss, he lifted his bourbon and toasted the sunrise. It was going to be a good day.

. . .

Sepp woke up and ran his hands along his belly. He stopped. He felt around his torso, a sense of panic rising. The chiseled cut of his abs had rounded. They were still there, he could feel them, but the sharp definition was gone. It was like a soft blanket of smoothness had been laid over them. Dude. He was fat.

Sepp climbed out of bed and pulled on his shorts. He was going for a run. Even if it was in flip-flops and Bermudas, he was hitting the road. He had to do something. A slow jog to burn off some fat. He wished he had his fancy ASICS trainers, but they were sitting in his bedroom in San Diego.

He heard the water bed slosh and turned to see Harriet waking up.

"Where are you going?"

Sepp shook his head. "I'll be back in an hour. I've gotta go for a run before things get out of hand."

Harriet heard the RV door shut. She heard Sepp saying something to Roxy and the Ninja outside. She was alone in the RV. A perfect time to look for the hard drive. She tried to hop out of bed, but her sudden movement only caused the water to slosh violently, turning the bed into choppy surf. She had to roll off onto the floor.

Harriet went into the living room of the RV and peeked out the window. She could see Roxy standing in front of the camera, waving her hands in the air, screeching about something. The Ninja was with her, looking through the viewfinder, goading her.

Harriet began to search. She knew enough to be methodical. She started in the first cupboard and worked her way across one side of the van. She had to be quiet—no banging of doors or rifling of drawers. But she knew she was looking for something specific: computer gear and telltale cables and electrical outlets.

Harriet finished one side, the kitchenette part, and went to look under the front seat, in the glove box, and below the dashboard. Harriet felt her heart leap into her throat when she heard Roxy shout. She looked up, out the front window, expecting to see a manicured digit pointed in accusation at her, but Roxy was just shouting, spewing obscenities like a crack-whore Krakatoa.

"Cocksucking motherfucking bitch!"

The Ninja took his eye off the camera and straightened.

"Roxy. Please. Every other word can be a profanity, but they can't just bleep the whole sentence."

"I don't see why the fuck not."

"No one will know what you're saying. They need context for every 'fuck' and 'motherfucker.' You need words in between. Trust me. We've tried this every which way."

Roxy folded her arms over her chest and cocked a hip out to the side. Then she did it. Hair flip. Head snap. Snarl. "How would you say it?"

The Ninja shrugged. "Try 'That stuck-up, fucking librarian.'"

"Librarian?"

Hair flip.

"Librarian? Is that the best you can do?"

Louder this time, followed by a head snap.

The Ninja took a sip from his paper cup. He looked at Roxy. "Bookish?"

"What does that mean?"

"She likes books."

Roxy thought about it. Flipped her hair. "Lame."

"How about school marm?"

"What's a 'marm'?"

The Ninja drained his paper cup, crumpled it, and dropped it on the ground. "Just stick with 'librarian.'"

"How about I say 'flat-chested motherfucking book bitch cunt'? Is that okay?"

...

Jogging in flip-flops on a road of hard potholed concrete and gravel is not the smartest thing a person can do. So Sepp adjusted his gait from his normal loping stride to a more flip-flop-friendly shuffle and then veered off the road onto a hiking trail. It helped, but he could still feel blisters forming in between his toes where the plastic strap was chafing. But it felt good to move, good to feel his heartbeat increase, his pores open, and sweat start to slick his skin. Maybe he should just keep moving, put some serious distance between himself and the crazy shit Roxy was stirring up.

But that would mean leaving Harriet behind, and Sepp couldn't do that. Harriet was the first woman he had ever known to give him a reality check. Not only that, she cured his erectile dysfunction the first night he'd met her. She was like a sorceress or something. Sepp realized that while he thought he'd been in love with Roxy, Harriet was the one who showed him what real love was like. If it really was real love. How can you be sure? It, like, freaked him out to realize that the people he thought he'd been in love with weren't real relationships. Those were reality TV relationships and while they looked and felt real while you were on TV, once you weren't on TV then the feelings and stuff weren't real anymore even if they felt super real. It was confusing.

Sepp saw a lizard scamper off a rock as he jogged on. He wished he was smart enough to understand the book that the cool bookstore dude had given him but it was just too hard. Big words and sentences that, like, didn't make sense. Maybe he wasn't smart enough to know what reality was. Was there one big reality that everyone in the world shared? Or were there different realities, like individual pizzas? Sepp wondered if his reality was different than Harriet's. They probably were, he figured, like *they* probably were really totally different until they came together and had sex. During sex they seemed to share a reality. What if sex was the one big reality for everyone? We all live in our heads, everyone is the star of their own show, until we hook up with someone and then that's how we know what's real. Because that reality is something you can share. Sepp was pretty sure that was true, that that was what Dr. Jan meant when she said to be authentic.

Sepp winced as a piece of rock bit his foot. He kept running.

...

Harriet had tried to push the couch away from the wall, but it was bolted to the floor, so she pulled off the cushions and began poking around. She reached her hand under the back of the couch, through a little gap she'd found in the upholstery, and felt around for any sign of electronic devices.

Her arm was buried all the way in the sofa when Roxy and the Ninja came back. Roxy stopped, crossed her arms, and cocked her head. But it was the Ninja who spoke first.

"What the fuck are you doing?"

Harriet blinked up at them. She could tell the Ninja wasn't happy. "What?"

"What the fuck do you think you're doing?"

Harriet pulled her arm out. "I lost something."

Roxy made a snorting sound. "Your mind."

Harriet stood up and put the cushions back. She decided honesty might be the best policy in this instance. "I'm a techie. Okay? I wanted to figure out where you put the server. I might want to rig my car up like this."

The Ninja narrowed his eyes. "You can't get to it. It's locked up in a special shockproof casing inside the wall."

Harriet tried to look thoughtful.

"Wow. Cool."

The Ninja looked at her, then turned to Roxy. "I need a couple hours of snooze, then we'll get back on the road."

Harriet watched as he picked up the laptop and went back into the bedroom, pulling the accordion partition shut with a magnetic snap.

She turned to Roxy. "I'm going for a walk."

Roxy flopped down on the couch and sneered at Harriet. "Hey, while you're out, do us all a favor and walk off a cliff."

...

The gap between Sepp's big toe and second toe had been rubbed raw by the plastic thong of his flip-flops and had now started to ooze blood. It felt sticky between his toes, like he'd spilled syrup on his foot.

Sepp stopped running. He stood in the middle of the trail and looked out at the alien terrain. The thick black rock looked like piles of foam. Like shaving cream or mayonnaise. It was like the volcano barfed and rocks just blasted everywhere. He sucked fresh air deep into his lungs, his body shiny with a slick varnish of sweat, his muscles feeling tight and springy. He could've kept running, maybe gone ten miles, but his toe was a mess.

Sepp sat on a rock and tried to rip a piece of his shorts off. He succeeded in shredding a good hunk, enough to give his shorts a tattered, Robinson Crusoe look. He had to laugh at himself—he was starting to look like a contestant on *Survivor,* one of the few shows he'd never wanted to go on. Who wants to starve in a jungle when you can have sex in a Jacuzzi?

Sepp tied a makeshift bandage over his wound, giving him some padding against the flip-flop, and looked out at the scenery. It was then, as the heat of the day began to build, that he realized he needed water.

He heard the sound of someone running along the trail, shoes crunching in the soft dirt. He looked over to see a monk, or at least it looked like a monk, like the guys in the kung fu movies, wearing a red and yellow robe, running up the trail. The dude wasn't Chinese or anything. He was American looking. A white guy with a shaved head and some really nice New Balance running shoes on his feet.

The man ran up to Sepp and stopped. "Are you okay?"

Sepp nodded. "Am I on TV?"

The man's expression changed. He looked at Sepp. "Do you need some water?"

Sepp shook his head. "I just thought maybe you were part of the show. I'm just not used to seeing . . . what are you? A monk?"

He nodded. "Buddhist monk."

"But you're American."

The monk smiled. Sepp noticed that his eyes were friendly. "There are lots of American Buddhist monks."

"So you're not part of the show."

"What show would that be?"

"Reality."

The monk chuckled. "That depends."

Sepp didn't know how to respond. Did the monk think he needed a SAG card to be on the show?

The monk continued. "The reality you're currently experiencing is just an appearance to your mind so maybe I *am* on the show."

Sepp blinked up at the monk. "Dude. You lost me."

The monk caught his breath. "Think about your dreams. The things that happen when you're dreaming seem real, don't they?"

Sepp nodded. "Is that why I wake up with a boner?"

The monk smiled. "Exactly. Your mind creates a reality that seems as real as this reality." The monk waved his hand in the air to indicate everything around them.

Sepp nodded. "My dreams do seem real."

"And when you wake up, where does that reality go? Is the reality that your mind creates in a dream that different from the reality your mind creates when you're awake?"

Sepp pondered that for a moment. "Not really I guess."

The monk nodded. "Both are versions of reality. Both are appearances to your mind."

"So like my mind just makes stuff up?"

The monk pulled a cloth from under his robe and wiped the sweat from his forehead. "That's the basic idea. Everything depends on the mind."

"What about love?"

The monk looked out over the vista for a moment. "If you looked for love outside somewhere could you find it? Is it a thing you could touch?"

"No."

"We would say that if love truly existed, if it was a thing you could find in the world, it would be solid and unchanging. But everyone knows love changes."

"So it only exists in my head?"

The monk shrugged. "Is that so bad?"

Sepp stuck a finger in his ear and scratched. "No. That makes a kind of sense. I see that." He looked at the monk. "But what about, like, reality TV?"

The monk smiled.

"Buddha would say that television is inherently empty. It only exists in conjunction with our mind perceiving it."

Sepp nodded. "Like a dream."

The monk smiled. "Like everything."

...

A festive pop echoed through the RV as Roxy let the cork fly on a bottle of bubbly. She licked the foamy spew as it ran out the top and down the side of the bottle, then poured herself a big glassful. She took a sip, letting the bubbles tingle her tongue, and pulled a small paper rectangle out of her purse. She unfolded the rectangle and, using her long pinkie fingernail, scooped out a bit of white powder, held it to her nose, and hoovered it. One clump for each nostril.

She carefully refolded the paper, put it in her purse, and then sat back on the couch to begin texting in earnest.

...

The Ninja lay back on the water bed and propped the laptop on his chest. A couple clicks of the mouse and he had the footage he'd shot of Sepp and Harriet on their first night in the RV. Even though the picture was slightly grainy, with a green-gray hue, he could clearly make out Harriet's body as Sepp's head bobbed between her legs. The image was hot. He captured fifteen seconds of it and uploaded it to his personal website. He wanted to make it available to all his friends and fans. A little taste of the show to come.

The Ninja couldn't put his finger on why Harriet had such sex appeal. Sure, there was something hot about her girl-next-door figure, and there was something to be said for her amateurish enthusiasm in bed; there was nothing staged or made-up or porn star about her. But what really turned the Ninja on, the single thing that stiffened his cock in no time, was the look on her face. It was an expression of pure pleasure. Her mouth open, gasping, her eyes wide. It wasn't the thrusting of their bodies or the wobble of her tits, it was the look in her eyes that caused the Ninja to get up and see what Roxy was doing.

...

Harriet stood on the edge of the cliff and looked down at the rocky floor below. She halfheartedly considered jumping, but she just wasn't the suicidal type. She didn't want to pull a John Kennedy Toole and have her book win the Pulitzer posthumously. If there was a big prize she was going to be there, in a cute black cocktail dress, to accept it.

She thought about Franz Kafka, a writer she hadn't thought about since college. He was the overused cliché when things got weird. But, when she thought about how to describe what had happened, and what was continuing to happen, the first word that popped into her head was "Kafkaesque." Circumstances conspire, misunderstandings emerge, and the next thing you know people are dead and you're a giant cockroach. Harriet knew she'd behaved badly, she could admit that to herself. She wasn't proud of what she did. But, fuck it. It had happened. It was an accident. A horrible, terrible, *Kafkaesque* incident. It wasn't an excuse, really; just the way it was.

Now she was trapped in this constructed reality TV reality where the normal rules didn't apply. How could they? You can't go putting secret cameras everywhere, record every intimate moment and confidential conversation, and then broadcast it to the world. After a moment's reflection Harriet realized that the internet—her turf—was filled with exactly that kind of thing. Was the World Wide Web only built to humiliate people with YouTube videos of them kicking each other in the nuts and to sell self-published books?

Harriet found herself with the unappealing options of going to jail because she'd incriminated herself in Curtis's death by being on a reality show—and honestly, how could she explain *that* to the literary world—or destroying the hard drive that held Sepp's confession. One way or the other she'd have to force the Ninja to turn over the drive. She didn't know how to do it, exactly. Threaten legal action? Convince Sepp to walk off the show? Hit the Ninja with a tire iron? She had to do something.

Harriet looked at the RV and noticed a cargo hatch on the side. Maybe that would provide access to the hard drive.

She tiptoed over and tried the latch. It opened. She hesitated, not wanting them to hear her, until she realized that someone was playing the stereo. Harriet was no music aficionado, but it sounded like a band her college roommate used to listen to called Mott the Hoople. Harriet swung open the cargo hatch and stuck her head inside.

...

The Ninja didn't usually get involved with cast members. It just never turned out good for anybody, it wasn't good for the show, and it could hurt your reputation as a reliable shooter. But the speed and bourbon combined with watching his homemade porn had got the better of him and now he found himself sitting in the driver's seat with his pants around his ankles as Roxy straddled him. Her breasts were shoved in his face and all he could see was bouncing flesh as she worked her body up and down, riding his cock like a porn star. All he'd had to do was ask and Roxy was up for it. She even seemed mildly interested in the sex. Not like he was rocking her world, but she was tolerating it in a friendly and professional way. She drank slugs of champagne from the bottle she held in her right hand and in between gulps would talk dirty to him.

As the Ninja got more and more turned on and increased the power and tempo of his thrusting, Roxy fell back, leaning against the steering wheel, accidentally honking the horn. The horn was loud and the shock of it caused her to drop the champagne bottle. The bottle hit the parking brake and caused it to pop up, releasing the brakes. Despite its weight, or perhaps because of it, or maybe because the Ninja's thrusting had caused Roxy's elbow to put the gearshift into neutral, coupled with the fact that the RV was pointing downhill and susceptible to the force of gravity, or maybe it was some combination of all these factors combined, the RV began to roll.

The Ninja felt the vehicle move and was caught in two minds—he was on the verge of climaxing and yet he needed to hit the brakes. He didn't stop thrusting as he tried to stomp on the brakes but Roxy's legs were in the way and he ended up kicking her before frantically jamming his foot on the gas pedal while having one of those orgasms that leaves you breathless.

...

Harriet had climbed halfway in the cargo hold, following several thick cables that led to the main cabin. She was sure they led to the hard drive. A loud honk startled her and she was scrambling out when she felt the RV lurch and begin to roll. Harriet jumped out of the way, slipping on the gravel and falling on her ass. She looked up in time to see the RV roll toward the lip of the overlook, picking up speed as it went, until it broke through the wood guardrail and plunged off the cliff.

Harriet ran to the edge and watched the RV face-plant into an outcropping of sharp rocks, bounce off the cliff face, flip, and fall two hundred feet down into a dry arroyo, where it landed on its roof, crushed like a stomped beer can. The RV sat there for a moment, silent except for the rattle and clatter of falling rocks, and then it burst into flames.

...

Sepp saw black smoke drifting in the cloudless blue sky and thought that the Ninja had broken out the grill and was barbecuing steaks. He was famous for that, had some kind of special spicy rub he put on the meat before he threw it on the fire; Sepp had eaten barbecue with the Ninja at least once a week on *Love Express*. But as Sepp walked back he noticed the smoke getting thicker, blacker, and not looking at all like a barbecue.

42

Colorado

While Sepp filled their rental car with gas, Harriet went into the minimart to buy a couple of coffees for the drive to Denver. Sepp had convinced his publisher to spring for the car, as long as he promised to get back on schedule with his tour, take the flights he was supposed to take, and not go driving off into the boondocks on a whim. He was happy that Brenda wasn't mad at him. In fact, she seemed to be thrilled by the fresh burst of national media coverage the book was getting now that Roxy had died in a freak accident. "Tragic for Roxy, but great for the book." That was something Brenda had said to make him feel better.

It was a new rental, a Chrysler 200 with a convertible top and, although they never discussed it, the top stayed up; neither of them were in the mood to be exposed and Sepp had warned her that once the paparazzi found them it would be like a feeding frenzy.

Harriet looked out the glass door of the minimart and watched as Sepp meticulously cleaned bugs off the windshield with a squeegee. "Squeegec." That was an awesome word. She thought it probably began as some kind of nautical slang. Perhaps related to, or derived from, "squeeze."

An unhealthy smell emanated from a machine that heated hot dogs, the meat product glistening with sweat, rotating on metal cylinders under hot lights. For some reason it made Harriet think about the trail of dead she'd left across the American Southwest. It was weird. She didn't really feel bad about it. Well, that's not true, she did feel bad about Curtis. He had so much promise as a writer. Could his accidental death be some kind of karmic retribution for selling out? The kind of thing that happens when you don't honor your gifts? Harriet had thought she'd be racked by guilt, but really, she wasn't. Maybe the guilt would come haunting her in the night like she was a character in some B-movie. But she didn't think that would happen. Curtis had slipped in the shower, the Ninja and Roxy had died when the RV's parking brake failed. Accidents happen.

Harriet filled up two large cups with scalding hot coffee, leaving a little room for sugar and milk in Sepp's; she preferred hers black. She put the lids on them and carefully slid them into corrugated cardboard sleeves so she wouldn't burn her fingers. All that preparation didn't keep her from almost dropping the cups on the floor when she turned and saw the cover of *Us Weekly* perched by the cash register. Under the headline "Sepp's New Love" was a glossy color photo of her and Sepp holding hands as they exited the bookstore in Phoenix. A subtitle said: "Who is the mysterious writer who's captured his heart?"

She paid for the coffee and then stood there, frantically checking the internet on her iPhone. News about her and Sepp was everywhere. *Gawker* was the first to break the story of her identity; they had a snarky profile on her and ridiculed her for "self-importance in overdrive." *Perez Hilton, Go Fug Yourself, Jezebel, Celebitchy,* and *TMZ* all followed with articles or links. Someone had even fished photos off her Facebook page. She did not look cute in any of them. It wasn't just celebrity gossip sites that were pumping the news, everyone else piled on too; book blogs like *GalleyCat, Jacket Copy,* and *Bookslut*—which seemed fitting—had all run pieces. *The Huffington Post, E! News,* and MTV had reported the story; even MSNBC had mentioned them. It was unbelievable.

Harriet wonder what it all meant. She checked the metrics on her site and discovered she'd had almost a hundred thousand hits yesterday and more than three hundred emails. That was unheard of. What was happening?

She was about to put her phone in her pocket when the ringtone began playing its marimba rhythm. The call was from the 212 area code.

"Hello?"

There was a pause on the other end of the line and Harriet wondered if she'd accidentally disconnected for a second before a robust voice crackled through the phone.

"Hey! Is this Harriet? Harriet Post?"

"Yes."

"Hi. This is Amy Evanston calling from New York. You sent me your amazing manuscript a few weeks ago and I just had to call and talk to you about it."

Harriet remembered her—she was one of the agents who'd asked to see her massive manuscript.

"That was six months ago."

"Well, I do get busy. But listen. I think it's terrific and I'd like to work with you on it."

"What?"

"I'd like to represent you. Your writing is just brilliant, your book is amazing, and I think I can find an editor who will give your book the TLC it deserves."

...

Sepp was standing next to the car, checking the air pressure in the tires, as Harriet walked up to him and handed him his coffee.

"What took you so long?"

Harriet looked at him. "I think I just got my fifteen minutes of fame."

Sepp looked at the minimart. "In there?"

Harriet nodded. "Yeah."

"That's so cool."

Harriet wondered if it was cool. She wasn't sure. "Do you mind if I drive?"

Sepp handed her the keys. "Be my guest."

...

It felt good to put her hands on the steering wheel, to put her beeping and chirping iPhone in the backseat, and just drive. It was relaxing. The scenery was changing, the mountains in the distance looking pretty instead of the oppressive and foreboding hills in the desert. Of course that might've been because she didn't have a dead writer in the backseat. That kind of thing can color your perception.

Sepp reached over and patted her knee. He seemed happy. Content. It was amazing. He could just go with the flow no matter what was happening.

Harriet didn't know if this thing with Sepp was going to work out in the long run. Opposites attract, obviously, but do they stay together? When the infatuation and sex wore off, what would she be left with? An amiable lunkhead? A trophy husband? Would she be okay with that? Maybe that's the thing about love—you don't know, nobody knows.

Sepp turned to her. "I'd like to read a book."

"What made you think of that?"

Sepp shrugged. "Well, you really like reading books so, like, I thought maybe I should check it out."

Harriet reached over and ran her hand through his hair. "I'll pick out a couple of books you might like when we get to Denver."

. . .

As they neared Colorado Springs, Harriet noticed a big mountain in the distance. "That's Pikes Peak."

"Yeah? How do you know?"

Harriet tapped the GPS. "It's on the map."

"What do you know about it?"

Harriet thought for a moment and realized that she didn't know a thing about Pikes Peak; she didn't know it was named after Zebulon Pike or that it was made of pink granite and stood more than fourteen thousand feet above sea level, and she didn't know that it was famous for having the world's highest cog railway. Pikes Peak was a mystery to her. A complete blank.

"Nothing really."

Sepp leaned forward to get a better look out the window. "I've never even been to Colorado."

They drove in silence for a while, up Interstate 25, heading north to Denver. The sun was beginning to set in the west, the golden rays streaking across the sky, the mountains turning slate and indigo as they withdrew into shadow. Harriet knew it was a cliché, a conceit made famous in every western ever made, but she couldn't resist it.

"You want to check it out? We've got time."

Sepp grinned and flashed her a thumbs-up. "Hell yeah. Let's do it."

When they got to the junction with Highway 24, which is the road to Pikes Peak, Harriet took it, leaving the main interstate and heading west, into the sunset, toward the mountain and something she'd never read about in books.

Acknowledgments

I'd like to thank Julie Buxbaum and Cate Dicharry for their early reads, insights, and encouragement; Marc Weingarten and Lamar Damon for giving me a behind-the-scenes look at the world of reality television; Gen Rigpa for dharma lessons; Brian Lipson for being the best lunch companion a writer could have; and Mary Evans for everything she does.

Big ups to Judy Hottenson, Deb Seager, Isobel Scott, Hilary Baribeau, Amy Hundley, Dara Hyde, Charles Rue Woods, Gretchen Mergenthaler, and everyone at Grove/Atlantic for their continued enthusiasm and friendship. Also thanks to Rachel Vogel, and Bart Heideman, and Baker Montgomery.

And special thanks to Diana Faust, Olivia Smith, and Jules Smith.